BILLY BLACKSMITH
The Demonslayer

The Blacksmith Legacy Book 1

BEN IRELAND

Ireland, Ink

Ireland, Ink

BISAC: Young Adult/Urban Fantasy/Monsters/Adventure/Humor/Friendship
Paperback:
ISBN-10:0-9977860-2-7
ISBN-13:978-0-9977860-2-6
EBook:
ISBN-10: 0-9977860-3-3
ISBN-13: 978-0-9977860-3-3

I dedicate this to Kaelten, Koen
and the fourteen year old in everyone
that's holding out for that win.

I also dedicate it to astronauts.

You guys are out of this world.

Contents

"Agoston," the warm, gentle voice pulled the spider from his sleep. He opened his eyes and blinked at the luminous angel standing at the edge of his web.

"It . . . it's you," he said as he scrambled to his claws. "I didn't think I would ever see you again."

The angel smiled. She looked nothing like a spider, but he could not help himself from thinking she was the most beautiful thing he had ever seen.

"Of course," she said. "I told you, we always keep our word."

"Is it time?" he asked, scurrying out of his web and down the wall. He grabbed the supplies hiding in his chest, slipped his scabbard over his shoulder and sheathed his sword. "Of course it's time. That's why you're here, isn't it?"

"It is." She nodded, her smile deepening. "It is time for you to kill William Blacksmith."

1

The Watcher

William Blacksmith—Billy to his friends—stepped onto the baseball field. He kicked the baseball bat as he walked, bouncing it off each cleat. The bright afternoon sun peered over the ball park illuminating the words *Bleakwood Devils* painted above the half-full bleachers. Beside the words, the grinning red face of a devil in a baseball cap stared mischievously over the field. Billy tilted his cap to shade his eyes as his team cheered, chanting his name.

A ruckus rose as Billy stepped onto home plate. He glanced over and saw the Oakdale Sparrows fans pounding on tin trashcans. The high schoolers shouted enthusiastically in their attempt to distract the star player.

"*Silly Billy, bumbling batter,*" they chanted. The coach gave a half-hearted order for his supporters to stop. They didn't.

The players whispered the other verse.

"*Stupid. Ugly. Couldn't be fatter.*"

Billy smiled to himself. The teasing wouldn't impact his game. Only four months had passed since he first picked up a bat. He walked onto the JV team and became the clutch hitter. After a month, he was practically dragged onto the varsity team—a first for any sophomore in Bleakwood High's history. There were not many things Billy considered himself good at, but he was no sluff at baseball.

Billy inhaled and took in the scene around him. The thick green turf had been cut that day, leaving a rich, sweet scent in the air. In the distance, he could hear the rumble of traffic on the freeway. To his left, a clump of oaks grew by the wide dirt path that lead onto the field. To his right the clamor from the visiting team's supporters grew louder.

Billy looked to his two best friends, Ash-Lea Grey and Greyson Ash, spectating from a large oak beside the field. Greyson, wearing a button-down shirt and with his chocolate colored hair glued to his head, had his nose pressed into another Castles and Demons monster manual. He licked his finger and turned a page, oblivious to the game.

Ash-Lea, in contrast, sat perched on a branch of the oak, her hand gripping the limb between her feet. Her black hair streaked with purple covered one eye and hung over her black karate outfit. She flipped Billy a thumbs-up, but started to totter; her arm pin-wheeled furiously for a second before she grasped the trunk again. Greyson and Ash-Lea almost always came to watch him play and he loved them for it.

The pounding and shouts continued from the bleachers.

"Hey Tubby," the catcher sang as Billy gave a practice swing. "Tubby, Tubby, Tubby."

Usually comments about his weight bothered Billy, but not when he was playing. Baseball brought him a sense of confidence and calm he had never felt before picking up a bat. The catcher continued with his onslaught of ridiculously clever insults.

"Don't blow this one," a harsh voice called from third base.

Billy looked up and saw his teammate, Belle, glowering at him as she smacked her gum. The girl's thick shoulders, short hair, and large cheek bones gave her an intimidating quality. She was always chewing gum. Even if the teacher made her spit it out, she had another piece in as soon as his head was turned.

Belle wasn't happy when Billy joined the team. True, they hadn't lost a game since he'd donned the Devils' jersey, but he'd replaced her during her big senior year as star player. Belle dusted her hands on her legs, adjusted her cap, and crouched, prepared to run.

Billy squatted at the plate and took in the field. The outfielders were too far to the left so Billy decided to hit it into the gap on the right. He crouched, the bat behind his head, ready to swing. His bulk crowded the plate easily, leaving a very small strike zone. At fifteen, he was already six foot three inches tall—and not small around the waist either, a fact many of the kids did not miss an opportunity to point out.

Coach Schnurrbart stood frozen, his arms folded across his chest, watching Billy intensely from over his thick, caterpillar-like mustache.

In the opposite dugout the Sparrow's beer-bellied coach paced back and forth. He repeatedly touched the brim of his cap and forearm with two fingers in a precise pattern. The pitcher—a senior who was endeavoring to grow a beard, but only managed patches of spotty fur on his cheeks—nodded, acknowledging the play.

Billy could hear the catcher breathing behind him as he took his position on home plate. The wind rustled the trees on the side of the field as the banging and shouts from the dugout faded to a white buzz. He slowed his breathing, listening only to the throb of the pulse in his ears. Everything else in the world disappeared. There was nothing left but the senior on the mound in front of him and the bat in his hands. The pitcher wound up, lifting his leg as he pulled back to throw, then in a whirr he let the ball fly.

Billy smiled and thought, *Ball.*

"Ball," the umpire shouted, and noise returned to the world. The Devils sighed collectively from their dugout. The Sparrows banging and shouts reached his ears once more.

Letting the bat swing to his side casually, Billy kicked the dirt, and took his stance again. He concentrated on the fuzz-faced pitcher before him. Once more, the pitcher wound up and sent the ball sailing towards him. Billy shook his head, it was another ball.

"Ball," the umpire shouted once more.

The Sparrows cheered triumphantly. *"Billy, Billy, bumbling batter,"* the chorus of voices jeered.

Billy straightened and bit his lip, growing suspicious. The bases were loaded and the pitcher did not look the least bit nervous that the best batter in the school district was up to plate. If Billy hit a home run it would add four runs and they would win, no question. Everyone knew that whenever Billy hit the ball he got a home run— and everyone knew he never missed the ball. Billy scowled at Fuzz-Face. He shot a glance over to the Sparrow's coach too, who had stopped pacing and was now flashing his tobacco-stained grin. Billy grimaced as it all became clear. The pitcher had been instructed to walk him. Gritting his teeth, he smiled back.

Not today, folks.

Billy planted his feet as the rustling trees, traffic, and the cacophony from the Sparrows all faded to the background. The pitcher wound up, leaning to the right and threw the ball. As he honed in on the small white blur moving towards him, Billy compensated for the misaimed pitch and pulled the bat in as he swung. His palms itched in anticipation of hearing the solid crack of ball against aluminum bat.

Billy felt his heart jam into his throat as the sky above the bleachers tore in two. A giant crimson-black *thing*—like a mix between a human and a bird—descended through the tear. Billy's eyes grew wide with horror. The monster flapped its massive, dark, school-bus length wings to slow its descent, perching on the top row of stadium chairs. Long, impressive talons bent around the seats. Its human-shaped body was covered in deep crimson colored skin, loose robes of black cloth wrapped about its chest and legs. The eyes in its human-like face were narrowed and serious. The creature pressed his mouth into a line, neither smiling nor frowning, never shifting his gaze off of Billy.

"Strike?" the umpire asked. He turned to Coach Schnurrbart. "Strike?"

Billy snapped back to the game and glanced around, wondering why everyone wasn't running away in terror. The noise from the Sparrows' dugout had ceased completely as they gawked at Billy, a row of glossy wide eyes and open mouths—for the first time ever, Billy had missed a hit.

Nobody seemed phased by the monster that had just appeared. It was still there but the game was all anyone seemed to care about. Even the catcher, usually so colorful in his taunts, was at a loss for words. Belle stomped her feet on the ground and mouthed curses at Billy as if expecting that to happen. Everyone stared at him with amazement, confusion, or anger on their faces. Hadn't anyone noticed a giant, half-human, half-pterodactyl had just joined the audience?

Billy looked to his friends in the tree for corroboration. Greyson only turned a page in his book, unconcerned by any supernatural spectators. Ash-Lea gave a questioning shrug, as stunned as anyone.

"What happened?" she mimed, inaudible from the distance.

Billy tilted his head and pointed one finger in the direction of the dinosaur-man, hoping Ash-Lea would get the idea. She squinted in the general area, then back to him, shaking her head. The creature remained in the bleachers, with its black, shiny eyes penetrating Billy. He stretched his great leathery wings. A crack, like a canopy in a strong breeze, echoed through the grounds as the monster flapped his wings before folding them in once more.

And Ash-Lea couldn't see it. *Not a good sign.*

The catcher threw the ball back to Fuzz-Face, and the racket rose once more from the Sparrow's dugout, louder now they knew the unbeatable-Billy could make mistakes.

Billy looked around. Had no one else seen what he had seen? Did anyone care that giant monsters suddenly took an interest in high school athletics?

Belle shook her head and glowered, a look that threatened exquisite pain if Billy missed the ball again.

He lifted his bat and pointed it at his new target. "Here it comes, big guy," he whispered.

In response, the creature may have raised an amused eyebrow.

He could already tell the pitch would be a ball by the way Fuzz-Face wound up. The Sparrows fell into a hush again as they anxiously watched Billy. The pitcher smirked, attempting to mimic the technique he'd just employed. The ball whizzed towards Billy and he swung. This time the bat made a resounding crack. The Sparrows groaned in disappointment. The ball whistled through the air, heading directly for the giant beast sitting in the bleachers. Without taking his gaze off Billy, the creature leaned casually to the side as the ball whipped past him, bounced off the wall, and disappeared somewhere into the rows of chairs.

As soon as the crack sounded, the Devils rushed the field, ecstatic about another win. The Sparrows took off their gloves and started heading in, not bothering to watch where the ball landed. Billy's teammates ran up to him, punching him jovially on the shoulder, shouting things like, "You had us for a second, there," and "Always gotta put on a show, Billy-boy." The players on the bases came into home one by one, jumping victoriously on the plate and slapping Billy on the back. Except Belle, she just shook her head at him and scowled. It was another victory.

Billy jogged to the oak. Ash-Lea dropped behind the branch to swing down to the ground. She stumbled as she landed, but quickly regained her footing and brushed her hair back into place. Ash-Lea handed Billy his camera and he slipped it into his bag.

"Is it over?" Greyson asked, closing his Castles and Demons manual. "That felt quicker than usual."

"Yeah, we have two players out today," Ash-Lea explained. "The other team had one kid missing. Something must be going around. Great game, as per usual." She reached up and punched him in the arm.

"Hey, Ashes," Billy turned, pointing to the giant creature. "Look at the bleachers up there." The monster stretched its giant wings, seemingly in response, and flapped them once more.

"Yah?" Ash-Lea asked, nonplussed.

"What do you see?"

"Bleachers, dude," she shrugged.

"No, well, yeah, but do you see anything else?"

"Chairs, concrete, girders."

Billy took her around the shoulders and pointed to the massive human-like bat. "Do you see anyone?" It flapped again and the crack of his wings hit Billy in the ears. The motion seemed somehow taunting; it knew Billy was the only one who could see and hear it.

"There's a dude in a hat."

"What?" Billy asked, looking back to the creature. He couldn't tell for sure, because of the distance, but he thought he saw it laughing. "There," he pointed. "Right there."

"Yeah, there's a guy in a hat. So what?"

Billy blinked and shook his head. She could see someone there he couldn't see, someone who was not the creature. "Come on," Billy said, taking her by the arm and leading her across the diamond.

Seeing them approach, the creature opened his mouth and spoke. Despite the field between them, Billy felt the cavernous voice rumbling in his chest and pressing against his ears. The sound made Billy stumble and he stopped walking. "We shall speak later, William Blacksmith."

Billy froze and Ash-Lea bumped into him. "Dude, you ok?"

"Did you hear tha . . . that?" Billy stammered.

"Hear what?" Ash-Lea asked.

The creature spread its wings and lifted into the sky. It waved a clawed hand above its head and a tear appeared in the atmosphere. The creature lifted into the fissure and was gone.

Billy shook his open hands toward Ash-Lea. "HOW ARE YOU NOT SEEING THIS?"

Ash-Lea faced Greyson, looking the opposite direction of the bleachers. "You coming?" She turned back to Billy. "See what? The man? Yeah, he's gone, so what? Did you know him?"

Billy's mouth fell open and he stared at Ash-Lea. "Never mind," he said, his whole body trembling. He gripped the bat in his hand tightly trying to distract himself.

Keep it together Billy. He thought. *You're just going crazy. No need to let anyone else know.*

"Greyson, dude," Ash-Lea shouted. "Are you coming or what?"

"Yeah, I'm coming," Greyson sighed longingly as he leaned back against the tree. He wasn't looking at Billy as he spoke.

Billy followed Greyson's gaze to Quinn. The painfully stereotypical cheerleader had come to watch her boyfriend play baseball. Her long, silky black hair bounced, shining in the setting sun as she jumped up and down by her boyfriend Patrick, kissing him on the cheek. Her red, white, and black cheerleading skirt revealed the skin above her knees. Her shirt, depicting the grinning Bleakwood Devil, cropped just short enough to expose the slightest sliver of coffee-colored stomach. Greyson hadn't remembered to stand up. He sat there immobilized by the site of Quinn. Billy could almost hear the soundtrack playing in Greyson's head as he watched the sun sparkling off her eyes in slow motion.

"Why don't you just talk to her?" Billy tried to keep his voice as normal-sounding as possible.

Greyson shook his head, returning to reality. "Are you kidding me? She's a state champion marksman, so is her dad. From what I've heard their whole family is into shooting. And on top of that, her boyfriend Patrick is big enough to be a stinking linebacker. He would kick my butt as a warm up for mopping the floor with me. No thank you."

State champion? I didn't know that. Okay, not as stereotypical as I thought.

"Boys are stupid," Ash-Lea declared. "She's not worth your time, Grey. She's a total bimbo."

"That's your opinion." Greyson stuffed his book into his backpack and swung it over his shoulder.

"It's a pretty good one," she retorted. "Can anyone with brains actually date a jock like Patrick?"

"Technically I'm a jock now," Billy offered.

Greyson ignored him. "Can you blame her?" his voice forlorn as he looked at his bike chained to the nearby fence. "He has a car. A really cool car."

Ash-Lea slapped Greyson on the shoulder. "Grey, if that's the only thing she cares about then she is stupider than I think."

"Leave her alone," Greyson said softly.

"Okay, okay, lover boy." Ash-Lea held up her hands in surrender. She turned to Billy. "Do we need to go looking for the hat-guy before we leave?"

"Nope," Billy popped the P at the end of the word. The winged monster had opened the sky and simply disappeared. *Yup. Pretty sure I'm losing it.*

"You really should talk to her," Ash-Lea continued. Greyson raised a skeptical eyebrow. "When Patrick beats you up, she'll feel so sorry for you that she's bound to fall in love with you."

Greyson growled and started running towards Ash-Lea with arms outstretched. She twisted out of the way laughing.

Billy let Greyson and Ash-Lea banter and chase as they walked towards their bikes. He had to agree with both of them. Quinn was good looking and pretty nice from what he could tell, but she had to have some screw loose if she thought Patrick was worth dating. From playing ball with him, Billy could tell he was a decent enough guy—just painfully dim. Patrick played on every sports team—tall, dark, handsome, and pretty darn good at baseball. His black hair was shaved, and even through his letterman jacket you could tell he had muscled arms.

As Billy pulled his key from his pocket and started unlocking his bicycle, he watched Quinn climb into Patrick's car; a fire-red mustang with a black racing stripe painted off-center. She caught him looking and waved.

"Goo . . . ood game," Patrick called. He had this odd way of extending words when he didn't need to. It just added to the mystery of how he managed to get a popular girl like Quinn. "See you tomorroo . . . oow, Tubbers."

Patrick obviously thought *Tubbers* was an endearing nickname. They were, after all, *friends?* Patrick had never said anything deliberately hurtful to Billy, he was just one of the guys.

"It was all you," Billy called. Patrick smiled broadly and climbed into the driver's seat. *Poor guy thinks I was being serious.*

"Be nice to the lug heads," Ash-Lea slipped into her backpack.

"Why?" Greyson bitterly watched Patrick and Quinn speed away.

"Hey, chubby," a voice called.

Two seniors from Oakdale marched down the sidewalk towards them; a tall lanky one not grown into his body yet, and a stockier, pimple-faced one. They had silly rhyming names, Billy thought, Biff and Cliff, or something like that. Apparently, they'd waited until everyone had cleared out before making their appearance. Ash-Lea stepped in front of Billy, a scowl on her face, her fists clenched tight.

"Just ignore them," Billy put a hand on her shoulder.

"Great game," Biff, the taller one mocked in a tone that indicated the opposite. "You going to go celebrate with a pizza or three?"

"Sure, anything's possible."

"Shut up, Tubby," Cliff, the pimply one said. "We know you're juicing. Just need to prove it and you'll never set foot on a diamond again."

"Good luck, guys," Billy shrugged. "Look, I'm just trying to get home, if you wouldn't mind getting out of my way."

"Juicing?" Ash-Lea growled. "You think Billy is cheating? You are just a pair of sorry, jealous S.O.B.s. Why don't you run off home with your stupid little sparrow tail between your legs?"

Billy wiped sweat from his forehead. *Boy, hot afternoon,* he thought. "Just leave it, Ashes. These guys are harmless."

"Harmless?" Biff growled. "I'll show you harmless."

"Bring it, bat-for-brains." Ash-Lea stood nose-to-nose with Biff, despite the fact he was five inches taller.

"You wanna see my bat?" Biff slipped his hand into his sports bag and dropped it, leaving his baseball bat in his hand.

"Hey," Billy shouted, his knees shaking.

Ash-Lea grabbed the bat and twisted. She easily yanked it out of the thug's hand and threw it across the street.

Billy stepped between them. "Hey, guys. Let's just . . . not. Okay?"

"Come on, man," Cliff said. "Let's beat him on the field, 'roids and all."

"We are going to utterly demolish you, Blacksmith." Biff pointed a threatening finger at Billy as he walked away. "You're a cheat. And we're going to prove it."

Billy turned back to his bike and started unchaining it. "See you later." He paused with his trembling fingers on the lock, letting his racing heart slow.

Ash-Lea squatted next to him. "Why do you put up with that?" she asked. "Those guys are just jerkwads. We could have taken them."

"Probably," Billy said. "But I don't like fighting."

"You can say that again." Greyson laughed stiffly. Billy looked up to see his friend's face was white, his glasses shaking on his nose. He had obviously taken the encounter worse than either Ash-Lea or Billy. "I've never seen you fight Billy. Ever. Even with your brother."

There were a few reasons he hated fighting; but that wasn't a story he liked sharing, even with his best friends. "It's just not worth it." Billy shrugged.

He pulled the chain from his bike and dropped it into his back pack, his mind already drifting away from the bullies back to the pterodactyl-monster-thing he had seen at the game. For a moment he thought about telling his friends what he saw. Behind him, Billy could see the bleachers; empty and innocent.

What was that thing?

He pulled an Electrolyte-tastic from his bag and took a swig, his face twisting as the liquid hit his tongue. The energy drinks his big brother insisted he drink were horrible. Ash-Lea had seen someone in the bleachers. Maybe he was dehydrated and just hallucinated the giant monster that called him by name.

"Hey, Ashes," he said.

"Wuzzup?" she replied in a gruff voice.

"Who did you see in the bleachers?"

She pushed out her lower lip and raised both shoulders. "I didn't recognize him. He was some guy wearing a hat."

"It was a fedora," Greyson said.

"Whatever, a hat is a hat." Ash-Lea rolled her eyes.

"He looked like a talent scout to me," Greyson said. "I think you may have gotten the attention of some pretty big people. I imagine you're going to start seeing them at most of your games, the way you play. You should go out of state to UCLA with me. Their baseball team is one of the highest ranked in the nation. Apparently."

"Yeah, some pretty big people." Billy pictured those school-bus size wings. "So you did see someone?"

"Sure." Greyson mounted his bike. "Did the coach tell you a scout was coming? He didn't stay long. But there was definitely someone in a fedora watching the game."

"Huh. Okay. Yeah, that must have been it. Thanks guys." Billy swung a leg over his bike and adjusted his backpack.

Ash-Lea scrutinized Billy as she climbed onto her bike.

Billy attempted what he hoped to be a nice, normal, not-insane smile. The afternoon had been far too exciting as it was. "See you guys tomorrow."

"Don't be sad," Greyson added.

"Don't feel bad," Ash-Lea said, pouting artificially.

Billy smiled at the memory that started their silly tradition and waved over his shoulder as he rode away.

2

The General øf the Spider Hørde

◆————————————————————◆

General Krios stood beside the throne, a long darkwood spear gripped tightly in his claws. He watched with wariness as thousands of spiders, of all sizes and colors, swarmed into the audience chamber. A spider himself, Krios stood taller than three grown humans on one another's shoulders—the largest of the race of spiders known as an Arachnis. He shifted his stance, his dark-steel platemail reflecting the many torches in the room. Adjusting the swords crossed under his thorax ensured the circular hilts were still within easy reach. If any fool caused trouble in the stronghold of the Spider King, he would be ready for them.

Twelve Arachnis were stationed around the thrones. The armored, spear-bearing, eight-legged guards under Krios' command were the strongest warriors in the kingdom. He would trust the life of the king to any of them.

Upon the throne sat the king, his eight, hairy spider-legs drumming the floor in anticipation. The king was an Arameous, a being with a human chest and a spider's body. He leaned forward; his spiked crown inlaid with rubies glinted in the torchlight. A crimson robe with white woolen trim hung open, exposing his pale chest, before cascading over his hairy spider thorax. He bore a satisfied glint in his eye as he watched the spiders spread like black smoke over the floor and up the walls.

Krios looked at Jaimie, the beautiful, light-skinned Queen of Spiders who sat on the throne made especially for her small human body. She watched with interest as the spiders took their places in the chamber. The green silk dress she wore shrouded her diminutive frame. Upon her throat she wore a necklace of beaten gold, and on every finger a golden ring, each sparkling with a different precious stone. Her hand traced a tender line across her swollen belly in an unconscious, motherly gesture. Her gaze met the king's and she gave him a warm and wicked smile with her bright red lips.

"You seem happy, Theron," Queen Jaimie said. "It's been a long time since I've seen you smile."

The king grinned and winked at his wife. "I am very happy."

"You can't even tell me what this is about?" she said in a teasing voice.

"You shall see."

The queen frowned in pretend disappointment and put her arm around the small human girl beside her. The princess Patricia had her mother's golden hair and blue eyes. She was perhaps six or seven in human years, Krios could not remember the child's age. Despite being the child of an Arameous, she had a human body like her mother. The little girl regarded the spiders about the room with nervous glances, clinging closer to her mother's side. Krios smiled. Humans should be afraid of the spiders. He never said such things to his liege, but always believed the Palace of Hidden Corner was no place for a human.

Thousands of years ago the ancient spiders who crossed the Sulfur Sea carved the smooth, granite walls of the grand hall. Each stair of the tall, pyramid-shaped dais depicted heroic stories of the greatest spider warriors and their victories over demonic enemies and the armies of men.

The spiderkine continued to swarm through the wide, circular doors across the chamber. Spiders of all size were in attendance, from small younglings to those taller than a human house. Spiders on the roof spooled webs so they could drop below the mass of hairy bodies in front of them and see their king. Hatchlings clung to their father's back to hear what would be announced. Some were large and black others were small and white, some bore red or green or sometimes blue patterns on their abdomens, some glowed with a glittering luminescence. Several wore the torsos and faces of men, like Theron himself. The gathering was a beautiful sight to Krios. Never had there been such an assembly in all of his time as General of the Spider Hordes. It pleased him to see happiness among the spiders he swore to protect.

King Theron flicked his hand. Seeing the gesture, the guards clad in the blackened steel armor of the royal guard forced the circular doors closed, pushing away more than a few disappointed spiders. The door slammed, silencing the chittering of a thousand mandibles.

King Theron rose, his eight legs lifting his human torso high above the throne, his arms raised in the air. The room waited eagerly.

"Subjects," he began, a smile in his voice. "Your excitement at this historical moment is understood. For thousands of years we have dwelt in the darkness and shadows. We have been considered lesser than our companions that rule this Realm."

Krios grit his mandibles in sympathetic frustration as the room began hissing in agreement.

The king paused, waiting for the noise to subside. "The strength of those who pretend to rule over us prevents us from taking our rightful place above the humans. We have been subjugated to the will of the *greater* demon races." His voice grew louder, his vehemence glowing in his eyes. "This has been under the pretense of our protection from the humans. They feign that this is to keep us safe from their guns and tanks. But the spiderkine do not fear human weapons as they do."

Krios felt a burning frustration at the truth in his king's words, the spear in his claws creaking as he tightened his grip.

"We could take the whole human race as slaves if it were not for those that oppress us. We could rule the Earth and have food and drink to spare. We would have endless forests in which to spin our webs and dark caves in which to sleep. My beautiful spiders, I have found a way that we need not fear the humans, nor the demons, the dragons, nor the angels." He paused, letting the significance of his words settle on the gathering. Krios inclined his head towards his king and furrowed his eyebrows. "For I have discovered the location of the Demonblood."

The room exploded with noise. Krios felt a cold chill run down his back, and all the hairs on his thorax stood on end. Spiders hissed and spat in fury at the name. Thousands of clawed, hairy legs stomped the walls and roof, the chamber shook with the thunderous noise.

"The Blacksmith," some shouted.

"The Horde Mind," they whispered.

"The Bloodied Blade."

"Demonseed."

The king raised his pale hands for silence. "The blood of the demon descendant will imbue he who drinks it unimaginable power. And this time we will not let it escape us. I grant any of you who find a path to the human realm permission to bring his body to me. Bring the Demonseed to my throne and you will be permitted to drink an ounce of his blood."

Again the room was filled with excited hisses and clacks. Krios' grip on his spear tightened. Finding the Demonblood was one thing. But capturing it—if all the stories were true—was all but impossible. From the shouts of excitement, it sounded as though few of the spiderkine shared his hesitation.

"The Demonblooded resides on Earth. In the northern area of the continent that the humans call the Americas." Few spiders nodded, understanding what *The Americas* were. "His name is William Blacksmith."

3

The Cave
Under the Bed

Thick purple clouds hung low over the city, darkening the twilight as Billy rode home. He stood on the bike pedals and leaned sideways, bouncing over the low curb and drifted into his driveway. Before his bike stopped moving, he hopped off and dumped it onto the concrete next to the car, running a couple of heavy steps as he slowed. He unlatched the creaky gate and let himself in the back door.

Billy lived in the uncomfortably neat suburban rambler with his foster parents, Steve and Belinda. They were tolerable and more lenient than his last. They'd even let his older brother stay two years longer than they had to—on the condition he pay rent. They were strict about things like chores and curfews, but Billy could live with that. Other than the light flickering from the television in the living room the house was dark. The pop and fizz of a beer bottle opening came from the front room.

The house appeared ridiculously clean as usual. The chairs at the dining room table were tucked in and placed at measured intervals. No dust had time to gather on the running boards, and the plastic plants always looked freshly plucked from the garden. It was clean enough to make Billy feel crazy. He checked behind him as he walked to the kitchen to make sure he didn't leave any evil footprints on the shiny white tile.

Billy dumped his bag on a chair and went straight to the fridge. He recovered four cupcakes from the pack he'd been saving, and poured himself a glass of milk. He gulped down the glass and then topped it up again. Dinner in hand, he began to make his way to his room.

Steve and Belinda sat on the couch in the living room watching the news and drinking beer, just like they did every night. Their socked feet rested on the coffee table, a case of beer tucked in between them. The finished bottles were lined in a perfectly straight row on the glass tabletop between their feet. The pack was already half empty.

"I'm back," he announced as he walked in front of the TV heading for his room, cupcakes and milk in hand.

"You left your bag on the chair?" Belinda asked sharply.

"Oops," Billy paused. "Let me just put this in my room and I'll—"

"No bags on the table," Steve snapped then took a swig from the bottle in his hands. Neither of them bothered looking away from the screen.

"Okay," Billy mumbled as he stomped back to the kitchen, making an effort to not roll his eyes in front of his foster parents. He carefully slipped one hand through the back strap while balancing his milk and cupcakes in the other. He shuffled past the grownups, careful not to interrupt them again.

The cupcake plate teetered precariously on his arm as he maneuvered to open the door to his room. He barely managed to hold onto the drink. The fear of Belinda's reaction to a cup of milk on the carpet kept his fingers glued to the glass. He slipped inside, closed the door, and breathed a sigh of relief.

His room contained a bed and a desk with a very nice, although old, computer. Chris, his big brother, had pieced together the sweet rig for him a few years back and it needed some upgrades. The wall beside his bed was one large window. It gave him a sweeping, panoramic view of the neighbor's fence, and a glimpse of the mountaintops in the distance. If Billy lay on his bed right up next to the wall, he could see the roof of the neighboring house and the occasional star. Above his desk were two posters, one partially covering the other. The first, a poster of his favorite Shinigami, on top of him was a more recent baseball poster Chris had given him as an attempt to cure Billy of his nerdiness. Billy guessed it was appropriate, now that he played baseball.

He placed his meal on his desk, discarded his bag on the floor and slumped onto his bed. He let himself lie there for a minute, trying to decide if he was going to need more cupcakes for dinner. *Probably.* He sat up and pressed the power on his computer. The red glow from the case light filled the room. It had almost slipped his mind that he had a stupid Greek history report to write. Billy snagged a cupcake and lay back down on the bed while he waited for the ancient PC to boot up.

His mind wandered back to the bleachers during the game, and the dark, winged creature. Whatever that thing was, it was massive. It saw him. It smiled at him. It *spoke* to him. It dodged the ball Billy hit right at him. All Greyson and Ash-Lea saw was a man in a fedora. Was it just a talent scout checking out Billy? *Nope. I know what I saw. The only reasonable conclusion is I'm going insane.*

Billy flinched in surprise as someone knocked on the door.

"Hey, Big-guy, you in there?" Billy's brother Chris whispered from the hall.

"Enter, if you dare," announced Billy as he sat up.

The door opened and Chris stepped into the room. Chris was much thinner than Billy, but in a toned, athletic way, with short brown hair and eyes like Billy. He stood as tall as Billy, despite being five years older. The foster parents let him stay at the house after he had aged out of the program; on the condition Chris worked, went to school, and paid rent. And also, like Billy, he loved baseball. It was Chris' love of the game that made Billy pick up a bat in the first place.

"Hey, how was the game?" Chris asked, closing the door carefully behind him. Neither of them wanted to hear from Steve again about how impolite it was to slam doors.

He considered telling the whole the story, but thought better of it and kept the hallucinations to himself. "I swung and missed."

"Bull-hockey," Chris folded his arms and sat on the corner of the desk.

"No, seriously. I missed one."

Chris raised an eyebrow. "Huh. First time for everything. Did you still win?"

"Yeah."

"Then it doesn't matter. If you win in the end, it doesn't matter what happened." Chris scrunched up his lips in thought. "As long as you don't cheat."

"Yes, *dad*," Billy said with a smile. "How was your day?"

Chris shrugged. "I worked, dude. Don't grow up too fast. There is nothing to look forward to. You wake up, go to work and then do it all again until you die."

Chris was being playful, but Billy wasn't convinced. A job meant cash. Billy gushed at the thought of what money implied. Maybe he could get a PC that had the guts to play some of the newer M.M.O.R.P.Gs.

Chris sat down on the bed next to Billy, suddenly serious. "I'm sorry I act like your dad sometimes."

Billy shook his head. "Don't be. It's not like we have much choice. Those stand-ins out there don't count." He waved a hand in the general direction of the living room.

"Steve and Belinda are okay." Billy glared at his brother until Chris broke and laughed. "Okay, maybe they're not ideal foster parents, but they've let me stay here two years longer than they had to. They give you a place to sleep and food to eat." Chris's gaze fell on what Billy planned to eat for dinner and grumbled.

"I'm sorry, did you want one?"

"No, dummy." Chris shook his head. "Mom would kill me if she knew I let you eat cupcakes for dinner."

"Was mom a good cook?" Billy asked softly, his elbows resting on his knees, studying the carpet between his feet.

Chris looked away from the cupcakes and smiled. "She *was* a good cook. She never did anything fancy. But man, her lasagna . . . and she'd make this spaghetti sauce that's nothing like any I've ever had. And she did this thing where she grilled up cheese sandwiches and turned them into like these gourmet deals with meat and avocado and this seasoning she'd make herself." He sighed, drooling over a delicious sandwich in his hands that wasn't there. "She was really good to us, Billy."

Billy smiled, imagining the grilled meat and avocado sandwich. He hated not remembering their parents, and it hurt Chris to think about them. But Billy was glad when he could get Chris to talk. He wasn't sure how it worked, but sometimes he missed that *something* which he never had.

"Don't they have anything else to eat?" Chris tore his eyes away from his imaginary sandwich and eyed Billy's meal again.

"There is some cereal left."

Chris growled. "I'll go get some groceries tomorrow after work. Let me know what you want."

Billy bounced a fist off his brother's leg gently. "Chocolate cupcakes, thanks."

Chris made a disgusted sound. "I'm headed out. Don't stay up late," he ordered as he stood.

"Yes, dad," Billy laughed.

Chris socked him in the arm.

"Night, Big-guy. Congrats on another win."

"Thanks, have a good time."

Chris closed the door behind him and Billy began to remove his sweaty clothes. He slipped into his pajamas and took another bite of cupcake. Dressed in his loose flannel pants, Billy sat at his desk staring at the computer. He sipped on the milk. Before he knew it he'd finished half the cupcakes and the milk but still hadn't written a single word. He flopped onto his bed with a frustrated sigh. The paper could wait.

He looked out at the orange sky, the lights of the city glowing off the clouds. A single star broke through the clouds and Billy felt himself smiling. His eyes traced the silhouette of chimneys, trees, power lines and roofs stretching into the distance.

One of the roofs moved.

Billy sat up, peering out the window. It could be his imagination, but he swore he saw the silhouette of a roof, or something as big as a roof, move and settle back into position. He knelt on the bed and stared harder at the shadow; probably a trick of the dimming light through the fly screen . . . Or it could have been a giant demon with red skin, stretching his wings. If the man in a fedora was a talent scout, Billy had no interest in playing for the team he represented.

Billy rolled over and retrieved his baseball bat from his bag. Turning back, he tucked it into the sheets next to him. As he squinted out the window again, he could no longer see the roof stir—it was gone. The electric-orange sky filled the void where it had been.

Staring intently at the rooftops, Billy gripped the bat with both hands, positive he was not going to be able to fall to sleep after such a weird day. *At what point do I call the cops for something like this?*

Hours later Billy woke with a start, the baseball bat still clutched in aching hands. He wiggled his fingers, each popped loudly as he opened his hand. Billy grasped the bat once more and closed his eyes. His heart skittered with panic and he tried to slow his breathing. He couldn't remember the dream that woke him, but it left his hackles raised.

Then his bed moved.

Billy sat bolt upright, a bead of sweat running down his face. In his dream, something huge hid under his bed trying to get out. His bed shuddered violently and Billy gripped the sheets as the frame scraped several inches across the floor. He could hear the distant howling of wind, as if he were deep inside a cave while a gale blew outside.

Looking to the foot of his bed, two long, black poles, almost tall enough to reach the ceiling, curved around from underneath. The hairy poles bore sharp claws on the end, and knobs in the middle like knees. The knees bent and the claws dug into his mattress. Billy started to gasp in panic as he realized these were legs—giant, hairy, disgusting *spider* legs. The bed jostled again. Two more legs emerged, one digging into the wall, the other thrusting into the carpet.

"William Blacksmith," a wheezing voice spoke from under him.

"What the—?" Billy leapt to his feet, bouncing on his mattress, his bat in hand.

Two more appeared, then two more legs from under his bed, digging into the wall and plowing a gouge in his carpet. His bed jostled as the body attached to those legs emerged from the too-small space beneath him. The hairy body was equal in size to Billy's chest, its long legs filling the room, resting on the walls and floor. The giant spider found Billy with its eight eyes and twisted unnaturally to face him, its body almost upside down. It spoke again, the razor-sharp spider teeth on its face clacking with excitement.

"William Blacksmith," the voice spoke with a hungry delight. "I have crawled through ash and smoke, through bog and swamp. I have supped at the tables of angels and hell to find passage to your realm. And I have found you cowering in your bed. This night, I will drink your demon blood and become more powerful than all my brethren." It rubbed its mandibles together—some distant part of

Billy's brain provided the name for the teeth-like things next to its mouth—like a diner rubbing his hands before an especially fine meal.

The spider swept up to Billy in a smooth motion, its legs thumping into the walls and floor. It leaned in close, eyeing Billy with its many glassy, wet eyes. For some crazy reason, it wore a sword on its back. *A spider with a sword. Of all the things I could see tonight.*

"Hey, uh," Billy stammered. "Look, the only thing that I just understood is that you're planning to drink my blood. I was wondering if you would not do that. Please."

The spider laughed, its breath thick and foul in Billy's face. It lifted a clawed leg and placed the tip against Billy's throat. Billy swallowed. "This is where the great vein is, correct? I puncture a human here and he will bleed freely?"

"I would love it if we could at least talk about this. Would you mind telling me why exactly you want to drink my blood? I mean, how do you even know who I am?"

The spider's head twisted to the side until it was almost vertical, an amused look on its fugly face. "Why all demons know who you are, Blacksmith. Though your fear . . ." It licked its face-claws with a wet, snake-like tongue. "I did not expect your fear to be so potent. So delicious."

Then the door opened and Chris walked in, rubbing his eyes.

"Chris, no." Billy shouted.

"Hey, big-guy, what's going on?" His gaze shot between Billy and the monster, his eyes widening. "Oh, no," he stumbled to a stop, his mouth dropping open. "Not again."

The spider twisted and cracked his foreleg into Chris' chest. He let out a shout as the wind was slammed from him and he flew backwards into the hall. He crashed into the wall with the muffled sound of drywall shattering.

Billy felt a fire burst to life within him, scorching every drop of his fear into oblivion. He reached up and took the spider by the hair under its neck and lifted it until he stared into its eyes.

"Nobody hits my brother," Billy growled. "Nobody."

The spider let out a ferocious howl as it twisted and lunged, the claws on its mandibles sweeping dangerously close to his face. Billy ducked and backed away as the spider turned and dove once more. Billy swung the bat upwards and it whacked into what would have passed for the spider's chin. The spider wailed and retreated, apparently not expecting Billy to resist. A clawed leg dug into the curtain and the railing popped off the wall. Billy sprang forward, swinging the bat at the closest leg, the spider saw him coming and withdrew, its hind quarters angling upwards, filling the top corner of his room. Billy fell forward as his bat connected with nothing but air. He summersaulted across the floor and came up behind the spider.

"What do you want with me, hairy?" Billy shouted and whipped the bat down.

The spider still faced the door as Billy's bat smashed into his rear leg. The joint snapped under the weight and the spider let out an inhuman scream of pain.

Unfortunately, it occurred to Billy then, giant spiders have eight legs, and breaking only one will not reduce its ability to kill you—it'll just make it mad.

"Stubborn human," it shrieked as it spun towards him. "You will pay for that."

"Stubborn spider," Billy screamed manically. "So, will you."

The spider drew his sword. The serrated blade sung as it came from the sheath. It swung the sword towards Billy but stopped abruptly as the blade jammed into the ceiling. The spider made a noise that sounded like a swear word, and focused on Billy once more. A clawed leg swung toward Billy. He dropped to his back, but wasn't fast enough. The wiry bristles of hair scraped Billy's face as the spider's shallow bone thrash him in the cheek. Billy landed on the bed and the frame gave way under his weight. The bed hit the ground with a crack just as another claw flew through the air mere inches above his face. The claw thudded into the wall, leaving a gash in the drywall ten inches long.

"Okay," Billy rolled off the bed and leapt to his feet. "I'm getting tired of this."

The spider scuttled forward, but Billy dove to the side. The monster's body collided with the desk and the wood shattered. Billy watched in horror as his PC flew, bounced off the wall, and fell to the floor with a crash.

"Now it's personal."

"Now?" Chris wheezed from the hall.

Billy stood by his closet between two of the spider's rear legs. If the spider turned, Billy would be thrown like his brother—he was running out of options, and out of breath. At the risk of making it more furious, Billy brought the bat down on the leg closest to him, next to the creature's body. The leg came off with a wet pop and green goo spurted from the wound. The huge hairy thing screamed again.

The spider spun to face him, but this time Billy expected it. Swinging the bat against the momentum of the thing, three more legs came off, splattering the walls with viscous ichor. The spider let out an agonizing scream and its body fell to the carpet with a thud. Billy backed away.

The spider only had three legs remaining. It started dragging its body across the floor away from him. The monster's leg furthest from Billy swept through the air and a familiar looking gap appeared—a hole identical to the one the demon made at the baseball game. A howl of a distant storm suddenly filled the room. With its remaining legs, the spider began to pull itself through.

"Oh, no." Billy gripped his bat and stepped towards the spider. "You don't come in here, attack me and my brother, break my computer, and expect to crawl off like nothing happened."

The spider inched towards the hole and considered Billy with eight eyes full of . . . of what? *Monsters attacking you in the night don't get afraid, do they?* The thing's eyes shimmered with what could have been fear.

"Truly, the Demonseed," it hissed respectfully.

Billy swung the bat above him and brought it down on the spider's head with a crack. The creature slumped to the floor. Immediately, the tear made in the air started to close, but not before Billy caught a glimpse of what lay behind—a deep, dark cavern rustling with the motion of several huge spiders. More sets of red spider eyes, full of rage, watched Billy through the closing gap.

"Blacksmith," a voice hissed. Then the fissure vanished.

Billy let out a long breath and wiped his forehead with his pajama sleeve. He took in the horrifying sight of the hairy body slumped on the floor. *How the heck am I going to get rid of that?* He thought. With a pop and an odd fizzing sound, the disembodied legs started to dissolve. Without thinking, Billy dove for his backpack, furiously zipped open the pocket and retrieved his camera. The body began disappearing into the carpet before the camera flashed. He scanned the screen. In the stark light of the flash, the half dissolved body looked like someone had puked up a rug.

Globs of fluff and pieces of metal squelched out of the spider's carcass. He lowered the camera and knelt down next to it, leaning close to get a better look. The spider's body appeared to be turning into . . . *cotton?* But there were other things in it—powdered concrete, bedsprings, carpet. As the body disappeared, puffs of concrete appeared, the hairy skin suddenly grew white and fell away in fluffy balls. Billy found the odd splooching noise it made both fascinating and stomach-churning.

A hint of movement outside caught Billy's attention and he spun around to the window. The creature, the same one who watched him at his baseball game, stared at him from the other side of the glass. He appeared like a normal man, except his head was the

..e height as the roof, and his eyes glowed a dull red in a leathery face. He watched the disintegrating spider, his eyes wide and full of anger.

"Oh, sad your pet couldn't finish me?" Billy shouted. "You're next." He started towards the window but stopped as the creature looked past Billy into the room.

Billy twisted, ready to beat the snot out of another spider as Chris limped through the doorway. He had one hand on his chest, the other holding the door frame. Billy turned back to the window but the creature was already gone.

"Billy?" Chris gasped. He grimaced at the spider on the floor. It was no more than a puddle of lumpy carpet, concrete and metal at this point, the one hairy leg left was quickly dissolving.

"You okay?" Billy panted.

Chris winced as he poked his torso. "Might have a broken rib, I'm okay."

"What's Steve and Belinda doing?"

Chris opened his mouth to laugh, his face growing white with the effort. "They're still on the couch, drunk to the world. You look like hell." His stopped and took a slow, pained breath.

"A giant spider just crawled out from under my bed and tried to drink my blood. I've had better nights." Billy attempted to slow his breaths before he hyperventilated.

"Your face is pretty messed up," Chris observed.

Billy raised a hand to his cheek. A cut dug deep across his jaw, he could feel wet blood running down his neck. His eye felt swollen and hard to move, now he thought about it.

"I've had worse." Billy shrugged.

"When?"

"In about—" he read his alarm clock, which now rested on the floor amongst the splinters of his desk, "three hours when Belinda and Steve see this."

Chris grimaced at the room. Billy took in the damage. The bed sat broken on the floor, one corner completely crushed somehow. There were more punctures in the drywall from the spider's talons than Billy cared to count. Both the baseball player and the Shinigami had been torn in half, the lower portions of the posters hanging solemnly from the pins that help them in place. The blades from the fan had snapped off at some point in the fight, the thing swung back and forth slowly. The sword was gone, presumably dissolved like the spider. But the hardest thing for Billy to see was the PC. He knelt next to its remains, picking up the hard drive with the data cable.

"Oh, that's not cool," he sighed sadly. "I can't even recover the case."

"Billy? Who were you talking to just now?" Chris quietly changed the subject. "Was someone else here?"

Billy watched his brother lean against the doorframe, holding his chest. He deliberated telling his brother about the demon bat thing. Could he tell Chris what he'd seen at the game, and then again, right now, just outside his window? Chris had seen the monster in his bedroom, so Chris would reasonably believe he'd seen one earlier that day. *If I can't trust Chris, then what's the point of even trying?*

"Yeah, there was. Outside the window. I think he set this little visit up. But," Billy discarded the hard-drive and stood, the baseball bat still in his hand. He faced his brother. "I'd like to know what you meant when you saw the spider."

Chris glanced at Billy from the corners of his eyes. "I said something?" He gave a half-hearted laugh.

"You said, 'not again.' What did that mean?"

Chris sighed, then winced, pressing two fingers into his ribs. "I'll make you a deal. Let's figure out what the hell we're going to tell Steve, and I'll tell you all about it tomorrow."

Billy wiped the blood from his cheek and groaned at the demolished room. *My foster parents are super cool with stuff like this. Right?* "Maybe I should have let the spider kill me."

4

The Demøn øn the Bus

Billy yawned as he wound his way through the school corridors. Kids scooted aside as they saw his towering form approach through the crowd. He received more than a few wide-eyed looks as passersby saw his bruised and swollen face. Chris had helped him clean and cover the gash, but his black eye was still fully visible. Gauze and adhesive bandages covered his entire left cheek.

Billy turned the corner arriving at his hall. The tall windows to the right wall of the corridor showed the yard to the parking lot by the street in front of the school. The morning sun shone in through, lighting the corridor a brilliant yellow. On the left ran row after row of battered lockers. The fresh coat of paint they'd received at the beginning of the school year wasn't enough to cover the eons of abuse at the hands of careless high school students.

The sound of Billy approaching made Ash-Lea glance up from where she knelt, stuffing books into her locker. Her head whipped around and she sprung to her feet. "What did you do to your face?" she asked, her lips twisting in disgust as she took in Billy's appearance.

"Just wait until you find out, Ashes." Billy removed his backpack, extracted a book and notepaper, and grinned, wincing in pain at the effort. "Ow. Remind me I'm not allowed to smile today."

She slammed her locker closed, scrutinizing Billy through dubious eyes. "Is it *The Fosters*?" she asked in a low voice, using the nick name she'd given Billy's foster parents.

"Oh, geesh. No," Billy said, shouldering his locker door closed over his protruding backpack.

Ash-Lea didn't look convinced. She pulled her black and purple hair over to one side letting it fall in front of one eye. She wore a black shirt with the words "Children should be scene and not herd" written in rainbow letters.

Greyson walked up beside her adjusting his glasses as he studied Billy's injuries. "A bruise like that has either a story you'd want to tell, or a story you don't want anyone to know."

"How about both?" Billy smiled awkwardly with the one, undamaged side of his mouth.

Greyson nodded, but Ash-Lea folded her arms. "Why wouldn't you want to tell us?"

Billy adjusted the books in his hands and laughed humorlessly. "Well, you're going to think I'm crazy."

Ash-Lea glowered. "People don't get to hurt my friends, Billy. If Steve is hitting you I am going to kick his can so hard he'll be using his butt cheeks as ear muffs."

Billy stepped back, a little surprised at her ferocity, and raised his hands. "I have good news. It's not Steve."

Greyson smirked. "His foster father couldn't even reach Billy's face."

"Yeah, well if he does . . ."

"Calm down, Ashes. Look, I'll tell you later. I just can't talk about it in front of—" Billy glanced around at the hundreds of kids walking up and down the hall. "—anyone." The first bell rang and the walking became a bustle.

Ash-Lea folded her arms. "Promise?"

"I promise." Billy crossed his heart, grinning unevenly.

"Well, lead the way. We're late." Ash-Lea gave a gentlemanly bow.

Billy attempted to smile and started down the hall, his friends falling in behind him. Ash-Lea and Greyson always let Billy walk in front and part the crowd for them. The hall was wide and worn, coated in layers of posters that had never been completely removed over the years, full of students elbowing their way to their lessons.

"Tubbers," a jocular voice called.

Patrick and a group of vaguely familiar seniors were walking the opposite direction. Patrick held up his hand for a high-five. Billy reluctantly obliged.

"My man," another senior said.

"Can't wait to see you play Saturday, Tubbers," said a third. "But stick it to the Ponies tonight, okay?" Referring to the Fallingcreek Stallions.

"You know it," Billy called back, not sure what else to say.

"It's so weird that you're cool now," Greyson said when the seniors had passed.

"Tell me about it."

"It's ridiculous," Ash-Lea grumbled. "They don't even care about the real you. All they care about is baseball."

"They're okay," Billy shrugged.

"Look at your face, Billy. They didn't even mention it. It was all about baseball."

"Okay, they're jocks," said Billy, "but they're people, too."

"The jury is still out on that." Ash-Lea gave a knowing look to Billy. "I mean, I want to know about your face."

"Not yet, Ashes."

They walked into the classroom and took their usual seats, one from the back, by the windows. Greyson, then Billy, then Ash-Lea. She kept glaring at him during the class, expecting an explanation, or a note. But this was something Billy did not want to write down. Even if he did write it down, what would he say? Every time he thought about giving in to Ash-Lea's nagging, it ended up just sounding like a joke. There wasn't a way a note could convey 'almost eaten by a giant spider in my bedroom' with the gravity such a statement required.

Even during lunch, Ash-lea pestered him, but Billy didn't give in. By the last period she had started giving him the silent treatment. She scowled her most sincere scowl and turned down the hall to art.

Billy started towards the tall glass doors to join the rest of the baseball team in the parking lot for an away game. His cover story was Billy had come off his bike onto his face, but other than that he was fine. Earlier that day, when Billy had relayed this, Coach Schnurrbart looked at him for a full minute without saying anything, then nodded and walked away. The coach wasn't going to risk losing a game just because Billy could barely see out of one eye. *Priorities, you know.* Billy thought.

"Break a leg," said Greyson.

Billy held up his hands imploringly to his friend, glancing at Ash-Lea as she stalked silently down the hall. "This isn't something I can really say in public. I'm going to tell you guys, I swear."

"I know man, but you know how protective Ashes gets over us."

Billy felt the truth of his statement deep in his chest and smiled. "Yeah."

An unexpected seriousness fell on Greyson and he took a step closer. "Is it *the Fosters?*" he asked quietly.

Billy laughed, as much at the accusation as being reminded that his foster father, Steve, was still drunk-unconscious when Billy and Chris snuck out at four in the morning. His laugh faded into a groan.

"No. I'll come by after the game tonight. I really need to tell you guys about this in private." *And avoiding Steve for a few more hours couldn't hurt.*

"Okay. We'll be at Ashes' place." Greyson nodded understandingly. As if saying, *'Hey, I'm being super cool about this, you know you can tell me, stop avoiding it.'*

"Be there as soon as I can."

Billy stepped through the glass doors into the parking lot. The Devil's baseball team stood around a bright yellow school bus. They wore white and red jerseys, the scowling devil on the front, and suddenly Billy realized the team logo was familiar. His memory flashed to the red, leathery face glaring at him through his bedroom window the night before. He shook the image from his head. *You need to sleep more . . . and get attacked less.*

The team cheered as Billy approached the bus, a reaction he still wasn't used to. The oddest part was the older kids would join in too. Older, smarter, and infinitely more popular than Billy, thought he was cool enough to cheer for.

Nope. I am quite positive I will never get used to that.

Everyone piled onto the bus as the coach confirmed the gear was accounted for and stowed in the underside compartment. The bus shuttered as the driver turned the ignition.

Billy sat near the front next to Mason, a blonde, shy outfielder with long arms, good for throwing. Absentmindedly spinning his baseball glove in his hands, he stared out the window. A hush came over his teammates and Billy instinctively turned his head towards the door.

Then a man in a fedora stepped onto the bus.

Billy gripped the rail in front of him with one hand and crushed his baseball glove with his other. He recognized the face; though not leathery and red as it had been last night through his window. Billy scooted forward in his seat, ready to jump out of the window if a spider or two showed up.

Up close Billy could see the man's outfit more clearly than the way Ash-Lea had described it. It wasn't cheap looking, despite being very outdated. He wore a tan trench coat over a dark suit, a black tie knotted about his neck. He dressed like he had stepped out of the 1930s. He removed his fedora and held it in his hands. The visitor's eyes traced across the expectant students, and finally fell on Billy. The coach followed the man up the stairs.

"Devils," Coach Schnurrbart shouted over the noise of the bustling team. A whistle hung around his wide, muscled neck. His face was worn, wrinkled and dark from spending a lifetime standing outdoors shouting at teenagers. From under his mustache he smiled in a way Billy had rarely seen him smile. He put a hand on the shoulder of the man wearing a fedora.

"This is Mr. Diomed. He's a talent scout for . . ." the name of the university he represented was lost in an explosion of excited talking and murmurs. Someone whistled enthusiastically from the back row. "Guys, guys!" the coach shouted through a laugh. "Guys, he's just coming to see the game and he wanted to ride with us. So, game faces on right now. And keep it P-G in here. Let's show Mr. Diomed that the Devils are savage players and gentlemen to boot."

The team started hooting and chanting the school song. Belle, a grin on her face, shouted in protest at the insistence she be a gentleman.

Mr. Diomed walked directly to Billy and the shouting died down. Of course, he was here for the star player. The brief moment of elation vanished in a sigh of disappointment and understanding. Billy did not miss the glares of displeasure, frustration and out-right anger directed toward him. Belle glowered at him with pure rage etched into her features. *This is not going to work out well for my new-found popularity.*

Mr. Diomed glared at Mason. He looked back, confusion written on his face. "Please vacate your seat," the man rumbled in a deep, rocky voice.

The powerful voice carried through the air, and despite the churning of the bus engine, hit Mason and Billy solidly in the ears. Mason bolted, scrambling into the aisle without even thinking about where he planned to sit.

Mr. Diomed sat down beside Billy. Billy's wide mass spilled onto the seat next to him, but the strange man did not seem to mind.

"William Blacksmith," he began, his voice perfectly clear despite the noise of rowdy high schoolers.

"This is not cool, dude." Billy glanced at the students on the bus. They were all staring daggers at him.

"I'm sorry?" Mr. Diomed raised an eyebrow at Billy.

"Not cool. I don't know what you are. But coming on here pretending to be a talent scout is not helping me make friends."

Mr. Diomed took on an unfriendly, serious expression, his mouth pressed flat. "I must needs speak with thee, I mean, with you."

Billy slapped his knees with both hands. "I'm stuck on this bus for thirty minutes, well played."

Mr. Diomed shifted in his seat and looked Billy squarely in the eyes. "There are matters of immense significance you must understand before it grows too late."

Billy's eyes roved around the bus in mock confusion. "Wait, I think you wanted William-the-guy-that-gives-a-toot. I just want to play baseball. And video games. And eat cupcakes."

"Your human games are of no consequence compared to what I must discuss with thee."

"Human? Okay, there is a good starting point," Billy chuckled. "What are you? I saw you at the baseball game yesterday, and then you stood by while your pet spider tried to eat me. And now you show up on the bus for a chat?"

"Yes, that was I."

"I just want to know when the spiders are going to show up. Because I'm so freakin scared right now and trying to not show it, that I'm laughing." Billy tried to clench his fists, and failed. "So, let's get this over with."

"To what are you referring?"

Billy lowered his eyebrows. "Are you going to kill me or not?"

"What? No. William, you misunderstand. The spider was no pet of mine. I apologize I did not arrive in sufficient time to avoid the destruction of your residence. Antagonizing your caregivers will not make our task any easier."

"It doesn't take much to bother the Fosters, but yeah, I bet they're going to be mad." Billy squinted at Mr. Diomed. "So, you're just planning to kill me yourself?"

Somehow Mr. Diomed found the question funny and snorted. "No, William. I do not intend to kill you."

Billy relaxed a little, but not much. His brain was cartwheeling with questions. "Okay, if you're not going to kill me, will you please call me Billy?"

He eyed Billy for a moment, as if it took time for the request to register. "As you wish, Billy." He nodded.

"So, what are you doing here? You don't like that spiders trashed my room and tried to kill me, and you have something super-duper important to say?" Billy raised both eyebrows and waited.

The man scowled. "Billy. I have found you, thankfully before those that would have you dead succeeded. You are the key to saving this planet from invasion by demonic forces."

Billy laughed and slapped the man on the leg. His laughing faded to a confused *huh?* when he saw the dark gleam in Mr. Diomed's eyes. "Holy cow. You're serious."

"This is most serious. I have been prepared to protect and train you for hundreds of years, before I even understood it was my destiny to do so. The battle for the universe is coming, William. And you must be prepared to win it."

Billy chewed his lip for a minute. The man watched him with deep red eyes that seemed very old, very serious, and very deep. "Dude, I don't have any friends who could be bothered putting in the energy to prank me like this. So, I really think you believe what you're saying. But," he raised his index finger, "you sound insane."

Mr. Diomed furrowed his eyebrows, a twitch of impatience in the corner of one eye. "You saw my true form at the stickball game yesterday, did you not?"

Stickball, ha. "I sure did. You looked like a giant bat with a face."

"How can you doubt me, knowing my power?"

"Fedora Man, I don't know squat about your power. Look at this," Billy waved his hand in front of his large frame. "I don't look like a baseball player, but you know what, it turns out I'm not bad. I don't care about appearances, man."

The man faced the front window. Billy glanced around. The team whispered amongst themselves as they peered at him surreptitiously. Billy wasn't keeping his voice down, but had the impression that nobody understood what they were saying.

"This method of mortal travel is crude. Is it not?" The man shifted uncomfortably in his seat.

Billy shrugged. "I dunno. It's what we have."

"Were you watching me as I departed yesterday?"

Billy nodded.

"I touched the sky and disappeared into it." He waved a hand in front of him in a gesture similar to the one Billy saw the monster make at the game. Billy folded his arms and waited. "And that glove you have in your hand." Billy tried to hold up his baseball glove, but it was no longer in his hand. He looked back up to Mr. Diomed. He now wore the glove, although loosely.

"How did you—" Billy said, impressed despite himself.

"These are just the powers I can show you in front of the other mortals. There are many more I am here to teach you. Many more that you must master."

That I must master? "Why?" Billy said slowly. *Here comes the sales pitch.*

Mr. Diomed watched out the front window again and didn't respond for several minutes. Billy could tell he was sorting silently through some deep thought.

"You could call me a human sympathizer," he said softly.

"A what?"

Mr. Diomed sighed, his voice low, more pensive. "I care about the humans, William. I care what happens to them. And if Aberdem does what he has promised to do, things will not go well for your kind." He met Billy's gaze with a curious look of sincerity in his slightly inhuman eyes.

Aberdem? What the heck is that? First things first. "So, you're telling me you're a good guy?" Billy cocked an eyebrow.

"Yes. At least I'm trying to be. It is not in our nature." He shifted his eyes away from Billy, uncomfortable at the confession.

He gave a pensive 'huh.' "I don't know a thing about where you come from, but doesn't that make you, like, unpopular?"

"I have had to keep my disposition secret from all my acquaintances and kin." Mr. Diomed spoke with a sadness reminiscent of Billy asking his brother Chris about their mom and dad.

"That must suck, dude. So, it's just you?"

"No, there are some who feel the way I do. Those who see humans not as an obstacle to obtaining this realm, but its rightful occupants." He fixed Billy with a serious look. "There are those among you that are indeed far more wicked than my kind. Wickedness which grows from the seed of something as naturally good as a human soul, can become one of the most bitter and vile elements in existence. But despite that there are many, many more that redeem your race. It is they who make humans worth fighting for. It is they who make humans worth saving."

He sighed deeply, looking out the window of the bus into the distance. Although he talked about humans in general, his voice sounded as if he meant someone specific.

"Okay. So, what does this have to do with me?" Billy asked.

Mr. Diomed turned to Billy, deep creases of sadness, sorrow, and weariness carved into a face much older than it looked. "The difference between the annihilation of humans and their survival hinges on your choices, William Blacksmith."

"Huh," Billy scratched the back of his head. "We're screwed."

5

Thanks a Løt, Billy Blacksmith

◆━━━━━━━━━━━━━━━━━━━━━━━━◆

The Bleakwood Devils won. Billy hit another home run, cinching the game eight runs to seven. Mr. Diomed did not ride home on the bus with them. Coach Schnurrbart had no idea where he disappeared to, although Billy suspected he'd split. What Billy didn't understand was why a giant man bat—slash—Indiana Jones hat wearing dude, would care about a high school baseball game—even if they were on a winning streak. Baseball couldn't have anything to do with saving humanity from Billy's choices.

The team arrived at the school and Billy endured the typical cheers and pats on the back, although less enthusiastic as they had been in the past. He hopped on his bike and rode straight to Ash-Lea's house, as promised.

He found Ash-Lea and Greyson in the small back yard as twilight wrapped up and night lay darkness on the world. Ash-Lea glared at him, then returned to her nightly activity of attacking the tree in her backyard with throwing knives. The tall tree was dead, as was the knee-length grass. Ash-Lea's three youngest brothers, Aspen-Cliff, Fir-Bay, and Birch-Dune, were running in circles, screaming louder than Billy thought was possible. The brother just under Ash-Lea and the youngest one were chasing Fir and hitting him with sticks. He swore at them and swung his arms wildly in defense. Music thumped from the other side of the wall where Ash-Lea's two oldest brothers, Hickory-Cay and Hawthorn-Cape, shared a room. One of Ash-Lea's two older sisters, either Maple-Key or Cherry-Pond, shouted something about being on the phone and they'd better turn the asinine music off now. All in all, a typical night at the Greys.

Ash-Lea let loose another throwing knife. It whistled through the air into the innocent tree. Most struck the thick trunk with the handle and bounced away harmlessly. Greyson sat on a cement bench next to the overgrown vegetable garden, more grass than vegetables. Although through the foliage Billy could see a small pumpkin struggling for life. A Castles and Demons book sat perched on Greyson's lap; he waved moths away from his face as they drifted to visit the flood light above his head.

Greyson glanced up at the sound of the closing latch. "The hero returns."

"Sorry to disappoint, it's just me. You guys ready to see how I cut open my face?" Billy smiled, then winced and scratched the bandage over his cheek.

"Sure," said Greyson, closing his book and placing it next to him.

Ash-Lea responded by looking away and viciously throwing another knife. It missed the tree entirely and landed with a *thunk* in the wall of the garage. She let out a frustrated grunt and moved to retrieve the blade.

"Hey, blackheads," Ash-Lea called.

The two youngest brothers in front skidded to a stop, dust rising from around their sneakers. The brother bringing up the rear didn't get the message in time and collided with them. They fell onto the ground in a screaming, swearing, laughing pile. More whacking of sticks followed thereafter.

"Scoot," she demanded.

The brothers extricated themselves, exchanging punches in any attempt to get the last shot in.

"Ash-Lea, mom told us to play outside," Birch whined. He tried to fold his arms and jammed Fir in the face with the stick. Fir snatched the stick and threw it across the yard.

"Then go play in the street. Just scoot." She motioned for them to leave. They looked at each other, then back at their big sister defiant. Standing shoulder to shoulder, each folded their arms accepting the challenge. Adversaries only moments before, now they were united against a common enemy.

Ash-Lea growled and held up the knife in her hand. Her brothers squealed and ran, opening the back door with a bang and disappearing inside where the screaming, and probably hitting, continued. One of the big sisters renewed her insistence that everyone shut-up-for-the-love-of-marmalade-I'm-on-the-phone. She then screamed in frustration and slammed a bedroom door. The back door was left to swing slowly closed on its own.

Billy joined Greyson on the seat and placed his backpack between his feet. He retrieved his camera and turned on the screen. Above being tempted, Ash-Lea resumed attacking the tree with her throwing knives.

Greyson glanced over with interest at the image Billy pulled up, then snatched the camera holding it close to his face. "What the—?"

Ash-Lea looked over, curiosity on her face despite her irritation.

Greyson slowly rose to his feet. "Is that . . . What is that?" He studied Billy's bandage with angled, concerned eyes.

Billy nodded. "That's what it looks like, man. Came into my room last night and attacked me."

"Attacked you?" Ash-Lea strode over and grabbed the camera, a skeptical glower on her face. Her eyes widened as she absorbed in the improbable image on the screen. "That's fake, right?"

"I like a joke, Ashes, but would I joke about this?" He stood, pointing to his PC that lay demolished in the corner of the image.

She stared at him, her mouth slightly open, her face stiff with fear and concern. Every trace of anger toward Billy evaporated. "Are you okay?"

"I'm okay."

Greyson leaned over to peer at the screen once more. "What?"

Ash-Lea grabbed the camera. "Look. Look at this," she pointed to the broken PC.

"Oh, your computer, man." Greyson lamented sympathetically and flashed Billy a frown. He looked at the image again. "That's a real . . . uh . . . spider?"

"I think so. It crawled out from under my bed while I was asleep and told me it wanted to drink my blood." Billy barely believed the words coming out of his own mouth.

"What?" they insisted together.

Ash-Lea's face dropped into an open-mouthed grimace.

"It *told* you it wanted to drink your blood?" Greyson asked. "It spoke to you?"

Billy shrugged. "Yeah. It wasn't a normal spider."

"I'd say." Ash-Lea stared at the camera screen. "What a mess. How did you kill it?"

"I had my bat with me." Billy pointed to his sports bag.

"In bed?" Ash-Lea raised an eyebrow, smiling despite every attempt to keep a serious demeanor. "You two sending out wedding invites any time soon?"

Billy tilted his head towards her. She grinned back.

Billy took a breath, ready to lay it all on them. "No. It's just. Well. That's the other thing—and just hear me out because I'm about to sound really crazy—I met the guy in the fandora."

"Fedora," Greyson corrected. "What does he have to do

with it?" He passed the camera back to Billy, a perplexed look on his face.

Billy felt his thoughts stumble, not sure how to explain Mr. Diomed. Stalling, he put the camera back in his bag.

"He's been following me around. No, not like that." He added, shaking his hands in response to their surprised, disgusted expressions. "He's a bat."

Ash-Lea's face scrunched up with confusion. "Is he the bat you had in bed with you?"

"No." Billy waved his hands at them. "He's like a giant, demonic bat." Billy held his hands out wide to illustrate the size of the thing.

They stared at him, their faces blank.

"Okay. I'll start at the beginning. Do you remember when I missed the ball yesterday?"

"Sure, yeah," they said.

"It's because I saw Mr. Diomed in the stands." Billy groaned in frustration. It made no sense.

Ash-Lea narrowed her eyes until she was practically squinting. "A man in a fedora made you miss the ball for the first time since I've seen you start playing baseball?"

Billy ignored the ripe skepticism with a sigh. "Yes, but when I saw him he didn't look like a man in a fedora. He was a dude with dark, red skin, almost black. And he had these gigantic wings. Like one of them would reach from here to the back of your neighbor's house." He waved his arms beside him in a feeble approximation of a bat flapping.

Ash-Lea frowned at Greyson, her eyebrows pressed low over her eyes. "So, he looked like a giant man-bat to you, but a regular guy in a fedora to us?"

"I told you it would sound crazy, but I am not kidding about this." He shook the camera at them.

Ash-Lea and Greyson considered the camera, then they looked at each other.

"It seems pretty legit," Ash-Lea twisted her mouth and shrugged.

"I would have to concur," said Greyson. "So, you were really attacked by a giant spider last night?"

"Scout's honor." Billy held up a three-fingered salute, despite never actually attending boy-scouts.

"And this Mr. Diomed guy," Ash-Lea began, "looks like Indiana Jones in a trench coat to us, but a giant bat to you?"

"Yes. Most of the time. He kind of went to our game today and we talked."

"A giant bat that likes baseball." Ash-Lea amended, sounding as if she were a zoologist discovering a new species.

"He said it wasn't about baseball. He said I'm supposed to save mankind." Billy's voice dropped away, embarrassed.

Ash-Lea glanced over her shoulders as if he had to be talking to someone else. Seeing no one there, she looked back at Billy, and then busted up laughing. The laughter continued as she fell to the ground holding her sides, an expression close to pain on her face as she gasped for air.

Greyson turned to Billy, ignoring his friend writhing on the ground beside him. "This is all pretty farfetched, man. I don't think you're lying, but it's hard to believe."

Billy held up his hands, helpless. "I know. I don't know if I believe it. But I know what I saw. I'll see if I can get him to come over and do the bat thing for you." He felt bad for springing the offer of having a man-bat over for tea on him.

Greyson absorbed the suggestion for a moment, his eyes wide. "Okay." His mouth pressed in a tight frown. "Just be careful. Lots of creeps out there."

"I know." Billy shook his head. "But this is . . . not that."

"Can I have a copy of that picture?" Greyson asked.

"Sure," said Billy. "Just need a Wi-Fi connection. What are you going to do with it?"

A bashful smile found its way onto Greyson's face. "At the risk of sounding as nuts as you do, I think I recognize that thing."

Billy felt a small amount of crazy dissipate. "Really? From where?"

Greyson picked up his Castles and Demons Manual. "In one of these."

Ash-Lea started laughing again. "You guys. I love you guys." She struggled to speak through fits of laughter.

"That's cool." Billy ignored his friend convulsing in hysterics at his feet.

"Yeah. Maybe the Mages of the Ocean were on to something." Greyson bobbed the manual in his hands.

"Who?"

"The guys that publish these books. Maybe the monsters are not as made up as we think they are. What if they actually know about spiders and fedora wearing man-bats." Greyson shrugged. "Worth considering."

"Couldn't hurt." Billy nodded vigorously, feeling encouraged.

Ash-Lea managed to pull herself to her feet. "Oh, I don't know, boys," she said, draping an arm around Greyson for support, her breathing finally returning to normal. "If you guys keep me laughing like this, I'm going to need to be attacked by giant spiders, because you are killing me."

They spent the evening talking about school and homework, Mr. Diomed, destroyed PCs, and the possible reactions of foster parents to demolished rooms. Ash-Lea passed the time throwing knives at the tree, and even managing to land one good hit. They agreed tomorrow evening they would convene at Greyson's house, this would allow them an opportunity to dig through his piles of Castles and Demons manuals. Greyson mentioned something about needing to cut up the old manuals for the Diorama contest; which was all well and good, assuming Billy's foster parents didn't disembowel him before then.

Ash-Lea finally stopped her laughing and finished out the evening looking at Billy with concern. Not like she thought he was crazy, but because she didn't believe he was safe.

It was just before eleven when Billy decided to go.

"No more giant spider attacks, okay?" Ash-Lea insisted. Billy side-hugged her in thanks. "And watch out for strangers. You don't know what this Mr. Diomed really wants."

Aint that the truth. "Thanks, Ashes." Billy said as he mounted his bike and pedaled into the darkness.

He wasn't supposed to stay out late, but he was okay avoiding The Foster's for as long as possible. He was not looking forward to their reaction to his demolished room.

Tightly gripping the handlebars, he flew around the corner and onto the main road. He loved riding late at night, racing down roads that were just his. The cool wind tugged at his t-shirt, chilling his chest and clearing his mind. His friends had taken the news better than he could have hoped. Perhaps they were just patronizing him, but the way Greyson studied the picture seemed to be more than just protecting Billy's feelings. Greyson said he recognized the creature. Billy found that both heartening, and a little disturbing. Then again, maybe Greyson was just as crazy as him.

Billy glided onto his street, enjoying the freedom of a quiet night. But as his house came into view he felt his throat grow dry. He brought his bike to a slow stop, feet resting on the asphalt as he watched. Something was happening, and he did not like the looks of it.

Chris' truck sat parked on the front lawn. Steve stood by the door, beer in hand, watching Chris carry an armful of clothes and dump it in the back of the truck. Steve still wore his work boots and coveralls, the words SENIOR SUPERVISOR printed in large letters across the left breast pocket.

Billy pushed on the pedals and was on the grass in a few seconds. He was talking before anyone knew he was there.

"What's happening? Chris?" Billy cut Steve off when he opened his mouth to respond. "What do you think you're doing?"

"Moving out, little guy," Chris said as he finished arranging something in the bed of his truck. He jumped down to the grass.

Billy felt his palms chill with sweat, the skin on his neck grew tight. *This cannot be happening.*

"He's twenty, Billy. We should have kicked him out two years ago. We had no legal reason to keep him around. Obviously, that was a mistake." Steve spoke with a wet smile on his face, relishing each word.

"But you can't . . . just . . . make him leave his home." Billy held out one helpless hand towards the house.

"This ain't your home, Billy, you just live here." Steve took another swig.

Belinda stormed through the front door wearing loose track pants and a pink sleeveless sleepshirt. She started speaking loudly, unconcerned about where the current conversation might be. "What on bleeding earth did you do to my grandmother's desk? I let you borrow that desk, and now it's *destroyed.*" She cupped her hands before her, as if holding a dead body. "You are paying for that, William."

"Belinda," Chris said in a calm voice, edged with tension, "I said I'd replace it."

"My Grandmother's desk, Chris. How are you going to replace that? I want him," she pointed to Billy, "to pay for it himself. I don't know what you two think you were doing last night, but you will pay for all the damages. It looks like you let a giant animal loose in there."

"Funny you should say that," said Billy, nodding and holding his hands up in explanation.

Steve pointed his beer at Billy. "None of your cheek, kid. So, that's what's happening, Billy. Chris here has to move out tonight, and you have to replace everything in there that's broken."

"You can't make him leave." Billy shook with the fear running under his skin.

"They can, Billy. They have no legal obligation to me. They really had no reason to let me keep living there." Chris stepped towards Billy and gripped his shoulder.

"Damn right, we didn't. And this is how you repay us for letting you two stay together." Belinda said quickly, her words blending together with frustration.

"Then why did you let him stay, huh?" Billy blurted, his anger overriding his commonsense.

"Because we actually *like* Chris," Belinda spat. "He's quiet, respectful, tidy. Then there's you. Trashing your room, and my grandmother's desk." At the last words her bottom lip shook and she visibly forced back tears.

Billy faced Chris, trying to keep the bubbling sense of hopelessness he felt inside from making him cry. "But what about me? I need you around."

Belinda hissed. "You should have thought about that before you two went disco-dancing in your room. We can't have him around when you encourage him like that."

"Where are you going?" Billy turned his back on Belinda and looked at the half-full truck bed.

"Tonight? I'll sleep in my truck tonight. I have a good enough job. I'm sure I can find a place tomorrow. As soon as I do I'll let you know so you can come live with me."

If ditching Steve and Belinda was an option, maybe this would turn out to be a good thing.

"Sorry, buddy," Belinda's head pivoted on her neck, moving side to side and she waggled a finger at Chris. "Billy is still our legal dependent. You take him and we'll call the cops for kidnapping."

She jabbed a finger at Billy, the ends of her t-shirt swirling with the movement. "You leave and we'll have you jailed for running away."

Billy wasn't sure it worked like that, but he didn't want to test the theory, at least not without researching it first.

Chris stepped towards her. "Then I'll file to have him made my legal dependent."

"Good luck with that," Steve smirked. "We'll fight you the whole way."

Billy's heart sunk to his shoes. "Why would you do that to me?"

Belinda held a hand in the general direction of Billy's room. "Why would you do that to us? You're not leaving until you fix that room. I have a feeling it's going to take a long time. Until then, you can sleep on the couch."

"On the couch?" Billy complained. He'd fallen to sleep on the couch once before. It wasn't long enough for him. He'd bruised his scalp on the armrest, and the sprain in his neck didn't ease up for a week.

"Yes, on the couch," Belinda said, "and you should be thanking us for that. We should make you sleep in the garage, the way you treat our home."

"Not next to the Tahoe, he's not." Steve took a pull from his beer and threw the empty bottle in the back of Chris' truck. He put an arm around Belinda. "You know, you should thank us. Thank us for not calling the foster association. Thank us that you still have a place to sleep tonight."

They both stood in front of Billy, expectant, unpleasant scowls on their faces. It took Billy a moment to realize that they actually wanted a thank-you, as if they deserved one after he'd saved them from being eaten by a giant spider.

Billy balled his fists, then felt a gentle hand on his shoulder.

"Hey, big guy." Chris shook his head once and glanced at Billy's fists. "Don't worry about it. We'll get this figured out. Just hang tight and I'll talk to a lawyer."

"Well?" Steve said sharply.

Billy glared at his foster parents. He breathed slowly, deliberately. Finally, he growled through clenched teeth, "Thank you for letting me sleep on the couch."

Belinda barked out a laugh and walked inside. Steve followed.

Chris put his arms around Billy. He forced down the tears threatening to erupt and swore at himself for being so stupid. He felt like a dumb, powerless kid.

"We'll get this taken care of. I'm just going to be a little further away than down the hall. This is stupid as hell. But the way that room looks, you're lucky they didn't call the cops."

The injustice of the thought filled him with frustration, he felt his fists shaking. "I hate them," Billy whispered.

"I know. Just hang in there. It could be worse."

"But it's not even my fault."

"I know," Chris held Billy a little tighter.

After a long moment, Billy stepped away from his brother, wiped his face on his sleeve and smiled. When he spoke, it was loud and light. "You're becoming a softy."

"It's my old age." Chris laughed once, showing his teeth. He then winced and put a hand up to his ribs.

Billy started inside. "Come on, I'll help you carry your stuff so you can get out of my house."

6

Keep Your Enemies Close

B illy gripped the small desk and leaned his head to the side until he felt his neck pop. Mr. Strict—or more commonly referred to as *The Strictmeister*—explained how numbers could equal letters, or something like that. Ash-Lea sat at the desk next to Billy. Today she'd gone with jeans and a t-shirt depicting a space elf. Underneath the pointy-eared face were the words, "Prosperity and Long Life." She looked at him quizzically and pointed to her neck. Billy sighed and shrugged. She raised her eyebrows and continued staring at him.

He leaned toward her, the small desk restricting his movement. "The Fosters taped off my bedroom and made me sleep on the couch. It's not exactly big enough for me. Think I hurt my neck again." He rubbed the aching muscles ineffectually.

"Billy," the Strictmeister snapped, pointing a red marker at him.

"Sorry, sir," he said, shifting uncomfortably in his too-small desk. A portion of one of his buttocks hung off the seat and he could see his knees protruding from the other side. He felt ridiculous.

Ash-Lea clenched her jaw and shook her head. This latest development had not improved her opinion of his foster parents. Once the Strictmeister started writing on the board, she leaned over, whispering, "What are you going to do to make back the money from the damages?"

Billy felt his stomach knot at the reminder. He groaned. "I don't know. Get a job, I guess."

"You're fifteen," she reminded him quietly.

Greyson, dressed as neat as his mother made him, shot them both a warning look from the other side of Ash-Lea. He liked math and he liked the Strictmeister. Billy and Ash-Lea ignored him.

Billy gripped the desk as hard as he could, trying to contain his frustration. "I'm doomed. It's not even fair. It's not like I invited that spider to attack me." The tabletop cracked with a sharp pop, Billy let go, alarmed.

"I know, right?" Ash-Lea whispered, apparently oblivious to Billy's accidental vandalism.

"Hey," Greyson leaned towards them, seeing the teacher's back turned to the whiteboard. "You guys coming over to help me with my diorama tonight, right?"

Ash-Lea shot him an incredulous look. Greyson was far too excited about the diorama competition. Billy suspected it had less to do with the chosen topic—Castles and Demons, of course—and more about how Quinn the Cheerleader was one of the judges.

"I'll come over and help right after school," said Billy.

"No baseball tonight?" he looked surprised.

Billy shook his head. "Not tonight."

Ash-Lea flipped him two thumbs up. "Count me in."

Greyson beamed at them.

"Now, Greyson," Mr. Strict said gently. "Please keep your eyes up front."

"Yes, sir." Greyson swallowed, his eyes wide with fear that he'd just been busted talking in class. He glared at Ash-Lea, eyebrows lowered, as if the reproach was her fault. She smirked in response.

Waiting until the teacher faced the whiteboard again, Billy leaned in. "The Fosters told me I have to go home first. Something about the room."

Ash-Lea curled her lip in distaste and grumbled with empathy. "That's going to suck."

Billy furrowed his brow. "Thanks for the encouragement."

"Now, does anyone know where Katy is today?" the Strictmeister asked, noting that the end of the school day was fast approaching. Nobody raised their hands. "Susan, you're friends with her right?"

Susan, a gangly girl with thin brown hair nodded. "Yessir."

"Will you please make sure she gets the homework assignment?" he handed an extra packet to her.

The bell rang and everyone moved.

"Homework, homework, homework," the Strictmeister said, tapping the place on the whiteboard where he'd written the assignment.

"Diorama, diorama, diorama," Greyson sung to Billy and Ash-Lea. "One must have one's priorities straight."

"I thought you liked math homework," Billy said.

Greyson shrugged. "I do. I did all the exercises in the book last summer. You know, just in case something important, like a diorama contest, came up."

Ash-Lea stood, swinging her backpack over her shoulder. "That is the most hardcore nerd thing you have ever done, Grey. And you're obsessed with Castles and Demons."

Greyson beamed. "Thank you."

Ash-Lea snorted. "But do you really think Quinn is going to care about your diorama?"

"If she didn't care, why would she sign up to run it?" Greyson stared at Ash-Lea, his logic obviously infallible.

She put her hands on her hips. "Because she likes it when people look at her, and it gives her an opportunity to talk in front of the school. She is a year ahead of us, man, give it up."

"Never!" Greyson declared, raising a defiant fist above his head.

"Hey, that's another kid out," Billy said as they shuffled through the crowd into the hall. "Whatever is going around must be bad."

People bustled past them, Ash-Lea and Greyson filed in behind Billy. Ash-Lea took a fistful of his shirt to avoid being swept away.

"But if there's some bug going around town you'd think we would have heard about it." Greyson pulled up short to avoid being trampled by a pair of girls running past them.

Ash-Lea stopped walking and tugged on Billy's shirt. He looked down at her. "What if it's not a bug?" She nodded toward the lobby.

A group of police officers stood at the end of the hall, talking to the Principal and several other teachers. A flood of students poured around the adults to the parking lot. More police officers were walking down the hall handing out fliers.

One approached Ash-Lea and handed her a sheet of paper. She started reading it as they walked. "Warning. Residents of Bleakwood Vale. A suspected predator is on the loose in your area. Almost thirty people have been reported missing in the last seventy-two hours. Please be vigilant . . . it goes on. Not much more detail."

"Thirty people?" Greyson choked on the question. "I guess there is something going around."

"Holy crap. I've never even heard of something like this. How do you make thirty people disappear?" Ash-Lea asked.

Students and teachers stood in clumps, talking with a loud excitement. Billy heard the words 'thirty people' and 'three days' repeated over and over. Susan ran past, Katy's homework clutched to her chest, a desperate look in her eye.

"We should get out of here," Billy said.

"Are we still on for tonight?" Greyson asked, his voice dropping in embarrassment.

Ash-Lea crumpled up the paper and threw it in a trashcan as they passed through the lobby doors to the front lawn. "Why not? No need to stop living."

Greyson's mouth pulled into a frown, his eyes worried. "Don't you think it's a little dangerous?"

"I'll protect you, Grey." Ash-Lea patted him on the shoulder. "Billy, you go get your butt kicked by your foster parents. We'll get a head start on this lovebird's completely foolproof attempt at winning the attention of a bimbo."

"You don't give her enough credit," Greyson said quietly.

"Yeah, yeah," Ash-Lea said through the shadow of a kind smile on her lips.

They walked to the bike racks. Billy knelt to unlock his before noticing the three police cruisers parked in front of the school. More police officers stood by the busses counting the students as they climbed aboard. They were taking the disappearances seriously.

"See you guys tonight," Billy said as he unchained his bike and mounted.

"Don't be sad," Greyson added.

"Don't feel bad," Ash-Lea clicked her tongue, winked, and pointed her fingers.

He smiled and waved goodbye over his shoulder.

Billy barely paid attention to the routine ride home, he usually made it home without incident. He bounced up on to the sidewalk and leaned into the turn heading toward the park. He rode his bike through the park every day, but this time he felt a cold shiver run down his spine. For some reason that he could not put his finger on, something was off. Billy rode to the fountain in the middle and stopped, taking in the still park around him. The warm breeze smelled like spring, the birds in the trees were . . . missing, now that he thought about it. In fact, there was no sound of wildlife in the entire park. He couldn't even hear a dog barking. In the pond around the fountain the fish pressed in a tight clump on the far side, desperately avoiding something.

"Super weird," Billy said to himself, as he mounted his bike again.

Heavy footsteps approached him from behind, coming from the opposite direction to the clump of fish. A tall, oddly shaped shadow appeared over him, spreading across the water and the fish started to freak out. They began jumping, trying to escape onto the pavement. Billy's stomach dropped into his feet.

Billy turned around very slowly. The bat creature from the bleachers loomed over him; his massive wings were folded and towered over his head, adding three feet to his appearance. He must have been at least ten feet tall.

Billy's knees started to shake; a small wheezing noise escaped his throat.

"William," it said in a deep, almost familiar voice.

Despite having heard this creature speak before, the magnitude of the sound startled him. Billy leapt from his bike, jumping backwards and swearing in surprise. His bike clattered to the concrete.

"Dude," Billy exclaimed, he continued stepping away from the . . . *demon*. No better word could describe him.

The thing held out a huge, viciously clawed hand in a gesture that was probably supposed to be reassuring. "I apologize. I did not mean to alarm you."

"Dude," Billy said again, taking another step back and clenching his fists in front of him. "You here to eat me?"

"I'm sorry?" the creature asked, looking genuinely confused. "William, you have no reason to fear me. I am an ally. We have discussed this."

"Okay. Okay." Billy put his hands on his knees and took a deep breath. "You're just, you know." He straightened and took in the thing from head to heal. "You look like a horrifying nightmare ready to peel off my skin. It's not something I'm going to get used to very quickly. If ever."

"I shall attempt to announce my presence in the future," his voice rumbled, flowing over Billy, penetrating the afternoon air like arrows.

Billy shuddered, trying to control the terror coursing through him. "Not sure that's going to help. We'll just have to work on it."

"As you wish." The thing nodded and folded its ridiculously muscled arms.

Billy looked up at the creature, a *real* good look close up. His proportions were normal, by human standards. Crimson skin stretched tight over his body. Despite his bald head, Billy was surprised to find his face could be considered handsome. A grey shirt and black cloth pants lay loose on his frame, tied with a length of black rope. On his feet he wore black leather sandals, belted up around his ankles. Again the word *demon* came to mind, but the thing didn't appear exactly how the stories had told him it should. This one, for starters, did not have any horns on his head.

"Okay, first things first," Billy said, craning his neck to look at the demon's face. "What's your real name?"

He grinned, showing a mouth full of white, sharp teeth. "Is Mr. Diomed not acceptable?"

Billy inclined his head. "It's obviously fake."

"Not entirely. Diomed is a title I have earned in my order," it explained.

"Order? You belong to like a demonic country club or something?" Billy shook his hands in a 'hold-up' gesture. "Okay, one thing at a time. What's your name?"

"My name is Selanthiel."

Billy smirked. "Selanthiel, huh? Can I call you Selly?"

The demons face darkened and he took a step towards Billy. "If you refer to me as Selly again, I shall tear your arms off, shove them down your throat, and make your own hands choke you to death."

"Oh, em." Billy coughed. "We'll put Selly in the 'maybe' pile."

"You may call me Seth."

Billy picked up his bike and leaned it against the fountain, then removed his helmet.

"So, Seth, I know your name. Secondly, and it should have been first now I think about it. Why is it okay for you and your ten-foot-self to be standing in the middle of my park in broad daylight?"

"I appear to you in my true form," Seth said, matter-of-fact.

"Okay, I've got that. But won't that scare the crap out of the locals?" Billy indicated the nearby swing set, then the road on which cars could clearly be seen driving. "I know it scared the hell out of me. And I know you're supposed to be a good guy." *I hope.*

"Do not interrupt," Seth glowered at Billy.

Billy raised his hands. "Geesh, kay."

"I appear to you in my true form, but to others I will appear as a man."

Billy squinted and looked at Seth. "So, are you just an illusion, or something?"

"No, I am truly here." His voice was gruff, and Seth sneered. Billy could tell he was becoming frustrated that he wasn't keeping up with the demon's oblique explanation.

"So, what form are you really in?"

A puzzled expression crossed the demon's face. "I do not understand."

Billy counted off the options on his fingers. "Are you actually a dude but just look like a bat, or are you really a bat and just look like a dude?"

"Dude?" Seth asked before his face lit up in recognition. "Ah. I am both."

Billy shook his head. "Now you've lost me."

"I am what I appear to be."

"To who?"

"To whomever I appear to." Seth grit his teeth.

"So, you're actually a ten-foot-tall bat?" Billy finally understood.

Seth took a deep breath. "I am as I appear to you."

"Okay, so you're actually here and you look like a ten-foot-tall bat-dude. But, back to my original question, won't that bother people walking through the park?"

Seth shook his head. "No, because I appear to them as a man."

Billy's head spun. He raised his hands and pressed his fingers into his temples. "And the man thing is an illusion and you're actually ten feet tall?"

"I am both." Seth explained, his voice rising as he repeated himself.

"How?"

Realization spread across Seth's face and he smiled. "Ah, human. I do not think you could comprehend how. I will explain it like this. If a mortal man saw me as a man, and another mortal man saw me in my true form and both thrust a sword through my head at the same moment, their blades would both run through my head."

Billy watched the fountain as he absorbed Seth's words. "So, you are literally both people at the same time?"

"Yes," Seth said.

Billy scratched the back of his head as he eyed the giant demon. "You're right. I have no idea how that works, but it's probably the coolest thing I've ever heard."

Seth smiled with one side of his mouth.

Billy put his hands on his hips. "Next, what is this 'Order' you mentioned?"

Seth's smile widened and he sat on the side of the fountain. The fish, which had calmed down, suddenly panicked again and renewed their attempts to escape. "We are an alliance formed in the interest of protecting the humans against those who would see you destroyed or enslaved."

"Why?" Even with his limited exposure to the demonic, that sounded unlikely.

"It is the nature of my kind to destroy, to hate, to make others miserable." Billy forced himself to keep a neutral expression on his face. He was pretty sure he failed. "But for some of us that is not appealing. We believe humans have a right to be here. As much a right as do we. We believe you should be permitted to enjoy your love and relationships."

Billy shook his head at the demon. "But what makes the members of your club different from the rest of your kind?"

"We were born and raised as any demonic being. But we reached a point in our lives where we lost the satisfaction that hurting mankind once gave." He looked at his hands, remembering something that he did not say—his mother's gourmet sandwiches, perhaps.

Billy watched Seth, he could see his mind working, thinking about things that he did not want to share. Seth hid many things behind his demon eyes. What goes on in a demon's mind, in their heart? What kind of things would a demon care about; or give up to be here, talking with a human, encouraging him to save the world? *And what is the catch?*

Billy shifted uncomfortably, not sure if he should sit or stand. Or run. "What made you change your mind?"

Seth glanced at Billy before looking at the ground in front of him. "Perhaps someday I will show you." Seth stopped talking and stared into the distance.

Billy felt more horror course through him than when the spider appeared in his room. *If the demon starts talking about his feelings, I'm out of here.* "Why do I have to wait?"

Seth peered into Billy's eyes, his face solidifying into a somber expression. "I need to know if I can trust you."

"Trust me?" Billy choked on the words, and almost laughed.

"You have the demon blood, William. But that does not make you a good person. We must see if you are capable of controlling it." He placed his hands on his knees, raising his eyebrows and inclining his head. "The Demonseed have let us down in the past."

"Demonseed? Demon blood?"

Seth shook his head, an exhausted expression crossing his face. "There will be time for that later."

"You think I'm supposed to be able to save the world, right?" Billy casually kicked a loose rock on the ground. It bounced off the fountain and spun away across the concrete. "What happens if I'm not? What's your plan B?"

Seth stared into Billy's face, resolution shone in his large, red eyes. "There is no contingency, William. If our training is not successful, the world will fall and burn, as will all mankind. Though I may not have been clear earlier. This world is the first of many. If we fail it is not simply Earth at stake, all the universe will be at the mercy of ravenous and evil wills." He clenched his fists, and it sounded like the limbs of trees creaking in a gale of wind. "I am not willing to risk *this* world, William Blacksmith. We will not fail."

Billy felt the gravity in his voice. "Pretty attached to it?"

"Indeed." Seth rose. His wings expanded behind him, effortlessly spreading through the air and throwing a shadow across Billy. He flapped them once and Billy had to brace himself against the wind produced by the movement.

A thought, or more of an instinctual impulse, occurred to Billy. "Hey, you wouldn't happen to know anything about people going missing lately?"

"Missing?" the demon asked, interest and concern coloring his voice. "No. Are there a substantial amount of people missing in this area?"

"There are."

The demon's face took on a meditative look. "That is troubling. There are many reasons why humans go missing, William. Let me think on that, and see if my associates can help me ascertain what, if anything, is happening."

"Thanks. So, hey, why are you sneaking up on me in the park? They make us watch videos on this sort of thing in school, you know." He took in Seth's giant, demonic, appearance again. "Sort of."

Seth raised his chin importantly. "I am here to begin your training. We are to start immediately."

"Not tonight, I have plans." Billy clipped on his helmet and mounted his bike once more.

Seth sneered, fury in his eyes. A growl emanated from the being's throat, vibrating the ground in such a way that Billy felt it through his shoes. "I have crossed planes of existence to be here. I am risking my life to speak with you. Have I not made myself clear on the importance of your training?"

"Sure," Billy said, holding out his hands, palms up. "But I've got plans tonight."

"Plans?" Surprise barely began to explain the wide-eyed look the demon gave. His arms trembled from tension.

Billy looked at Seth's clenched fists. The thick, red skin had nothing but tight muscles and hard bones underneath. He swallowed, but continued. "I promised Greyson I'd help him with his diorama. I was supposed to go home first, but I would not mind accidentally forgetting about that. You know, I wanted them to meet you, so you can come along."

Billy made to begin pedaling again, but stopped as Seth stepped in front of him.

"Excuse me?" the demon growled with a deafening rumble, his voice sounding as if it echoed off the very air.

"I want you to meet my friends." Billy ignored the weakness in his knees at Seth's sudden anger. He craned his neck to see Seth. His red lips were drawn back in a furious scowl, revealing a surprisingly well-maintained mouth of teeth. That did not stop Billy from trembling all over.

Seth pursed his lips then spoke slowly. "Have you been advertising my presence to your companions?"

Billy pushed out his bottom lip and shrugged. "Well, sure."

"Is that wise? Are you sure you can trust them?" Seth's eyebrows creased into tight leathery lines. He leaned closer, sneering.

The accusation made Billy forget his fear for a second. He gave Seth a square look and pointed at him. "That's a dumb question. I wouldn't be friends with them if I didn't."

Seth closed his eyes, containing a rage Billy was sure would end with him on a milk carton. He took a long, deep breath before he spoke. "If I find that any of the humans you have told are threatening our purpose here, I will destroy them."

Billy started pedaling across the park as quickly as he could, without looking like he was fleeing—which he was. He called over his shoulder to the giant, furious being. "That's cool. I have no problem with that." Billy stopped and peered over his shoulder. "You any good with a pair of scissors?"

7

Diørama-rama

◆————————————————————◆

The diorama-rama was in full swing when Billy arrived at Greyson's hundred-roomed mansion. Billy walked inside the wide, glass paned door without knocking. His shoes echoed on the tile as he stepped into the entrance. A long, curving stairway greeted visitors immediately upon entering. White, French doors lead into Greyson's dad's office on the right, although Billy had never seen Greyson's father use it. To the left, a large formal dining room lay untouched, two chandeliers hung over a dark wood table. Billy didn't think he'd ever stepped foot in that room, either.

He wandered through the entrance, down the short hall under the stairs to the gigantic room that took up the back of the house. An entire wall of windows displayed a gorgeous backyard. A rock waterfall cascaded into the swimming pool, lit by underwater lights, casting endlessly rippling shadows on the roof high above Billy's head.

Greyson sat on the couch set before the stone fireplace, two separate piles of books at his feet. Ash-Lea sat cross-legged on the plush carpet before the glass coffee table, the frame of the diorama before her. An open Castles and Demons book lay next to her, a twisting hole in the page where the image of some monster had been cut out.

Greyson's mother—who insisted they call her Meredith—hummed happily behind a grey granite island, a vast array of shiny pots and pans suspended from a stained wood rack above her head. She was busy working over a tray of something that smelled sweet and chocolatey. An apron with frills around the edge covered her simple, but obviously expensive, jeans and a t-shirt. She was good-looking for an older woman, with silver streaks coolly accenting her dark hair.

"Hey," Ash-Lea and Greyson said when Billy entered, only sparing him a glance.

Greyson's mother walked through the kitchen and into the living area, two tall glasses on the tray she carried. "Chocolate milk," she sing-songed. "Oh, I'm sorry Billy, I didn't know you were here. My, what happened to your eye, and . . ." She froze in place as she saw the man behind him, a scrutinizing expression lowering her face. The glasses wobbled precariously on the tray. "Who is your friend?"

Greyson and Ash-Lea's heads whipped up at the interrogative.

"Fedora Man," Ash-Lea growled accusingly.

Mr. Diomed stepped into the room and removed his hat. "Evening madam."

"Hi, I'm Meredith," she said cautiously as she placed the tray on the infantile diorama and extended a hand.

Mr. Diomed paused, as if trying to remember what to do in this situation. He finally extended his hand. "The honor is mine. And might I say you have a lovely home." He kissed her fingers gently.

Meredith blushed and placed her free hand on her chest. "Oh my, what manners."

"A little out of date, maybe," Ash-Lea said under her breath. Meredith didn't notice.

Ash-Lea stood and took a few steps towards the newcomer, her eyes focused on him like a laser sight. Billy had to get Ash-Lea out of there, before she started drilling Mr. Diomed in front of Meredith. And that felt like a bad idea.

"Guys, let's get some fresh air," Billy suggested.

"Great idea." Ash-Lea sounded like a woman presented with a challenge, more than one who thought it was a great idea.

"Oh, but what about the chocolate milk?" Meredith protested.

"We'll be right back, mom." Greyson snapped his book closed and stood.

Meredith gave a strained smile to Mr. Diomed. "Can I get you anything, Mister—"

"Diomed," he responded.

"Mr. Diomed. Would you like something to drink?" Meredith started walking back into the kitchen.

"Water will be fine, thank you."

"Backyard," Ash-Lea insisted as she walked toward the back door.

"Should I bring it out?" Meredith asked, her eyes tracking Mr. Diomed as he headed towards the back.

"Just leave it on the table," Greyson called as he stood and followed Ash-Lea.

Billy shot an apologetic smile at Meredith. She watched mutely as the Mr. Diomed walked out the back door, a look of unease stretching her lips.

They made the trek around the pool to the grassy knoll behind the waterfall. White string lights stretched across the underside of the awnings giving the scene a soft yellow radiance. A small pavilion stood beyond the large trees, bulb lights hung suspended from short chains, coloring the trees and grass a warm, subdued glow. They stopped in the center of the yard—a small, neatly cut circle of grass, boarded by low cut hedges.

"These two were present at the stickball game." Mr. Diomed looked between Greyson and Ash-Lea. "They are the human companions you spoke of?"

"They sure are," Ash-Lea confirmed, her hands on her hips.

Mr. Diomed gave Ash-Lea and Greyson a narrow glare as if he were dissecting them. "And you can trust them?"

"With my life," Billy said simply.

Greyson glanced between Billy and Mr. Diomed, his fingers twitching anxiously. Ash-Lea crossed her arms and tapped her foot. She did not take her eyes from Mr. Diomed's face. Billy caught the glint of a throwing knife in her hand, partially concealed by her arm.

"Humans," Mr. Diomed began. "It was never my intention to involve any mortal in this, other than the Demonseed. However, he has chosen you as his trusted companions. As a member of The Blacksmith Guard, I can understand the importance of companionship and love. I know what it means to have a friend. However," he gave Ash-Lea a disapproving tilt of his head, then moved his gaze purposefully to Greyson, "you betray this knowledge, and you will be destroyed."

In a rush of wind, Mr. Diomed disappeared and Seth, in his true form, erupted from the image, his wings unfolding, filling the whole back yard. Greyson squeaked and fell to the ground. Ash-Lea ducked and leapt backwards, the knife flying from her hand. It struck Seth's flesh, only the smallest fraction of the blade keeping it in place.

Billy stood his ground, suspecting the demon had some supernatural showboating in mind. He muted the surprise on his face and swallowed nervously.

The demon eyed Ash-Lea's blade, plucked it from his skin and offered it to her, handle first. "Already I see the value that William places in your friendship." The demon smiled.

Ash-Lea took the knife, staring at the face towering above her, and laughed once, although nervously. "William. Heh. I think I might learn to like this guy."

A whimpering sound from the ground caught their attention and everyone looked down to see Greyson on the grass. He leaned back on one elbow, his other arm held protectively in front of his face. "You're a, you're a . . ."

"Yes, little human?" Seth's voice rumbled. "What am I?"

"Po . . . Popobawa. A bat demon."

Seth nodded. "I am related to the Popobawa, but I am not Popobawa."

"No," Greyson panted. "Your face is . . . like . . . normal."

"Indeed," Seth said, almost laughing.

The backdoor opened. "Chocolate milk is ready, Billy. Mr. Diomed, your water," Meredith called.

Ash-Lea and Greyson reacted immediately.

"No, Mom."

"Go inside."

They shouted over each other.

Billy and Seth laughed.

"What are you guys up to?" Meredith asked playfully, squinting to see them in the dim light across the pool. "Greyson, dear. Why are you on the grass? You're going to get stains on your pants."

"It's okay guys," Billy whispered. "He looks normal to her."

"Geeze," Ash-Lea sighed in relief.

"I'm just relaxing mom." Greyson adjusted himself into a comfortable-looking position. "Go on in. We'll be right there." Meredith raised an eyebrow, shook her head, and disappeared behind the door. A moment later she appeared at the large windows, trying to squint through. Greyson looked back to Billy. "So, it's an illusion?"

"Nope. I'll explain later. Just as soon as I understand it."

Seth offered his long, talon-like fingers to Greyson. He reluctantly took them, his hand being enveloped up to the wrist with Seth's fist, and was helped to his feet.

"Ergo, companions of William Blacksmith. I hope you can see why it is important that he forego human interests such as dioramas and begin his training."

"I guess." Ash-Lea said, a note of disagreement in her voice.

"Heck no," Billy argued. "I promised I would help, and I'm going to help."

Seth's demonic eyes gleaming impatiently. "William. I have entered this realm to awaken your blood and train you. We do not have time for trivial activities."

"It ain't trivial if it means something to my friend." Billy folded his arms and glowered up at the demon.

"What am I to do as you cut and paste with your parchments?"

Billy raised his shoulders indifferently. "I dunno. Whatever you do when I'm at school, I guess."

"It is for the best that I do not interfere with your mortal education, but it is not," he thought for a moment, taking in a deep, swift breath through his nose, "natural for a demon to wait for that which he desires. This is important, William."

"Sounds like waiting will be good for you, then. You showed up at my place, buddy, and started following me around. It's not my job to babysit you. If you can't think of something to do for a few hours I can't help you." Billy pointed at Seth's chest. "I thought you were a grown up."

"A grown up?" Seth showed his sharp teeth when he spoke. "I am an ancient being of uncounted age."

"Exactly what I just said. You can help, or you can go sit in a tree. I'll start training with you when I have some time."

Seth breathed again. He spoke with deep, low, broken words, his forced patience rumbling from his throat. "And when will that be?"

Billy bit his lip as he thought. "Tomorrow's Friday. We can start after the game."

Seth looked at Billy, taking in increasingly quicker breaths. Finally, the demon balled his fists, opened his mouth wide, and *roared*. The windows of the house shook with the noise. The alarm of an unseen car began whooping. A flock of birds from a distant tree took to the air.

Ash-Lea's knife was in her hand again, too overwhelmed by the noise to take a clear shot.

Greyson bolted, he ran to the back door. Then, seeming to think twice about abandoning his friends, he stopped. His back to the house, his legs shaking in fear, he managed to make himself face the furious demon again. Finally, Seth stopped producing his deafening bellow and looked at Billy, his chest rising and falling in anger.

"Done with your tantrum?" Billy asked, sounding far more nonplussed than he felt. It took all his efforts to not let his legs buckle under him.

"The demonblood may have given you power beyond your comprehension. But it did not give you an iota of wisdom," Seth snarled quietly.

Billy help up his hands in surrender. "I'm not in a position to argue with that."

Seth shook his head. "To answer your earlier question, William Blacksmith—the Demonseed, he who is destined to defend mankind against incomprehensible evil and suffering—I am rather capable with a pair of scissors." As Seth walked toward the house his form melted into that of a man in a coat and hat as he stooped through the door. Greyson scooted out of the way as Mr. Diomed let himself in.

"Well," Ash-Lea said as she slipped her knife into her concealed pocket, her voice shaking only slightly. "I'm not a big fan of your new friend, Billy. But he does seem to want to help with the diorama. So, I guess he can't be that bad." She started towards the house.

The diorama-rama did not end up as productive as Billy thought it would be. Mr. Diomed began flipping through Greyson's monster manuals. The exercise apparently gave him a good laugh. Eventually, Greyson took a seat next to him on the couch in hopes of defending his beloved hobby. Mr. Diomed explained the inaccuracies in the descriptions of each monster: some were slightly off, some were simply incorrect, others just didn't exist. Once that started, Greyson's desire to build the diorama was abandoned, replaced with educational curiosity.

Ash-lea added another figure of a cut-out, cartoonish monster to her pile. "Hey, what are the requirements for the diorama, Grey?" she said, flipping a page in the manual. "It will help me know what to look for. What's your theme?"

"Requirements?" Greyson asked timidly, glancing up from his book with worry on his face.

Ash-Lea's eyes widened in astonishment, her mouth slightly open. "Yes, the requirements. You have to meet certain criteria if you want to place. The requirements are given to you when you sign up. You did sign up, didn't you?"

Greyson stared at Ash-Lea with a blank expression.

"Good golly, Miss Molly." Ash-Lea threw the book on the table in front of her. "You are both the smartest person I know and the dumbest person I know at the same time."

"I . . . I didn't realize—" Greyson said, looking more and more horrified. "Did I miss the deadline?"

"No," said Billy, trying to sound kind. "You have until Tuesday."

Greyson sighed a great sigh, then his eyes shot open wide. "Where do I sign up?"

"I give up!" Ash-Lea announced as she stood and walked into the kitchen.

"Quinn has all that. You can pick them up from her," Billy explained.

"Oh, that's good. She lives next door. I should just walk over there and ask." Greyson looked excited and terrified by that idea.

"Wait," Ash-Lea stalked back into the sitting area. "She lives next door?"

"Um, yeah," Greyson replied.

"And you've never talked to her? Ever?"

Greyson looked at the carpet in front of him. "I say hi when we're both in our front yard, I guess."

Ash-Lea shook her head and walked back into the kitchen. "I can't . . . it's just. You're hopeless."

"You should totally go over there and sign up," Billy suggested. "It's an awesome excuse to talk to her."

Ash-Lea's voice shouted from the kitchen. "Nope. Talking to her is a bad idea. If he's unlucky, she'll encourage him."

Greyson looked at the clock on the wall then back to the book in his lap. "Maybe I'll go tomorrow," he said quietly, then collapsed onto the couch and buried his face in a cushion.

Mr. Diomed gave Greyson a knowing look. "You are enamored by this human, Greyson?"

Greyson pushed himself up and grinned at his knees. His face had turned a bright pink color. "She is so beautiful," he whispered.

"Too bad you're not." Ash-Lea walked in from the kitchen with four fresh cookies in her hand. She handed one out to each person in the room then sat on the floor. She held her cookie in her mouth and picked up the next book in the pile of permitted-to-destroy manuals, searching for more cool pictures.

Mr. Diomed sniffed the cookie and then placed it on the coffee table. "Love is the very reason I am here," he said.

"Really?" Ash-Lea chewed her cookie, a doubtful scowl on her face.

"Yes. Love is the thing that makes humans worth saving." He stared into the distance, thinking of something he obviously had no intention of sharing.

"Mr. Diomed," Ash-Lea began, "you're the first demon I've ever met—"

"That is most likely untrue, little one," Mr. Diomed replied.

Ash-Lea lowered her eyebrows. "Ooh-kay. You're the first demon I'm *aware of* meeting and I'm pretty sure you're one of the weirdest."

Mr. Diomed returned from the distant memory he was momentarily lost in. "If I was not unlike most demons I would not be making dioramas."

Ash-Lea smiled widely, showing all her teeth and some half-chewed cookie. "Indeed," she said, in an approximation of the demon's deep voice.

Mr. Diomed winked at Ash-Lea and she blushed slightly. Billy shifted his eyes away quickly, an odd knot formed in his stomach, though he didn't know why.

Greyson nudged Mr. Diomed and pointed to the manual. "Don't get off topic, you were telling me about the Knights of the White Spire."

Billy picked up another book and started flipping through an old monster manual. It had demons, angels, leech wolves, ethereal cubes . . . page after page of pretty cool drawings and extensive descriptions of fictional monsters. He looked at Mr. Diomed on the couch. Perhaps these beasts were not as contrived as he thought. He flipped a page, and then felt his stomach leap into his throat as he recognized one of the creatures: eight hairy legs, eight eyes mounted above sharp, familiar mandibles.

"Guys," Billy said, his voice rising, "check this out." He held up the book to the room at large.

"I knew I recognized that," Greyson exclaimed. He leapt forward, slid on his knees and snatched the book from Billy. He passed the manual to Mr. Diomed.

The demon 'hmmed' in recognition as he scanned the page. "A Shadowlurk. Yes, that is the creature who attacked you the other night. The description here is fairly accurate. The Hidden Corner is close to this realm and is easy to access for a spider with the knowledge. Though I imagine a Shadowlurk would have needed some help. They are not significantly powerful."

"Hidden Corner?" Greyson asked.

Mr. Diomed nodded. "The spider's capital is the castle in Hidden Corner. It is closer to the Human Realm than the other demesnes."

"Damn-near what?" Ash-Lea asked.

"Demesnes. It means, area, place. It is where they reside."

She flashed him a 'thumbs up'.

"Hidden Corner is close, which makes the lesser talents able to breach this realm, but it is also more vulnerable to attack from human forces."

"Does that happen often?" Greyson asked.

"Not in my life time," he responded.

"Huh," said Billy. "And how long has that been?"

Mr. Diomed eyed him, a shadow of a smile reached one corner of his mouth. "A very long time."

"So, you said the thing that attacked Billy was a Shadowlurk." Greyson scratched his chin. "Are there like, other kinds of spiders?"

"Yes. Shadowlurks are the least of the lesser demons. I am surprised that the one who found you was so weak. There are four primary races of spiderkine, the others are Tremanchen, Balchen, and Arachnis. If an Arachnis were to have found you sleeping, he would have crushed you bodily before he had a chance to drink your blood. The roof would have come off your residence, ere he had managed to squeeze himself into your room." Mr. Diomed laughed, like that was some kind of joke. Billy and Ash-Lea eyed each other and politely chuckled. Greyson choked on his cookie. "They are very formidable. Even I have been challenged by the strength of the Arachnis."

"Yeah, about that," said Billy. "You kind of just stood there and watched the spider attack me. What's up with that?"

Mr. Diomed took on a patient expression. "I am not permitted to interfere. If I do, then the other demonic races will realize that I have betrayed them. It will undermine our purpose."

Billy furrowed his brow at Mr. Diomed. *But that does not stop me from being bugged by it.* "Getting my head cut in half by a giant spider will undermine our purpose anyway, won't it?"

Mr. Diomed held up a hand. "I may, however, stop them before they attack. It is common for the different demonic races to assault one another if we meet. We are not known for camaraderie. I was hoping to intercept the assassins before they reached you. I failed."

"The thing almost killed me, Seth. Look at my face." He held up a palm to his cheek by way of presentation. "I could have used some help."

"It was clever of him to appear in your room. He engaged you before I became aware of his presence. I will stop them from killing you, William. I hope to avoid any intervention for as long as possible."

"Well, at least we can agree that 'me being eaten' is not okay."

"You are most capable of defending yourself, William."

Billy knit his brow and glared at Mr. Diomed. "You're admitting that there are monsters out there waiting to kill me, and if I ever get into a fight, I'm on my own. And that giant spider was one of the 'least of the lesser?'" Billy couldn't stop the frustration from bubbling up. He glanced at his friends for support.

"Isn't hanging out with us going to give you away?" Greyson asked.

"Associating with humans is common for demonkind. It is how some of us feed," he said conversationally. "And sometimes we do it to lure our prey away from their companions so we may kill them more easily."

Greyson gulped.

"It's getting late," Ash-Lea said, interrupting the awkward pause. "I need to get going."

Billy sighed. Monsters were not the only threat he currently faced. "I guess I can't put off getting killed by The Fosters any longer."

"Good luck with that, Billy," Greyson said.

"Thank you for coming." Meredith emerged from the hall. She gave Mr. Diomed a dubious look. "I hope you were able to help with the diorama." Her tone left no doubt that she thought his presence was entirely unhealthy and unnecessary.

"Thank you for your hospitality," Mr. Diomed bowed.

"Yes. Not a problem," Meredith said slowly.

Billy followed Ash-Lea and Mr. Diomed out the front door. They retrieved their bikes from the porch and mounted.

"Do you think your mom heard us talking?" Billy asked Greyson as the door closed behind them.

"She did not hear a thing." Mr. Diomed spoke before Greyson could.

Billy was tempted to ask how he knew she couldn't hear, but suspected the demon did not want her to.

"What are you going to do now?" Ash-Lea asked Mr. Diomed.

"I will keep watch over William," he said.

"Don't you sleep?" Ash-Lea called as she pushed on her pedal and rode about the tree on the front lawn.

"Not as much as humans do. Your guard are taking turns keeping watch over you when we need to rest."

"Geesh, must be nice to be important," Ash-Lea snickered.

"I dunno." Billy thought of spiders trying to eat him, and Hidden Corners, and the world being devoured by demons. "Getting kinda tired of it already."

"How are you going to get to his house?" Ash-Lea asked, noticing the man's complete lack of transport. "You don't look like you'll fit on the handle bars."

In response, Mr. Diomed's human form evaporated and Seth leapt into the sky, his mighty wings beating as it lifted him into the darkened night.

"He can take care of himself," Billy said as he watched the figure disappear above the clouds.

After watching the sky where Seth had disappeared, Ash-Lea shook her head and returned to the present. "Hey," she said, riding up to Billy and slapping him on the shoulder. "Don't let The Fosters get you down."

Billy smiled wryly. "I'll try," then added, "Let me ride you home. Don't want anything happening to you with all those people going missing."

"Trying to avoid The Fosters a little longer?" Ash-Lea smirked.

"You know it," Billy said, his playful tone falling into something much gloomier as he remembered what was waiting for him.

Billy escorted Ash-Lea to her house and then turned to ride home. The evening did not bring the usual sense of blissful solitude that typically accompanied him on his nighttime rides. It probably had something to do with the large winged figure he could see in the corner of his eye.

The Foster's house was dark when he arrived. Steve and Belinda were passed out on the couch again, a common sight. Empty beer bottles lined neatly on the coffee table. Billy snuck through the living room hoping to not wake them. He reached his room and to his surprise the door was not taped closed. As he placed a hand on the door he noticed there was a piece of paper taped to the wood.

> *Billy. Because you don't have the decency to come home and talk to us like an adult, we felt it was fitting you find out this way. This is no longer your room. You may sleep on*

the couch. Until you pay off the repairs we had done today you MAY NOT move back in. Attached is the bill.

He opened the door and to his surprise the room was repaired; all the holes were covered and the furniture replaced. The smell of fresh paint hung thick in the air. New curtains drifted in the breeze that blew gently through the open window. All the furniture was new: a new bed, new dresser, new desk.

He looked at the bill. His heart sank a little more. Each item of furniture was included, in addition to the plastering, paint and carpet. One particularly large line item read 'emergency fee.' The only thing Billy really understood was the number at the bottom of the page.

$15,000

It took all restraint Billy could muster not to go into the living room and tell Belinda and Steve how unfair they were being. He scrunched the paper up in his hand, letting out a long, strained, muffled sound of frustration. He wasn't sure how long it took to reign in his breathing. He opened the door to the room once more. None of his things were on the bed. None of his stuff was on the floor.

Walking into the living room, Billy noticed his pillow and blanket in a crumpled heap next to the couch. Belinda and Steve continued to sleep soundly on what was supposed to be his bed. At least until he magically made fifteen thousand dollars appear out of thin air. He picked up his blanket and pillow, and stomped down the hall to Chris' room. He stopped at the note pasted on the door.

Don't even think about it.

84

He stormed into the small formal dining room and dumped his bedding on the floor behind the table. He flopped onto his blanket, buried his face in his pillow and screamed. When he was out of breath and energy, he rolled onto his back and stared at the ceiling, willing the carpet to be more comfortable than it could ever possibly be.

8

The Spider's Mission

◆————————————————————◆

"What do you mean Agoston was killed by the Blacksmith?" Krios, General of the Spider Horde, spat furiously.

Kees, a diminutive, brown Shadowlurk, bowed lower to his General. "It is as I say." The spider swallowed.

They stood in a small chamber in one of the towers of the Obsidian Wall, the long, narrow castle protecting Hidden Corner from incursion across the Sulfur Sea. A circle of couches wrapped around a fireplace. A nearby arch led onto a balcony with thick red curtains hung in place to keep the ocean wind at bay. The Spider King's royal garrison was stationed at the Wall while the army enjoyed a relatively rare time of peace. *The calm before the storm*, Krios thought pensively. Though which storm, he couldn't quite say.

The barracks were the best furnished in the entire kingdom. The bedchambers contained deep crimson pillows on which to sleep, and tall ceilings for the spiderkine that preferred the comfort of their own webs. What truly made the Obsidian Wall so safe, were the *feathers* lining the battlements—huge thorned spikes, designed to stop invaders from scaling the fortress. The cries of battle rose from the yard as his soldiers practiced with freshly sharpened sapphyril blades. He always made use of the smithy at the Wall when he could.

The ants who forged upon the anvils were unrivaled in their craftsmanship.

Sir Ursus, Krios' senior advisor, stood by the arch, watching him. He was a Balchen, smaller than Krios, but significantly larger than the Shadowlurk trembling before them. An older spider, his legs were bowed with age and the hair on his face had turned entirely white.

Kees mustered the courage to speak. "Agoston found passage to the human realm through one of the lesser gates. He appeared in the human's chambers whilst he slept. But was overcome by the Demonseed's cunning."

Krios paced away from his soldier, his eight legs drumming the ground furiously. He passed through the archway to the balcony. His brawny guards pulled the curtain aside as he walked. Outside, the dark body of the Sulfur Sea stretched out to the purple horizon. Krios stood a moment, listening to the distant wail of cyclone winds over the unsettled water. He watched as the wakes crashed against the black sand. A pair of white wyverns sat on the railing, their leathery wings flapping with excitement over the two-tailed rat they shared between them. The pale creatures' sharp horns extended backwards from the top of their skulls to end in pinkish points. Krios reached up and scratched one of the wyverns behind the ear. It stopped feeding for a moment and let out a satisfied squawk before returning to the rat with its razor teeth.

The words Kees had spoken played about his mind. Agoston located the Demonblooded. He should have reported it immediately to him, so word could be passed onto the king. And Agoston was neither clever nor powerful enough to have found the Demonseed on his own. Others must have assisted him. And the accomplice must have had a decent amount of power to open even a lesser gate. They all would be punished for betraying their king.

"The King will be furious when he learns of this," Kees said from within the castle, his voice shaking.

"Indeed, he will." Krios placed his second legs behind his back and interlocking his claws. He kept his back turned. "How did you come to learn of this?"

"I happened upon his companions as they attempted to retrieve his wounded body from the human. I watched as the human slew Agoston with a metal stick."

"Slain with a metal stick?" Sir Ursus exclaimed, his voice dry and old. "What a humiliating end for a soldier of Hidden Corner."

"It is. It is," Kees agreed.

"You say you saw his collaborators?" Krios asked, coming about and looking down at Kees, his legs trembled visibly. The image of a cowering soldier had never inspired pity in Krios.

Kees nodded slowly, his eyes shifting about the room quickly.

"I would have you name them for me. They must be punished for neglecting to tell their king that they had found the Demonseed. More so for attempting to drink the blood themselves."

Kees shook, his eight eyes darting to the guards about the room that stood watching him. "If I tell you, mighty General. I will be named a sneak, and the others will kill me."

Krios strode back into the room, ducking through the curtain. "If you do not tell, I will take your head to the king and tell him I have found Agoston's collaborator."

The Shadowlurk swallowed. "I understand, my General."

Krios nodded. "Guard, help Kees with the parchment so he may write down the names of our forgetful soldiers. And please see that he is thoroughly motivated to remember everyone that was present."

The guards moved, taking Kees by the foreleg and dragging him from the room. Kees looked between Krios and the guard, his eight eyes wide. "I came to you in good faith, General. I hoped that you would reward me."

Krios watched the spider as he was forced from the room, his hind-claws groping futilely against the stone floor. "You are a sneak, Kees. I do not tolerate sneaks in my army."

"But I am not yet a sneak. I have not betrayed any of my friends," Kees wailed.

"Before this evening is through," Krios' said, his voice thick with venom, "you will have betrayed your mother's deepest secrets."

The door slammed on the wide-eyed Kees before he had a chance to respond.

"Sir Ursus," Krios turned. "Agoston has done us a significant favor. He has narrowed down the search for the Demonblood. We may be able to find him before his blood is awakened and we face even greater difficulty subduing him."

Sir Ursus nodded. "If the location is accurate, in Ixachitlān Mictlāmpa, then we already have a great number of our soldiers there gathering materials for the ritual."

"They call that area North America now," Krios corrected.

"Humans," Sir Ursus shook his head. "So incredibly inconsistent."

"They are indeed. Which is one of the reasons why they are such dangerous animals. They are highly unpredictable."

Sir Ursus nodded. "I agree with you whole-heartedly. I'm sure the fool Agoston must have found the Blacksmith by accident while hunting for ceremonial ingredients."

"It is likely why that location was chosen for the ritual. The Demonseed's scent would have made the place seem an attractive target."

"That is a potentially disastrous mistake the mages have made."

Krios snorted. "Those brittle fortune tellers would not know their spinners from their mother's eggsacks. But I am never afraid of a fight. I welcome the challenge"

Sir Ursus tutted and shook his head. "I have fought against a Demonseed whose blood was not awakened, young soldier, and he was not easily defeated. If the rumors are true that the Blacksmith Guard already move against us, then we fight against time. If the Blacksmith is permitted to awaken, we shall not be safe even here, behind your feathered stone walls."

"Then I shall destroy him before he awakens. Gather the Tremanchen garrison. We shall strip the skin from William Blacksmith's bones and make a bowl of his skull from which our king will drink his demon blood."

9

The Discøvery

●━━━━━━━━━━━━━━━━━━━━━━━━━━━●

The sun shone warm on Billy as he waited outside the school, his backpack slung over one shoulder. The mountains, vigilant brown-green giants watching over the valley, were visible in the distance. There came the rush and murmur of students calling goodbyes and hellos from the drop-off area. Billy raised his head at the sound of approaching footsteps, somehow distinguishable among the hundreds of other footfalls of students around him. Ash-Lea marched toward him across the yard. She joined him under the covered walkway. Her t-shirt today was black and bore the words '1337 g4m3r5 d0 1t 0nl1n3' in white characters across her chest. She had a determined gleam in her eye, the quiver of something important to say on her lips.

"I have something important to say, Billy," she announced.

Billy adjusted the straps of his backpack and raised his eyebrows. "I see."

"But I can't tell you, not in public," her mouth pinched into a frown, an insincere apology on her face.

Billy understood and held back his smile. "Okay, if you insist. But you promise you'll tell me?"

She looked at him from the tops of her eyes, her eyebrows drawn down in a grave expression. "I promise, as soon as I can." Then she grinned.

Throughout the morning Ash-Lea kept glaring at Billy in class, her mouth in a flat, solemn line, her eyes angled. She would then shake her head slowly and mouth the words, "Not yet, sorry."

Billy nodded, trying to appear genuinely hurt by her unwillingness to share something so very important. She was enjoying her light-hearted revenge, and Billy had no problem allowing her that. Greyson, on the other hand, huffed, his pen gouging the paper as he ignored her.

After fifth period, Billy blinked in the sunlight as Ash-Lea led them onto the lawn by the cafeteria, lunch tray in hand.

"Now do we get to hear what you've been so anxious to keep from us?" Greyson snapped.

She scanned the yard, taking in the clump of trees on the far side, the tables by the tall cafeteria windows. "Let's find a private spot first, then I can tell you."

Ash-Lea led them around the grass. Some kids were playing soccer across the field, shouting and laughing as they did. She moved away from the game, stopping at a tree they'd passed on the first lap, then walked around the tree three times before sitting on the ground, placing her lunch before her.

Greyson and Billy looked at each other, then sat in front of Ash-Lea.

Ash-Lea sighed. "No, this isn't quite right," and made to stand again.

Greyson slammed his tray on the ground. "Ashes, so help me, if you start walking around again I'm going to put superglue in your karate mitts."

Ash-Lea laughed and sat down again. "Okay."

She started arranging her lunch on her tray. She made no effort to hide her enjoyment at Billy and Greyson's expense.

"Ashes," Billy said gently.

"Okay, I'm done," Ash-Lea said, dangerously close to laughing. "But seriously. Seth was married."

It took a moment for what Ash-Lea said to sink in.

"What?" Billy asked.

"Seth? Mr. Diomed?" Greyson furrowed his brow.

"The very same. Seth Diomed was married seventy years ago," she raised both her eyebrows quickly twice, impressed with her own detective skills.

Billy's mouth dropped open, an assortment of curiosity and disbelief twisting his face in a dozen different expressions. Greyson popped a carrot stick in his mouth as he mulled over the news.

Billy chewed his cheek. "Seth married a human? Legally?"

"Yep. In the Cathedral of the Madeleine, to a young lady named, get this, *Rose Bloom*."

"I didn't know he was Catholic," Greyson jutted out his lower lip and raised his eyebrows.

Billy smirked. "No, he never mentioned that."

Ash-Lea gazed up at the tree, a dreamy gleam in her eyes. "Don't you think that's the best name ever? Rose Bloom. How sweet." She was coming dangerously close to swooning, in Billy's opinion.

A gentle gust of wind rustled the leaves above them. A leaf fell from a branch, quietly landing on Billy's tray. One of the teachers on Lunch Duty joined the soccer game and it quickly disintegrated into 'get the ball away from the teacher'. He kept flipping the ball up onto his head and running around with it balance there.

Billy pondered over Ash-Lea's revelation. Seth stated last night that love was the reason he came to earth. Is this what he was talking about, a woman he married almost a hundred years ago? It might be, it made sense. But if he loved a woman, why should he care about what happened to Billy? Greyson's voice brought Billy back to the present.

"How do you know it's our Seth Diomed?"

Ash-Lea shrugged. "I don't. But Diomed isn't a real last name. I only found one reference of it in the marriage records."

"Seth said that Diomed is a title," Billy reminded his friends, pointing a carrot stick at them. "I wonder what it means."

"Could mean he really likes horses." Ash-Lea shrugged one shoulder.

Billy and Greyson eyed her blankly.

"It was a famous horse too," Ash-Lea appended.

"How do know that?" Greyson asked.

"My dad is really into horse racing," she took a bite of her sandwich.

Greyson rolled his eyes. "No, about the marriage."

Ash-Lea spoke before she'd finished chewing, her words muffled with bread. "Oh, that one's easy. There's a ton of that crap on genealogy web sites. Weddings, deaths, kids. I didn't even hunt very long. Just had a crazy idea. I searched his name to see if Seth Diomed had ever been recorded anywhere. And he has—seventy years ago."

Billy stood up and jumped towards Ash-Lea. She stiffened at the sudden movement, looking at Billy with wide-eyed horror that he might be planning to crush her. She let out a muffled squeal and dropped to one elbow, accidentally kicking her food tray at the same time. There was a sudden, loud slapping noise, she gasped and dropped her sandwich in the dirt. He moved his hand from behind Ash-Lea's head and showed her the soccer ball he'd just caught. He threw it back to the kids playing with it.

"Sorry," someone yelled in apology.

"Sorry?" Ash-Lea twisted and called, "you can go shove your 'sorry' up yourrr . . ." she slurred her 'r' as she saw the teacher, waiting for her to finish, ". . . rrr quite alright, carry on." Ash-Lea turned back to her friends and made a disappointed face.

"That marriage stuff is crazy. What are we going to tell him?" Greyson said, bringing the conversation back around.

Ash-Lea eyed him in disbelief, breathing heavily, not quite recovered from almost being clocked in the head. She picked up her soil covered sandwich and tossed it lackadaisically in Greyson's general direction. It fell short of hitting him. He picked up his sandwich from his tray, gleaming untouched in the transparent plastic wrap and offered it to her. Ash-Lea squinted at it for a second, then took it.

Billy sat on the grass again and picked up another carrot. "What do we tell Mr. Diomed? Nothing. If he wanted to tell us, he would. He's obviously kept it from us for a reason."

Ash-Lea frowned with one side of her mouth, disappointed.

Greyson shrugged. "If you say so. I mean, are we even sure we can trust that guy? He is a demon. I don't know much about demons, but they don't have a reputation for being the trustworthy type."

Ash-Lea unwrapped Greyson's sandwich, tore it in half and offered one half to Greyson. He took it from her without looking and bit into it.

"He seems to be on the level." Ash-Lea waved her sandwich in Greyson's direction. "But I'd still be careful. You never know with these demon fellows."

Billy laughed. "Yeah? How would you know?"

Ash-Lea smiled. "Exactly. But being married to a human is like, I dunno. If not innocent enough, it's," she thought for a moment, "less suspicious."

Billy mulled over the odd news. "It does make you wonder."

Greyson nodded in agreement. "Makes you wonder what else he's keeping from us."

Billy shrugged. "Being married doesn't make much of a difference. It was seventy years ago. Maybe she's dead and he doesn't like talking about it. He said love is the reason we're worth saving. I think that's enough information to go on for now without having to know the details."

"Yeah, maybe," said Greyson. "If I were you, I'd want to know as much about Seth as possible."

"Have to agree with Gray-matter there," Ash-Lea said. "We need to know more. Problem is, Seth is the only source of information we have on Seth. I don't like that."

Billy twisted his carrot on his tray. Ash-Lea was right, but he had no idea what else to do. He took stock of everything that had happened over the last few days. Loads of demons were anxious to drink his blood. Seth—Mr. Diomed—wanted to train Billy, but he wasn't going to help him fight off any monsters coming after him. Seth was a member of a club of demons that thought humans were a-okay, and used to be married to a human. He knew where Billy and his friends were and how to find them. If he planned to hurt any of them, Billy doubted he could stop him. He looked at his friends and felt a cold fear rise in his stomach. He had to keep them safe, but he didn't know if he could.

"And," Greyson added, "what did Mr. Diomed mean when he mentioned *awakening your blood?* That sounds dangerous. And he glossed over it like it was no biggie."

"I was thinking about that," said Billy. "I haven't actually had much of a chance to get the details of this plan of his, yet. We've only talked about training me, but awakening my blood sounds much more. . ."

"Invasive?" Ash-Lea offered.

"Yeah, invasive. Like he's going to fiddle with my guts. No thanks to that."

"Just don't let him do anything to you that you don't understand," Greyson said. "This is all so *weird*. He didn't even help you out with that Shadowlurk."

"Hey," Ash-Lea popped up, as if remembering a question she forgot to ask. "What's the damage on your place?"

Billy felt his head swim at the sudden reminder. He closed his eyes and grumbled, letting out a long, low, pained sigh. "Fifteen thousand big ones."

His friends stared at him with gaping mouths for several moments. Birds chittered in the branches above them. The vice principal had wandered over to the soccer game and was now speaking quietly with the teacher. The kids with the soccer ball had all vanished.

Ash-Lea finally closed her mouth, swallowed and asked. "They're not making you pay that off, are they?"

"All of it." The words felt heavy. Billy had to squeeze his insides to force them out.

His friends fell into silence once more. The joy in Ash-Lea's demeanor at her discovery evaporated. "That's a fortune," she whispered.

"I know." Billy closed his eyes and dropped his head.

"Hey, my dad could set you up with a job," Greyson offered, a note of optimism in his voice.

Billy felt hope rise within his chest. "You think?"

"Sure. He owns like a hundred salt plants. He can do whatever he wants with people that work there."

"Well, not exactly," Ash-Lea differed. "Billy is fifteen. Not really allowed to work in a factory."

"He doesn't look fifteen," Greyson argued.

She scowled, eyeing Billy with her jaw twisted in thought. "No, but I think there are laws about this stuff."

Greyson shrugged. "It couldn't hurt to ask. My dad would know better than either of us."

She nodded in agreement. "He would."

Greyson started flipping his fingers and muttering to himself, his eyes practically buried in in his eyebrows.

"What's Chris doing?" Ash-Lea ignored Greyson's lapse into deep concentration. They were both used to it.

"Oh. He got himself a place downtown. He loves it. I know he likes being away from The Fosters, but he's trying to act like he's super sad to be away from me."

"I'm sure he hates being away from you," she said. "You guys are the only family you have. It's probably tearing him up."

"Okay," Greyson cut in. "If you make ten dollars after taxes and pay it all to The Fosters, it will take you about three-point-two twelve-week summers to pay it off."

Billy almost fell backwards onto the ground. "Three summers? I'll be out of high school in three summers. And do you think he'd pay me ten dollars an hour? After taxes?" His voice rose in disbelief.

Greyson shook his head sadly. "No. That's not very likely."

"Taxes? That's so disgustingly grown up. How do I even pay taxes?" Billy grumbled and buried his face in his hands. "My life is over."

Ash-Lea scooted over and patted him on the back gently. In a soothing, friendly tone she said, "It sure is, big guy."

10

The Lessøn

After another winning game, Billy biked home, following his usual path through the neighborhoods. He rode into the park as the sky started to darken in the oncoming twilight. Again, there was no sound of birds chirping in the trees, no chipmunks chasing each other through the branches. Noticing the lack of wildlife in the park once more, Billy knew who he would see as he came around the corner. Seth stood by the fountain, his muscular arms folded across his chest. Billy was surprised at how normal it felt to see the demon waiting for him.

Billy rode up and stopped, placing one foot on the ground. "You're not subtle."

"*Subtle* is not one of my stronger attributes," Seth spoke without smiling.

Billy took in the serious, bleak demeanor of the demon. "I suppose you're here for my training."

Seth nodded once. "It is imperative that we begin as soon as possible."

Billy sighed. "Not what I typically like to do on my weekends, but, no time like the present."

"Excellent."

Seth reached for Billy and spread his wings. Before Billy understood what was happening he felt himself being swept into the air, the ground disappearing below him at a gut churning rate.

His bike was already a dot in the distance before it toppled to the ground. "My bike," he squeaked, lamenting having no opportunity to lock it up.

Seth let go of Billy with one hand and tucked him into his chest, holding him against his torso with one iron-strong arm. Billy squealed as he looked at the ground fading beneath him, feeling like he was strapped into a rollercoaster with no seat. Somewhere beside him he could hear the deep, rhythmic thrum of the demon's wings. Seth dove and they began soaring forward. Billy grabbed onto Seth's arm with both his hands and tried to keep his mouth closed.

Houses flashed below them, lights and streets and cars all growing smaller. He could see the specks of light gathered around the glow of the movie theater's marque, teens congregating for a spring evening movie and make-out session. Somewhere the red and blue lights of police cars raced down a black street to some emergency. His legs were not held by anything, and they flapped around uselessly in the wind. He gripped the demon's arm tighter and stifled a scream of panic.

Despite the warm night, the wind above the mountaintops whipped against Billy, making him shiver. Finally, after what felt like an hour, but probably no more than twenty minutes, the rows of houses below him stopped and he watched the ground nearing. Billy chanced a look up and saw that they were flying into the mountains. He tried opening his mouth to speak, but couldn't hear himself over the roar of the wind.

"We are almost there," Seth rumbled. Though Billy heard it through the vibrations in the demon's chest, more than over the gale of wind in his ears, there was something about the way the demon talked—he was always audible when he wanted to be.

Eventually, the wind started to die down. Billy felt the pressure hiss in his ears as they descended. He jolted as the demon's feet hit the ground, and he tumbled onto the grass. Shaking with adrenaline and fear, Billy gasped for breath.

"You sure know how to show a guy a good time," he stammered.

Without responding, Seth started to walk away. Billy rolled over onto his stomach, supported himself on shaky hands and took in their landing site.

Seth dropped him onto the side of a high, forested mountain. Tall quaking aspen covered in new season green surrounded him. Too many blue spruce, grey and dead from beetle damage, speckled the cusp. In the far distance, he could see the lights of the city winking below.

"Where are we?" Billy asked.

"This is the place I have been preparing for your training," he said over his shoulder. "Follow me."

Billy scrambled to his feet and started after the demon. After a brief walk through the woods they entered a clearing where a tall, pointed-roof cabin stood in the middle. Tall, glass windows covered the two walls Billy could see, trimmed with a deep, brown stained wood; a fire flickered inside, though it wasn't cold enough for one. Near the back of the residence rested a wide, four-car garage, the wooden doors stained to match the cabin. Billy looked behind him at the glorious view, the remnants of a fiery sunset visible on the high clouds over the distant mountains across the valley.

"Did you make this?" Billy asked.

"No," said Seth as he walked with his demonically long legs. "The humans that own this residence only come here during the winter."

Billy struggled to keep up. "Think I'll be ready by then?"

Seth grunted derisively. The two continued through vibrant flowers that bloomed in manicured beds. Someone obviously came up here to take care of the place during the summer. Though now he looked closer, Billy could see wanton blades of grass encroaching on the landscaping. The landscapers were probably due back any day. His eyes shot up to the towering demon and hoped they weren't here now.

Stepping up to the wide wooden veranda Seth faced Billy. "As you will learn this night, there are many stages to your training. These stages will take years to progress through. And while the process will change your body fundamentally, your relatively short life will not permit you the time to master any of them. So, no. You will not even start to glimpse the dawn of your training come winter."

Billy looked up at Seth, his mouth pressed flat in disappointment. "Oh, that's a bummer."

Seth narrowed his eyes. "This will not be easy. This will not be quick. This is not a free gift. It comes at the price of your tears and blood. Should you expect this to be a fast road to power, you will be disappointed. If you abuse what I am about to grant you, my brethren and I will destroy you.

"Our purpose here is to save humanity from a fate you cannot begin to understand in your current state. If I were to tell you our failure will result in pain equal to ice-hot needles being driven into your eyes for eternity you would not have a shadow of what may await your kind."

Billy looked at Seth, his eyes wide. "I'll take that as a 'no'."

Seth scowled and ducked to open the door. As Billy followed him inside he stopped, his mouth open. The source of the fire was clear now. Four holes had been bashed out of the expansive wooden floor and lined with sheets of concrete, marking the four corners of a square with the makeshift fire pits. Billy glanced through the window at the driveway, large chunks were missing. The items on fire appeared to be the furniture missing from the room in which they stood. Billy could see a couch and several smaller chairs stuffed into the holes, burning merrily.

Surrounding the fire pits were four circles. One was made of what appeared to be sand, one of salt, one of black ash, and one sparkled with what appeared to be crushed glass, though more brilliant.

Billy bent and looked closer at the fourth circle. "Is that . . . diamonds?"

"Yes," said Seth. He indicated the four rings and the four fire pits with an outstretched hand. "This is a circle of power designed to draw the energies from my realm and return it to where it has yearned to be since it was conceived."

"Um . . ." said Billy.

"This is how we awaken your blood."

"Yeah, I figured that. But, do you think the owners might be upset with the . . . vandalism?" Billy looked around the damaged room. The image of the bearded cabin owner kicking down the door and opening fire with a twelve-gauge shot gun made his neck itch. He eyed Seth and wondered if he was bullet proof.

"Do you recall what I said about needles being thrust into your eyes?" Seth reminded him.

Billy nodded.

"Do you think they may agree that eternal torment is less pleasant than finding their second residence, which they rarely use, transformed to a place of power, in order to save mankind?" Seth looked at Billy from the tops of his eyes.

"Well sure, but we probably could have found a less destructive way to do this," Billy said under his breath. He moved to kick the outer most circle with his shoe.

Seth zipped in front of him and placed an iron hand on his shoulder. "Take care to not break the circles or we will need to begin again."

Billy froze. "How long will that take?"

"Three of your weeks. And this time I'll make you help."

"But I don't know how to do this stuff. And it took you three weeks?"

"Longer," Seth responded and pointed to the open area in the middle of the fire pits. "We will sit here."

"Why did it take longer than three weeks?" Billy asked.

"I needed to find you, Demonseed." Seth looked at Billy, a deeply serious tilt to his eyes.

"Haven't you run into the grounds keeper in that time?"

"I have. Do not fear. He will not return." Seth sat cross-legged on the floor, a small smile on his face at the memory, and did not volunteer any more information.

Billy was pretty sure he didn't want to know why. "Oh," was all he could think of to say.

The demon indicated the space of floor before him in the middle of the four fires. Billy stepped carefully over the circles and sat in front of Seth. He could feel the heat from the fire pits baking the air about him. Despite the chairs he saw burning, skinned in leather and upholstery, there was a very different, distinct smell to the flames that reminded him of the time he'd visited Yellowstone Park years ago. *Brimstone.*

A sudden seriousness crossed the demon's face. "We begin."

Seth closed his eyes, took a deep breath. The hairs on the back of Billy's neck stood on end, as if the air had become charged with electricity. Wind suddenly burst into movement around them, like a door had been abruptly slammed open by a storm and blew in tight circles around the two. Billy felt an odd concern for the circles of sand, ash and diamond. Glancing at them he saw they did not move at all. In fact, it seemed like the gale was contained within the four rings. Red light began to glow on the ground and a fifth circle appeared, crossing through the fire pits and Billy realized that they were not in a square, but the pits marked places on a circle drawn with something he could not see. *Is it made of spirit? Heart?* Billy wondered.

Seth produced a small silver knife from his belt. At least it looked small in the creature's hand, it was at least the length of Billy's forearm.

"Wait, wait," said Billy. "Stop. How do I know I'm not like selling my soul to Satan or something?"

"You are thinking of being very different than I."

Billy wasn't sure how he felt about that.

Holding the knife before him, Seth took on the tone of an instructor talking to an apprentice. "There are many gateways from my Realm to the Earthen Realm. All but one are lesser gateways, cracks in the fabric between our worlds. Minor powers may use the lesser gateways because the cost to pass through is small. Much like the Shadowlurk that attacked you. His negligible power took little energy to pass to this dimension. The greatest powers are barred from this world because of the Demonseed—because of your blood. However, the greater powers, like myself, we must use the Threshold. Explaining the Threshold to a mortal is difficult. It is much like how I appear. I am what I am to whom I appear; it is the same for this gateway. It is not so much a physical door, as an immaterial passage of magic. Although, it is founded on a specific, physical object that exists in a specific place and time. It is through this portal that the superior of my kind can torment your kind. We have used this passageway to plague your people for eons. I feel it is—" he thought for a moment, "inappropriate for my kind to use humans in this way."

"Use us, how?"

"The best of us use manflesh as food. It is a delicacy."

Billy swallowed. Seth sounding more familiar with that topic than Billy was comfortable with. "That's the best?"

"The worst, and the reason why the war against humans began, was for those of us who are Animusphagous. Do you know what that means, Billy?"

Billy shook his head.

Seth lowered the knife. "They feed on flesh, as do all creatures, to maintain their bodies. But to feed their magics, they consume life energy. Specifically fear, terror, hopelessness. And humans are a rich, rich source of these emotions. Can you begin to understand why the pain of needles would be small in comparison to a creature that wants you to suffer eternally? And as you suffer, they gain in strength. And as they gain in strength, their ability to make you suffer increases?"

Billy blinked involuntarily at the thought, his mouth feeling dry. The wind continued to billow about them, but still he could hear the demon's rumbling voice.

"It is these darkest of creatures that we wish to keep from you. They have ways to prolong a human's life long after it should have ended. There will be untold torment for your kind if we fail." Seth inclined his head and continued to look at Billy, straight into his eyes.

"Oh. That sounds unpleasant." Billy wiped a nervous hand across the back of his neck.

"And once Earth falls, one by one, every planet in this universe will fall."

Billy nodded, understanding.

"Are you ready to proceed?" Seth raised the knife once more.

"Actually, I was wondering." Billy held up his index finger. Seth sighed. "You look like a normal dude sometimes."

"Yes, a normal dude," the demon said dryly.

"And you only appear to people in your—*normal form*," Billy framed the word with his fingers, "when you want to?"

"I do," Seth nodded.

"So, you're saying there could be demons all around us and they just look like regular joe-shmoes?" Billy grimaced as he asked the question.

Seth's frown faded a little, into an expression of sadness that reached his eyes. "Not could be, William. There are."

"There are?" Billy shifted uncomfortably. "Do you know of any? Will I be able to see them?"

"You will not be able to see them at first. But as we awaken your blood you will come to know the demons that walk among you."

"Spooky." Billy wiped his sweaty hands on his knees. He couldn't tell if he were sweating from the heat or from the way Seth held that knife.

"It is, isn't it? Are you ready now?" Seth raised the knife.

"Wait," said Billy. "I have another question. Why did the spider disappear? He just dissolved into like powder and fluff and stuff once he was dead."

Seth slammed the knife into the wooden floor beside him. He held out his palm to Billy. "Our bodies are made of material from this world, bound together by the will of the demon possessing them. As we pass through the gate the matter surrounding the portal is used to create the coils with which we walk this plane. There is no will to maintain form after the will is rendered inoperable, ergo the matter returns to its original state."

"You said just his body couldn't hold form, is he dead-dead, or did he just go back to your . . . realm?"

Seth nodded. "Indeed, the Shadowlurk that attacked you is dead."

Billy looked at Seth, an unexpected feeling of unease crept into his chest. "Does that mean you can die?"

Seth shook his head. "No, not I."

"Well that's not fair."

"I am a much more powerful being," Seth stated matter-of-factly.

"You're modest too."

He gave Billy a level look and continued. "I am a demon, boy. I am far more powerful than the lowly Shadowlurk. I have the ability to keep a foot in either world. If this manifestation of my body is destroyed, my will would return to the Threshold."

Billy nodded appreciatively. "Geesh, must be nice. Does that, you know, make you tired?"

"No. If I were not as strong as I am it would, but it does limit my abilities here." He flexed the fingers of one hand slowly, seeming somehow disappointed in the powerful, dangerous claws.

Billy looked at Seth, a thought occurred to him. "Could you bring yourself completely over? So, you know, you're at full strength, but also vulnerable?"

Seth looked up, a serious tint to his face. "If I chose to do so, yes."

"But not the spider demon." Billy adjusted himself. He could feel his legs starting to fall to sleep.

"No."

"So, his mind can't live without his body."

"Yes."

"Just like in the Matrix?" Billy raised his shoulders.

Seth seemed surprised at the comment. "No, the Matrix is a place where-- Oh, wait. That's a human reference." Seth pointed at him and Billy smiled widely. "Good movie. I liked the trilogy more than most, though."

Seth plucked the knife out of the floor and held it up. He shook it back and forth expectantly.

As he opened his mouth to speak Billy interrupted him. "One last question."

Seth let out a low stream of what may have been cursing, but in an ancient sounding language Billy did not understand.

Billy cleared his throat, waiting for Seth's frustrated muttering to cease. "If demons are sealed from this realm because of my blood, why are you here?"

"Only the most elemental and powerful demons were bound permanently. The arcane magics involved in the spell that granted your line the Bindingblood knew the hearts and minds of all demons. Think of it as a dam. It holds back great power, but also lets some trickle through."

"If you're as great as you say you are, how did you trickle though?"

"This is an ancient dam, William. It is cracked and leaking."

"You're saying we need to awaken my blood so I can fix it?"

"No. The powers and will that built this dam are long dead. We must awaken your blood so when the waters flow forth, someone is standing on the other side with the strength to hold the torrent at bay."

Holding back a dam's worth of water sounded just a little too impossible for Billy. He opened his mouth, but was cut short as Seth slammed the knife back into the floor with a frustrated shout.

"William," he barked. "I see your questions could flow until after this eternally enchanted fire dies." He took a deep, calming, breath. "Allow me to explain the machinations that brought us here, to this cabin upon a mountainside. I shall tell you a story of the deepest love, and most selfless sacrifice." Seth intertwined his fingers and lay his hands, palm up across his lap. The wind about them died quickly, like a door to the storm had been temporarily closed. "The Patriarch is the father of my Order. He was the first demon to ever love."

11

The Demøn Whø Løved a Maid and Saved Mankind

◆————————————————◆

illennia ago, all demons spawned from within the Demonic Realm. With their insatiable thirst for blood and suffering, it was expedient that a barrier be placed between the Demonic Realm and this one, to seal demons away from this plane. The door, known as the Threshold, was bound to the Earth and wizards were sent to stand guard. Their duty was to be ever vigilant and ensure this universe could not be encroached upon by the powers of evil. Darkness, sadness, wickedness remained the humans' constant companions, but the source of evil itself had for a time, been stayed.

My kin never forgot what had been done to them. With singular purpose, they raised an army and built machines of war. While on the Earth, the wizards grew apathetic. As the years went on, they abandoned their duty. The wizards bore children and spread across the face of the Earth. Eventually, they forgot from where they had come. The progeny of the wizards had no purpose. Instead, they built cities and civilizations and began to fight amongst themselves. Meanwhile, the gates that sealed the Demonic Realm were forgotten and fell into ruin.

One day, when the demonic hosts had rebuilt their strength once more, Aberdem, the God of Dragons, led his armies against the gates. For four hundred years his soldiers battered themselves against the arcane spells, against magics and light. Millions of Aberdem's armies fell, lost in flame and ice. But finally, the spells protecting this universe from the demons were broken. Aberdem stormed into this realm, prepared to commence the war against those who bound them. But to his amazement, he found no resistance. No wizard stood ready to defend against them. No angelic host barred their way. So they emerged unchallenged into the Earthly Realm.

Aberdem and his armies swept across the face of the Earth as a tide of death. Though the humans fought bravely, cities and kingdoms fell easily before a foe they could not defeat. Man after man in his platemail and boiled leather were slaughtered by the demonic blades, severing them crown to heel in a single blow. The demonic dragons burned their cities from above, while the sulfur-forged scales of mighty sea demons dragged their sailors to the depths of the oceans.

But one of us that never raised a blade against man was the Patriarch, Master of Demonspells. He was the greatest blacksmith that all Three Realms has ever known. He wove magics into the metal he worked. He forged blades that would never dull, maces that would never shatter, armor that could never be pierced by demon nor man. He took pride in his work, and always delivered the best he could to Aberdem's armies. If there was ever a crack, or flaw, the metal would be returned to the forges to be remade a hundred times before being marked with his sigil.

But fate, it would seem, took mercy on the beleaguered humans. As a reward for his efforts, Aberdem gifted the Patriarch a human maid, one who would be used as a meal, or whatever he chose. Yet when they brought the child to him it changed the Patriarch in a way Aberdem could not foresee.

The child was bound and brought to the Patriarch's private table. As she lay on the plate before him—for my kind prefer their meat to be fresh—she watched him without fear. As the Patriarch prepared to tear off her head, the girl said a simple word that redirected the destiny of this doomed world.

"Why?"

The question drove like a sapphyril blade into his heart, for he had never truly considered the question before. He did not answer her, but left her at his table and retired to his chamber. All night he pondered that question.

In the morning when the Patriarch returned, he was surprised to find the maid still in his meal hall, sitting in a chair too large for her small human frame. A dirty dress hung loose around her little shoulders as she sat eating the bread laid out for him the night before.

In response to his confused look, she answered. "I have nowhere to go. My family is all dead, my kin have been slain. If I were to escape your chambers, I would be killed by the guards in the hall. I wait at your pleasure, to eat me when you please."

When the Patriarch called for his breakfast, he ordered a serving of grain and cow's milk for his human. He had chosen to keep her as a pet, he told them.

For twelve Earth years, she lived in the chamber of the Patriarch, eating his meals and telling him stories of life before the demons swept over the land. She spoke of the beauty of a sunrise over a forested valley; the joy of a child, newborn and mewling in its mother's arms; the warmth of a kiss from the farmer's boy behind the barn.

After many years of many stories that made him laugh and cry, the Patriarch recognized he could no longer keep her against her will. He had learned to care for her and wished her to be free from within the stone and volcanic rock. He bade her leave and offered to sneak her back to this realm.

But she refused.

The Patriarch insisted she go, for he had found within himself something that he did not know his kind could possess. He

112

did not truly understand what the feeling was. He simply wished for the maid to be happy at any cost to his time and efforts. He longed for her to be safe and warm, for her to see sunrises once more. Never had any demon explained to him how true love felt, for no demon before had ever known.

But still she refused. In her time with the Patriarch she had in turn grown to care for him also. All her heart wished for him to feel nothing but joy, and she desired to spend her life dedicated to his joy. It was at that moment Patriarch understood what love meant. They embraced, and he wished to die before he ever let her from his arms.

They decided to leave together.

The Patriarch never left his forge, or the thousand demons that worked for him. There was never a reason to. He forged blades for the armies of Aberdem, and for that he was given great riches, comfort and revere.

He explained to the guards by the gates that he wished to see the armies of Aberdem, to see his work in action. They were surprised, but had no reason to stop him. With him, he took twelve carriages in case any of his brethren required their armor repaired or swords sharpened—an odd thing, for swords that never dull, and armor that never breaks.

Within one carriage he hid his maid, whom he had grown to love, and whom had grown to love him in return. Over continents they searched for the survivors of mankind. But all they found were the bones of men, scattered and broken. Here and there they found the body of a demon, its blood soaked into the soil. But, for every one demon corpse was the corpses of ten thousand humans.

After three years two weeks and one day, when the maid had given up hope, they found the last of the human kings. When the last human city came into sight, the demons pulling the Patriarch's carriages drew their swords, desiring a taste of sweet, human blood.

The demonic carriage bearers rushed towards the gates of the last human city.

Seeing the hunger of his companions, the Patriarch drew his sword too and gave his demons a choice. Return to the city of Aberdem, or die.

That day, the Patriarch fought against his brethren while his maid watched, horrified that she may lose her lover. Her tears soaked her gown as she hid within the carriage. She gripped the bars over the window so tightly blood ran from her palms and down her arms. Her heart tore with the thought that they had come so far and she might lose him, for hate was all that remained within the hearts of demons and humans.

For twelve days and twelve nights the demons fought beneath the gates of the last human city, all while the last men watched from atop their wall. The Patriarch fought with a ferocity that no man and no demon had ever seen. The fire of sincere love burned within his demonic heart, imbuing him with a will and focus that until that time, had never existed in all reality. He knew that if he died, all humans would be lost, and with them, his lady and his love.

Finally, the Patriarch was victorious, and his twelve brethren lay slain about him. There he fell to the earth, bleeding from many wounds. The maid emerged from her carriage and ran to the side of her lover. Kneeling over his dying form, she pled with the men on the wall to bring the Patriarch behind their gates, for he was grievously wounded. He would not survive if not for their distinctly human emotion, compassion.

The men who witnessed the battle told the Last King of what they saw. The Last King decreed that the Patriarch be bound and brought before him.

The Patriarch gathered his strength and walked, bleeding as he was, through those gates to the throne of the humans. Weakened and near to death, he bent the knee to the Last King, pledging his service in creating demonforged weapons. The Last King accepted his servitude and loyalty.

After they tended to his wounds, he went to work the following night. He did not stop forging blades for one hundred days and one hundred nights. Finally, as the forge cooled that evening, the final human was armored with demonforged metals. As the sun rose on the one hundred and first day, the horns of Aberdem's hosts could be heard beyond the walls of the city.

A flood of demons came against them, seething like tar before the walls of the city. The human armies resisted Aberdem with their demon swords and sapphyril arrows. For the first time in the war, the humans stood their ground. The demonic forces were driven back, their skins cut by the blades, their armor smashed, the arrows pierced their helms, and their dark blood soaked into the earth.

Yet it was too late. The hosts of the Demonic Realm were too many, and Aberdem had called for his dragons that they may burn the city on the morrow. Humans, all but for one city, had been destroyed. And no city can stand against a legion of dragons. The Patriarch admitted that the war was lost. He had learned to love his maid too late.

That night the Patriarch lay in the arms of his human lover and wept for her. He wept for her kin that had been slain. He wept for the human children that would never run through the grass. He wept for the sunrises.

So, the Patriarch, the Master of Demonspells made an offer to his human liege—a final spell, that Aberdem and all those pledged fealty to him, be sealed behind the Threshold once more. This spell would not be dependent on any physical construct, but on blood. Blood is powerful and fluid, and cannot be broken. The Last King understood what was required and offered his blood to the Patriarch. He then asked all the remaining people in his kingdom for volunteers to seal the Demon God.

A thousand soldiers came forward. Their lives could end meaninglessly on the morrow at the point of a demon's blade or a dragon's hellfire. Or their lives could end with purpose, saving mankind in truth.

The night Aberdem was driven back, he returned to his forge in rage. He wished to understand how the humans had learned his magics and created demonblades. But he found the forge abandoned and realized the betrayal of his kin. His scream of rage shook the Earth's two moons, and caused them to collide.

The Patriarch circled the city with ash, salt, sand, and diamond. In the courtyard of the city, gathered together at the center of the circle of power, each volunteer stood with the Last King, their heads held high. In their eyes were tears of pride and fear. They wore their finest battle robes, the brass breast plates polished to a high shine. All around them their spouses and children wept for them. As one, the thousand fell on their swords, offering their blood and souls to the spell.

The maid approached her demonic lover and they kissed one last time. The wind of magic blew about them, the energy of one thousand souls mingled with the demonic blood within their child. The babe lay at the center of the circle, squalling, not understanding the sacrifice of his parents. The maid and her demon thrust the demon blades through the other's hearts and the spell was complete. Before Aberdem could return to Earth the Threshold had sealed against him.

Now that demon waits patiently on the other side of that door. For each volunteer, the Demonblood is kept alive for one generation. Each life sacrificed represents a human that must carry the burden of the Demonseed.

~*~

Billy looked up at Seth sitting before him. His eyes were wide, his mouth open, trying to absorb what he had just heard.

"It has been one thousand generations since this came to pass, William. You are the final barrier between hope and the annihilation of your universe."

Billy shook his head slowly.

"If we do not awaken your blood and teach you to fight against darkness, all mankind will be obliterated when the seal falls away. And the seal will fall away. Aberdem is coming to reclaim this earth no matter what you chose to do, young Blacksmith. Our only hope is to be prepared for him when he comes."

Seth held up his own hand and moved the knife quickly across it, cutting a deep gash in his palm.

Wind exploded about them in a tumultuous roar. Billy could hear nothing but the scream of a thousand souls. The flames burst to life, turning white and furious, reaching up to the vaulted ceiling. Seth turned his wide, red hand over and a drop of blood gathered on the tip of the demon's pointed claw.

Despite the deafening gale of wind, Billy felt Seth's low voice speak as if he were whispering in his ear. "Awakening your blood is easy compared to what awaits you."

The fires about them flared more violently, the roar of flames sounding like that of jet engines, the concrete holding the fires in place began to blacken and crack. Seth reached towards Billy and touched the blood to the tip of his gaping tongue. Billy jolted once, every muscle in his body convulsing as if he had been electrocuted. A soundless scream came from him, muffled by the thunder of flame and howl of wind. A sun of fire burned from the point where the demon's claw had touched him. The blood tasted of pain and sadness and hot sauce. Ice descended on him, crawling under his skin, covering his body in agony. He felt his soul peel away, layer by layer, as pain that he could not put into thought overwhelmed him. Then Billy fell to the floor, remembering no more.

12

A Walk
Through the Woods

◆————————————————————◆

B
illy woke up and lay still for a moment, looking at the wooden ceiling. It felt far away and unfamiliar. There must have been a fire once big enough to leave scorch marks on the high beams. Light fell on his face and he turned his head towards the source. The bright sun rose high above the distant line of trees. It had to be late morning, he must have slept in.

Billy surveyed the destroyed room around him, memories slowly seeping back into his skull. He sat up with a start. His head spun and he grabbed it with both hands. It took a moment before the room stopped doing cartwheels. He poked at the bandage on his face and his face itched. He pulled the gauze away and tossed it to the floor, the skin underneath felt whole.

The four fire pits still surrounded him, the flames gone, the holes lined with crumbling chunks of charred concrete. The rings that had encircled the enchanted flames were removed as well, but Billy could see the smudges from the ash, the scattered grains remaining from the sand. He looked up to the scorched roof above him. It might have actually caught fire in a few places.

"Seth?" Billy croaked. His voice felt weak, his throat dry.

There was no answer.

Billy stood, shaking. His back ached from lying on the hard floor all night. Limping to the glass doors, he slid them open.

"Seth?" he wheezed again. The only response was the warm morning breeze and the rustle of the trees. "You know you were my ride, man?" Billy shouted, his throat tight and hoarse.

Turning back into the cabin, Billy called the demon again. Nothing. Walking to the kitchen, he opened the fridge. It was empty and powered off. He checked in the cupboards. Nothing. He turned on the tap in the sink, hoping to parch his dry mouth. No water came out.

Billy glowered at the empty room. He stomped back to the fire pits and retrieved his backpack from the floor. Rummaging inside, he found a warm Electrolyte-tastic and took a long drink. The liquid wet his mouth but sat heavily in his stomach. Swinging his pack over his back, Billy stepped outside and slid the door closed behind him. He stretched and yawned, then flicked his head from side to side popping his neck.

"Seth?" he called, trying to not let his irritation into his voice.

Cursing the demon under his breath, Billy started walking. There was nothing else for it.

"Damn it, Seth," he shouted. "You are lucky it's a Saturday or I would just—" He kicked a stone. It went spinning down the mountain.

He could see the city far below him. The walk would take all day, and he had not eaten his morning cupcakes yet. Billy gritted his teeth and started moving his feet, cursing Seth the whole time.

Huh. I wonder if cursing a demon counts as a compliment, Billy mused.

It didn't take long for the temperature to rise to an uncomfortable level. His shirt started chafing his armpits as they became wet with sweat. Billy could feel it running down the small of his back. *But man, I'm thirsty. Really, really thirsty. I don't think I've ever felt this parched.* He started for another swig of Electrolyte-Tastic but stopped himself when he saw what remained in the bottom of the bottle. He considered the city, still a long hike away. Billy groaned and took a small mouthful before stuffing the container back in his pack.

The forest was serene, rustling with thousands of unseen birds above him in the trees. They chirped loudly, their beaks clacking. He'd never heard so many before. It wasn't the usual twittering he was used to down in the valley. *I wonder what kind of birds they could be.*

As he walked Billy thought about the night before—the fires, the circles, the long, weird story, the glinting silver knife and what Seth had done to his hand. Billy shuddered at the memory of the blade parting the demon's thick, red flesh.

Billy clacked his tongue where Seth's blood had touched. It felt normal, though he could definitely feel a small sore spot, like he'd burned it on a piece of piping-hot food. The memory made his shudder. He could not remember what the demon's blood tasted like, but the thought of having something else's blood in his mouth made his stomach turn.

Seth had talked about 'awakening his blood' like it was a big ordeal, but he didn't feel any different. He felt sore from sleeping on the floor, his feet hurt from walking, he was thirsty as a fish, but that was it.

But is he wrong about me? Can I really be the Demonblooded— whatever that means—or does he have the wrong guy? Billy looked at his large, unimpressive hands. *There is nothing special about me. I can hit a baseball, but other than that, I'm a normal kid.*

A sharp crack of wood snapping sounded behind Billy lifting him from his thoughts. It didn't sound like a careless person cracking a twig, it was a deep sound like a thick branch breaking high in a tree. Turning, Billy watched the branch fall through the foliage and land on the forest floor with a thump.

The clicking, chirping sound illuminated a dark memory. A shiver ran down his spine as he recognized the chirping—and it wasn't birds. That very particular sound was not something he wanted to hear again.

"Blacksmith," a low voice hissed above him.

Billy looked in the trees. Hundreds of hungry red eyes glared at him from the boughs. Hairy brown legs clinging to the trees all about him. The sound he took for birds chirping he now recognized as the rasping of mandibles. But these weren't the relatively small Shadowlurk-type that attacked him in his room, these were larger.

"Tremanchen, I think he called them," a disjointed, analytical part of Billy's brain provided.

Billy made a gargling squeal and started to run. The spiders burst into motion and clambered after him. The clacking noise swelled and almost sounded like laughter, enjoying the thrill of toying with him. He could hear them on all sides keeping pace as they leapt from tree to tree. Billy panted, his heavy body too out-of-shape to keep up. Tears of fear and embarrassment began filling his eyes, and he couldn't stop them. He put one foot in front of the other, ignoring how badly his chest ached from his heavy breathing.

Pain shot up his leg as his foot cracked into a root. Billy reached out to brace himself as he tumbled. He cried out as a rock, hidden under a carpet of old leaves, gouged into his palm. Trying to reduce the damage, he let his elbow buckle and began to roll. He found himself lying on his back, watching as thousands of red eyes glittered in delight at his pain and fear. A nearby spider took the opportunity and lunged. Billy scrambled away, but the monster's mouth snapped closed onto the leg of his pants tearing away the fabric. Billy looked at the spider, a shred of his jeans dangling from his mandibles.

"Run, fat human child, run," it hissed with glee. "Your fear is delicious."

Billy scrambled to his feet and ran; his chest burning, his face hot, flushed with terror and embarrassment at the taunts of the monsters. They would chase him until he fell to the ground and bind him in their sticky webs. Then probably fight over who got to drink the blood everyone was so excited about.

Sweat soaked his face as he gasped for breath, putting one foot in front of the other. He would never outrun them. The laughing followed him from tree to tree. They would tie him up and string him upside-down, nibbling bits off his bones while he screamed in pain, helpless. Tears blurred his vision, but he kept moving.

But what about Ash-Lea, and Greyson? And Chris? What if Seth was right? What if he was the only one that could stop whatever was coming? He couldn't give up just yet. He couldn't lie down and let the monsters take him. He needed to keep going for Greyson, for Ashes—and, if it came to it, the world. Billy pushed his feet as hard as he could to the ground, pumping his legs a little bit faster. He would not quit until he was dead, and he wanted to put that off as long as possible.

In the distance, Billy saw a gas-station, a small yellow thing resting on the side of a narrow mountain road, an old, rusted blue truck parked in front. If he could make it that far maybe there would be someone that could help, maybe they had weapons or something. It was about three miles away; he might make it if he ran as fast as he could.

The spiders laughed at him from the trees. Something hissed passed his ear and a glob of green goo spattered the tree beside him. The wood started to bubble and steam as the liquid dissolved the bark. He gulped and forced his legs to keep moving. Wind blustered in Billy's ears as he started running faster than he knew he could, he let himself hope just a little. More balls of the sweet-smelling acid flew past him, hitting the forest floor, dissolving the wood and leaves at his feet. The gas station slowly grew closer.

The gas station suddenly appeared right next to him. Billy slid to a stop, his feet skittering on the gravel, his breathing was heavy and labored. He stared up at the tall pole with the neon gas-can on it. He glanced back up the mountain, then at the gas station again. He spun around and saw the 1950s Ford truck parked by the trees on the far side of the pumps. A wash of nausea and exhaustion rushed up his back and over his head. He fell to his knees and puked Electrolyte-tastic all over the ground. Billy smacked his lips and his stomach gurgled. How had he ended up at the gas station so fast? His head twirled like a Gravitron and fell to his side in the gravel.

The sound of footsteps crunched towards him, moving quickly as they approached. He turned to see a grey-haired man standing above him.

"You okay, son?" he asked from behind a gigantic, coffee-stained mustache.

Billy felt the gravel digging into his arm, but didn't care. "Water," he managed to say.

The man nodded. "Sure, son. I'll be right back."

Billy sat up slowly and scanned the trees. He could see the spiders in the shadows at the edge of the trees across a clearing, not daring to come closer. Billy didn't know why, perhaps they disliked the idea of being close to too many humans. The man returned and handed Billy a bottle of water. He opened it and drank the whole thing.

"Thanks," Billy bent his knee and rested an arm across it. He let his head droop, waiting for the vertigo to pass.

"Where you coming from, son? Looks like you just came out of the forest. How did you get up there? You hiking?" The man tilted his head to the side to get a look at Billy's face.

"Um, yeah. I just, I need to go," Billy said. He tried to stand, but only managed to get himself onto his hands and knees again.

Billy looked back at the direction from which he'd come. There were more spiders now, pressing themselves into the shadows, waiting. A group of them broke free from the others and started towards forest that ran behind the gas station. Following that path, they could be on the back door of the building without having to leave the safety of the trees.

"How you plannin' on doin' that? You ain't in no condition to walk," he placed a hand on Billy's back.

Billy nodded. "I just, I need to go, sir. Thank you."

"No you ain't, son," the mustachioed man said as if Billy had just disagreed with him. "I'mma ask Carolyn if she's headed into the city today. Maybe you can hitch with her."

Billy stood, shaking. The man held out his hands, ready to catch Billy just in case he didn't make it. Billy leaned against the gas pump next to him. His legs felt like jelly. He wanted to protest but wasn't sure he could move anywhere else on his own.

"Thanks," he said finally.

The man walked away towards the small building, moving quickly for an older man. Billy examined the tree line once more. The spiders were gone, but that did not bring him any comfort. The trees swayed as a wave of hidden spiders snuck to the gas station. A minute later a squat woman in a large dress, with pink, round cheeks emerged from the building. She swung a set of keys around her index finger as she waddled towards him.

"Pete said you could use a ride, honey. I've got to hit the supplier 'nyway." She walked towards the ancient Ford pickup. "Come on." She waved a fleshy arm.

Billy walked as quickly as his shaking legs would carry him and climbed into the passenger seat.

"Where you headed?" she asked.

Billy strapped in his seat belt and leaned his head against the window. "I should go to . . ." he thought about where he wanted to go. Probably to Chris' new place. He hadn't talked to his brother since he was kicked out, at least not about what 'not again' meant. "Chris' house," Billy said wearily.

"I dunno Chris, love," Carolyn said.

Billy tried to answer, but his mouth didn't want to move. He needed to tell Pete about the spiders. He should get out of there. It wasn't safe. The man was just trying to help a kid that had wandered out of the forest and now he'd placed himself in danger. From what he knew about demonic spiders they didn't seem to care very much about things like collateral damage. He moved his mouth to speak again, but his lips were too heavy to budge.

"We're here," Carolyn said.

"Huh? What?" Billy said, sitting up and feeling more refreshed. He'd fallen to sleep almost as soon as he'd sat down. He wiped drool from his cheek.

Looking through the window he saw they were parked in the parking lot of a bulk supplier store.

"You fell asleep, love. Figured you needed it. We're downtown. You can find where you need to get from here?"

"Um, yeah. Sure. Thank you."

Billy climbed out of the cab and found himself in the crowded parking lot.

Carolyn climbed out of the car and slammed the door. "Take care, sugar," she said and started walking away.

"Carolyn," Billy called. The woman turned, a curious look on her face. "Give Pete a call as soon as you can. I just want to make sure he's okay."

Carolyn mouth twisted into a curious grin. "Well, aren't you a sweetie. I'm sure Pete is fine."

"Please," Billy said.

She pursed her lips, her curiosity sinking into suspicion. She pulled a cellphone out of her purse, pressed the screen a few times and held it to her cheek. After a moment a smile spread across her face.

"Pete. Hi. Letting you to know I got the young man downtown alright. He just wanted to say thank you."

Carolyn waved and turned towards the store, chatting happily with her husband. Billy sighed with relief.

He stood in the parking lot squinting in the bright afternoon sun trying to decide what to do next. A few cars drove slowly through the parking lot. One or two people pushed their carts laden with bulk goods towards their cars. A mother guided three young kids through the sea of cars. The store didn't seem as busy as it should have been on a Saturday.

He considered running after Carolyn and asking to borrow her cellphone, but he'd pressed on her hospitality enough. Billy stuck his hand into his pocket and felt the coins he usually kept there. Thank goodness his candy-change had survived the morning's activities. It would be enough to call Chris. Billy walked to the front of the store, frustration rising in his chest. He could see the outline on the wall where payphones used to be. He looked around and considered asking someone to borrow their cell phone, but decided that was too forward. A gas station was situated across the street from where he stood. Sighing deeply, he started the trek across the parking lot.

Two payphones were out the front of the gas station; one was broken, the handset cable hanging sadly. Billy picked up the receiver of the one remaining pay phone and pressed it to his ear. He slid the coins into the slot and heard the satisfying ping of a connection being made. He rapidly pressed his brother's cell phone number into the dial pad.

"You better pick up, you jerk," he muttered to the dial tone. The phone kept ringing. Billy felt a nervous itch on the back of his neck, worried Chris wouldn't answer.

"Hello?" Chris finally said, sounding hesitant.

Billy sighed with relief. "Dude, I am so glad you picked up. It's me."

"Billy?" Chris' voice was thin, almost panicked. "Where are you? Where have you been? I've been looking for you."

"Dude, it's okay. Seth just took me to, uh, show me something. It's cool. Look, I'm south of downtown. Could you come pick me up? I'm on. . ." he twisted to see the street signs from where he stood.

"Who the hell is Seth?" Chris shouted in response.

Oh, right. He hadn't told Chris about his newest friend.

126

"I'll tell you when I see you. Could you get me? I'm at the Maverick, seventeenth south, third west."

"How did you end up there? Never mind. I'll be there in twenty minutes." Chris hung up.

Billy sat on the warm concrete curb and waited. Fifteen minutes later a familiar red truck pulled into the gas station and stopped at one of the pumps. Chris jumped out and ran to Billy.

"Billy, where have you been?" he embraced his brother in a tight hug. "You smell terrible."

Billy smiled at the warm greeting. "Good to see you too. Where *have* I been?" Billy asked himself. "I guess I need to explain who Seth is first. Would you mind getting me something to eat? I'm kind of starving."

Chris held him at arm's length, inspecting him, looking from Billy's dirty shoes to his oily hair. "Have you had anything to eat since you disappeared?"

Billy shook his head. "No, I guess not. Wait, what do you mean 'disappeared'?"

"It's Tuesday. Nobody's seen you since Friday. People are vanishing like paychecks around here and you up and vanish too. I've been going crazy looking for you. Greyson and Ash-Lea are beside themselves. She's barely been sleeping."

"I'm sorry," Billy said slowly. *Tuesday? Greyson and Ash-Lea must be terrified.* Billy had no idea what he'd do if one of his friends went missing. *Go find them or go crazy,* he guessed. "No wonder I'm starving."

They walked back to the truck and Chris started pumping gas. His face darkened. "Did this Seth guy hurt you?"

"No, dude. Seth's cool. He's a friend," Billy said. But did he hurt him? He wasn't actually sure. "I just didn't know it was going to take so long."

"What was going to take so long?" Chris leaned against his truck, his mouth pursed tightly.

Billy's mouth twisted as he tried to figure out how to respond. "I tell you what. You tell me what you meant by 'not again' when you saw that spider in my room, and I'll tell you who Seth is."

Chris blanched and looked away. A seemingly simple statement had a deep impact on him, that Billy did not understand. Chris placed both hands on the roof of the truck. He looked between his arms at the concrete, and laughed once, but Billy got the impression he didn't think anything was funny.

"Does Seth know about the spider?" Chris said quietly.

"Yeah, he does." Billy put his back to the truck door.

"And he wants to help?" he asked without looking up.

"Yeah, he does." *I think.*

After a long while, the pump thumped and stopped. The noise startled Chris and he swore. He removed the pump from the gas tank and hung it in the cradle. "Pizza?"

Billy slapped his stomach. "Pizza sounds perfect. I haven't eaten since lunch on Friday."

13

Pizza With a
Side øf Løre

———————————◆———————————

The drive to the restaurant was quiet. Chris' concern over Billy's four day disappearance seemed replaced with a deep pensiveness.

"Mr. Blacksmith," the old pizza chef called warmly through a thick, middle-eastern accent the moment Chris walked through the door. He wore a large orange turban and sported an impressively full, black beard. He stood behind the counter working dough with his bare knuckles. "The usual?"

"Make that three," Billy said as they found their way to an empty table.

The pizza place wasn't busy. The lunch crowd had left and the families tired of cooking hadn't arrived. It was a small, out of the way place, with aged white linoleum on the floor and old acoustic tiling. The large cardboard pizza in the window was bent with age and probably hadn't been changed since it was strung up some time in the '90s. But for the price, the pizza was the best in the valley.

It wasn't until they were seated, the pizza in front of them before Chris spoke again. When the pizza did arrive, Chris stared at it for a long time. Billy had already finished a slice before his brother spoke. "Mom and Dad didn't die in a fire," he said finally.

Billy almost choked on his mouthful, and stopped his sputtering with a swig of soda. He coughed and thought about those words. He chewed on the next slice, unsure how to respond. "But I saw the newspaper clippings. The house burned down."

Chris nodded without looking up. "The house burned down, but they were dead before the fire was bad enough to kill them."

"It was a spider?" Billy guessed.

"It was two," he said, his voice a rough whisper. "I didn't really remember what happened until I saw that thing in your bedroom the other night. Mom and Dad died trying to save us, Billy."

He stopped and took a bite of pizza. Billy suspected it was an attempt to pull himself together before continuing.

"You were brand new, Billy. Just a baby. I was too young to really understand what happened. We were watching TV and they came out of the wall. Like the wall opened and there was a whole world on the other side. Dad jumped up and ran right at them. Mom started throwing things. She shouted at me, "Christopher, take Billy and run. Run.""

He stopped, his eyes full of tears. His body shook, as if the memory physically tore at him. Billy was too surprised to react. He felt a strange hollowness, but Chris just kept on scooping more out of him.

"Mom grabbed a lighter and some spray from the kitchen. She started spraying one of them with the flames. Everything caught fire and then it just bit her in half. She lay there in two pieces, her guts leaking from her, spraying that thing in its face until its hair caught on fire too. Dad picked up the TV and smashed it over one of the spider's heads. Then he ran to Mom and the burning spider. It was burning and could barely move, but it jumped at him and Dad fell into pieces, too. Then it stumbled, screaming in pain. I will never forget that demonic scream."

Chris shook his head and shuddered. "I had you in my arms and I ran out the door, but they didn't follow. I just stood in the snow watching the house burn and burn. And our parents were gone. I never knew why that happened. But after seeing that spider the other night I think I might know." He gave Billy a sad smile, his face wet with tears.

Billy had nothing left inside. Just a gaping hole where his parents used to be. "They're after me."

"I won't let them," he said through gritted teeth. "I won't let them take you too."

Billy shook his head slightly, tears in his eyes, too. "You don't blame me?"

"What could a baby have done to tick them off? I don't know why they want you, but whatever the reason is, it's not your fault."

Billy smiled at his brother. Chris patted his hand and took a bite of pizza. He chewed it without any enthusiasm. They sat in silence eating pizza for what could have been five minutes. Finally, Chris spoke.

"Now. Who is Seth, and why did he make you go missing for four days?"

"About that. Am I on the news or anything?" Billy asked, finishing off another slice.

Chris laughed humorlessly. "Belinda and Steve were starting to get worried, but they were more bugged that you weren't sleeping where you were supposed to, though. I went over on Monday after Ash-Lea told me you didn't show up at school. I was just about to demand they call the police to report you missing. The only thing they said was if they were going to call the police, it was to get you arrested for running away."

Billy rolled his eyes. "The Fosters are awesome," he said dryly.

Chris nodded in agreement. "Yeah. And so many other people from around town have gone missing the cops just added your picture to a pile and said they'd keep trying."

"People still going missing?"

Chris nodded. "It's getting worse. They don't know what's happening to them. People are vanishing from everywhere. They think it might be a drug cartel, or aliens. No one knows. About seventy so far. We were sure you were one of them."

"Sorry about that. Seth didn't mention the party he planned would last so long."

"Okay, who is Seth?" Chris dropped his pizza on his plate, he refused to be ignored again.

"He's a demon that's training me to fight the powers of darkness," Billy said, taking a sip of Mountain Dew.

Chris laughed heartedly, enjoying the reprieve from the sadness. His laughter died slowly when he realized Billy was not joining him. Chris gazed at Billy, his eyes growing to the size of pizzas. "You're not kidding."

"Nope. He's a demon. He came to help me learn how to be stronger so I can save the world," Billy said flatly.

"If I didn't know you, I would say this is the most insane thing I have ever heard." Chris took a pensive swig from his soda and eyed the water-stained ceiling tiles. He pointed his straw at Billy. "No, this is still the most insane thing I've ever heard."

Billy shook his head. "I'm still not sure about it. But this morning was . . . weird."

Chris held up one hand. "Okay, let's not skip to that just yet. Where have you been?"

"I've only been to one place. I thought it was Saturday morning. I've been asleep the whole time."

"You took a four-day nap?" Chris' eyes were wide, his eyebrows high. "That's long, even for you."

He gave Chris a level look before continuing. "I guess so. Look. He said I have demon blood and he needed to wake it up." Billy felt frustrated, he wasn't explaining this right.

Chris nodded casually. He took a drink of his soda. "Oh, okay. That clears it right up."

Billy grumbled and closed his eyes, thinking. "I'm not sure what he did to me. He took me up by Black Mountain to a cabin he'd set up. Then he did this ritual thing. Once he'd done it I passed out. I woke up this morning and started walking back home."

"He performed a ritual on you? Why on earth are you letting this happen?"

Billy shrugged. "I don't know. It seemed like a good idea at the time. I mean, he said he needed help saving the world."

Chris' face settled into a twisted half smile. "Far out, man. So your demon blood is awake now?"

"Well, yeah, I guess. When I left the cabin a bunch of spiders, I mean a *bunch* of spiders, started chasing me."

Chris shifted uncomfortably. "There are those spider things up in Black Mountain?"

"Yeah. I'd never seen so many. And they were huge. Bigger than the Shadowlurk that attacked me. I think it was a Tremanchen."

"A what?"

"Don't worry about it. The spiders come in different flavors, apparently."

"How did you get away?" Chris swallowed nervously.

Billy took in a deep breath. "That's the thing. I ran." Of all the ridiculous things he could have said, that sounded the most unlikely.

Chris raised one eyebrow very high. "You're not much of a runner, Billy."

Billy's voice dropped to an anxious whisper. "I know. But something Seth did to me allowed me to outrun them. I covered like three miles in just a few seconds." He picked up a piece of pizza and took a bite.

"Really? Think you could do it again?" Chris furrowed his eyebrows.

Billy spoke through a mouthful of pizza. "I don't know, man. I just wanted to make sure they wouldn't hurt you or Greyson or Ash-Lea so I ran. He said he was going to awaken my demon blood, and I guess that that's what it means."

"Means you should quit baseball and join the cross-country team?" Chris laughed sincerely.

"Exactly," Billy chuckled.

Chris started to stand, then decided not to. He picked up a slice and then put it back down. He was still on his first piece. "Alright, if he took you up to this cabin, what happened to him? Couldn't he give you a ride home?"

"I don't know where he went. I haven't seen him since he performed the ritual." Billy tried to sound bothered, but his voice sounded more afraid than anything in his ears.

Chris scowled. "If he really wanted to protect you from the spiders he's doing a lousy job."

"I know, right?" Billy huffed.

"I'm not sure I really get this, Billy," Chris said, sounding sad, apologetic and worried at the same time. "I'm supposed to protect you. It's my job, and I'll be damned if I don't. But this feels just so far out of my control. I can't just go buy you some groceries and fix this. And there're only so many times I can pull my baby brother out of a burning house away from demonic spiders trying to eat him." Chris studied his half eaten pizza slice as he spoke. "Billy, I want to help. But I don't know what to do." Chris gave a sad grimace, then shook his head.

Billy felt bad for his brother. Chris had always been there for him, always taken care of him. No one else had. Not their foster parents, no one. It had always been Chris. Billy didn't know what he was asking Chris to do either—so he didn't say anything.

"What now?" Chris finally said, shrugging once and raising his hands as if in surrender.

"You going to make me go to school?" Billy asked.

Chris smiled again. "No, you smell awful. Come back to my place and have a shower. You can go to school tomorrow. I'll write you a note."

Billy smirked. "You allowed to do that?"

"Probably not, but you think Belinda will?"

Billy laughed.

That night, after a shower and a change of clothes, Chris dropped Billy off at Greyson's house. He'd found Billy's bike in the park the night he went missing and dropped it off with him too.

Billy knocked on the door and opened it. Ash-Lea saw Billy from the back room, her mouth dropping open before she bolted towards him. She was fast when properly motivated and slammed into Billy with a mighty hug, coming as close to knocking him over as someone her size could. Tonight she wore a dark blue t-shirt depicting three wolves howling at a moon.

"Nice to see you, too." Billy laughed.

She dragged Billy into the back room by a hand. "Look what I found," she announced.

Greyson stood, he smiled widely when he saw Billy. His eyes were heavy from lack of sleep, his hair all over the place. Greyson rarely got away with having messy hair.

He placed a piece of paper on the table. "Guess we can stop the missing poster project and get back to my diorama."

"You guys weren't making missing posters," Billy said slowly as he stepped into the living room.

A hundred or so copies of Billy's face stared at him from the coffee table, grinning from underneath a Devils baseball cap. At the top of each page the word MISSING was printed in large letters.

"Guys," Billy's chin quivered, threatening to embarrass him.

"Shut up." Ash-Lea gave him a wet-eyed smile. "You would have done the same thing."

He took both of his best friends under his arms in a hug. "Yeah, I would have. You guys are the best."

"Hey," Greyson said, his voice muffled by Billy's shirt. "Let's get back to work on the diorama. You can tell us where you've been."

Meredith appeared in the living room and gasped when she saw Billy. She looked as relieved as Ash-Lea had at his reappearance. She gave him an awkward hug, her thin arms not hoping to reach around him. She gushed, wiping tears away from her eyes. "Oh, Billy. So many people have gone missing lately, we were so worried you had too. Oh, Billy." She hugged him again.

"Um, thanks. It's nice to see you too, Meredith."

"Muffins and milk," she announced, knowing that was Billy's favorite meal.

Ash-Lea and Greyson cleaned up the posters on the table to make room for the cupcakes. Billy picked up one of the pieces of paper with his face on it.

"I'm keeping this," he smiled appreciatively at the picture of himself. "It not every day that someone makes a genuine missing poster of you." *Plus, it's a pretty well made poster.* Ash-Lea had a knack for artsy things. He looked up and saw Greyson and Ash-Lea watching him examine the paper in his hand.

"Thought you were gone, man," Greyson said in a low voice.

Billy smiled and slapped his friend on the shoulder.

Over a ridiculously large plate of chocolate and peanut butter muffins Billy relayed the whole story. From the weird love-story that Seth had told him, about demons falling in love with girls and saving the human race, to the ritual that knocked him unconscious for four days. He finished with his life-threatening trek out of the mountain. Greyson listened with wide-eyed reverence to the part with the spiders harassing him in the forest. Ash-Lea just looked mad. At this point in the story she was standing, crushing the remnants of a cupcake in her hand.

"So, you just like . . . teleported down the mountain?" Greyson asked, his voice full of rich awe.

Billy shook his head. "No, it wasn't like that. It felt like that. I just ran really fast for some reason."

"That butt muncher," Ash-Lea grumbled. "Left you to get eaten. I just . . . I'm going to kill him."

Greyson watched from his seat by the table as Ash-Lea paced back and forth. "You should tell him what you found out."

Ash-Lea's face lit up with dark joy. She turned, pointing the messy wax-paper cup at him. "Well, until you told me that story, I was starting to think Seth was a decent guy."

"How's that?" Billy asked.

Ash-Lea nudged Greyson with her toe. "Go get it."

Greyson left the room and returned carrying a laptop. He placed it on the table and pulled up his email. He clicked on a link in one from Ash-Lea and an image popped up on the screen.

"There." Greyson handed the laptop to Billy.

Billy studied the image, it was a scan of an old photograph, a crease running through the center, the edges damaged by age and exposure. Although it appeared to be a very old photograph, he immediately recognized the man in the picture. Mr. Diomed, not looking a day younger, wore a dark suit with a white bowtie and matching black fedora perched on his head. He stood arm in arm with a beautiful young woman. She couldn't have been more than eighteen. The couple reclined in front of a wall made of large stone bricks with vines crawling up the surface—a church, perhaps. The woman wore a simple, elegant silk wedding dress with long sleeves, a fine veil on her head, and a wide, joyous smile on her lips.

"His wedding photo?" Billy asked, looking up at Ash-Lea.

"Yep," Ash-Lea confirmed.

"She sure looks happy; don't you think?" Greyson asked, leaning over to look at the screen.

She did. Rose appeared elated in a dozen different ways in the photo. Her smile was genuine, her arm gripped Mr. Diomed's tighter than it strictly had to, her body leaned into his just slightly. She was the very image of a euphoric newlywed.

"Think she knew who he really was?" Ash-Lea asked, crushing the paper cup like it was a demon's neck and dumping it on the table.

"I don't know," Billy said.

Ash-Lea scoffed, shaking her head and pointing at Billy as if it were his fault. "I doubt it. It doesn't matter if she was in love, if she didn't know who he really was." Billy didn't know how to respond to that. "But get this, she's still alive."

"What?" Billy asked.

"Ok, let me clarify. There is a Rose Bloom Diomed in a nursing home in Arizona."

"How do you know that?"

Greyson made an indistinct sound, something between a laugh and an embarrassed cough. "I did some, um, internet research." Billy gave him a questioning look. "It wasn't exactly legal internet research. But I found out her social security number and tracked her down."

A heavy knock resounded on the front door. Greyson moved to close the computer. Ash-Lea eyed Billy with a hard look on her face, then walked out of the room into the entryway. A moment later her voice echoed through the house.

"No thanks, we're not buying." Then the door slammed closed.

Billy and Greyson exchanged quizzical glances and ran to the front door. Greyson swung it open and Mr. Diomed stood on the stoop, his fedora in his hands. His face lit up in relief when he saw Billy.

"William, thank the flame you're all right."

14

The Rules

◆────────────────────────────────────◆

"Nice of you to finally show up." Billy said, folding his arms and leaning against the entryway wall.

"Where the heck have you been?" demanded Ash-Lea, blocking Mr. Diomed's access to the house with her small figure, one hand on the door knob and the other on the frame. "Billy almost got himself killed, no thanks to you, Mr. Ditchy."

Mr. Diomed made to step into the house, but Ash-Lea started closing the door again.

"Let him in," Billy said. "We could at least hear him out."

Mr. Diomed looked down at Ash-Lea. She scowled at him. After an awkward twenty second starting competition, she stepped aside.

"Why didn't you wait at the cabin?" Mr. Diomed asked Billy as he stepped through the door.

"Why did you disappear?" Billy retorted.

Mr. Diomed's lip quivered with frustration. When he spoke it was with slow, palpable control. "I was afraid you were not going to wake up. You were safe within in the cabin so I sought council with my associates. Naturally, I did perform the ritual correctly. However, when I returned on Monday you were still asleep, so I sought council once more. Lelansiel returned with me and we did not find you there. But we saw the spider tracks in the forest and feared the worst."

Ash-Lea stepped in front of him, her hands pressed against her hips. "Why did you leave him alone if you knew the spiders could find him?"

Mr. Diomed took a deep breath and gritted his teeth. Billy could tell he was holding back a lot of things; frustration and anger chief among them, but also something else. Could it be fear, or maybe even concern?

When he spoke, his voice was stiff and controlled. "The spells I placed at the cabin kept him hidden from beings of the Demonic Realm."

"Demonic Realm?" Ash-Lea asked. "Do you mean hell?"

Mr. Diomed shook his head. "Not at all. You must dismiss everything you think you understand about angels and demons, heaven and hell. It is grievously inaccurate."

"Rrrright." Ash-Lea frowned. "You kept him hidden at the cabin. So, how did the spiders find him?"

"He was hidden unless the ritual succeeded in waking his blood."

"Did the ritual succeed?" Billy asked and immediately felt silly. He knew the answer, he could, after all, run a mile in a split second, but he wanted to make sure. Maybe that was just puberty.

"It did. After a short time, we could start to sense your power from our realm," Mr. Diomed's frustrated tone smoothed into something tighter. "As can the spiders."

Ash-Lea gave a horrified, guttural, *ugh*. "So, you woke up his blood—whatever in bleeding heck that means—and that makes him easier to find?" She glanced past Mr. Diomed into the street, as if spiders might be swarming behind him. For all Billy knew they might be.

"Yes." Mr. Diomed inclined his head.

"Wait, wait, wait." Billy looked Mr. Diomed in the eye. He tried to keep his voice level, but could hear the anxious quiver in his

140

words that told him he was failing. "Being easier to locate by gigantic spiders is something I would have liked to know before I signed up."

Mr. Diomed's eyebrows fell, his lips held tight, his face solid and serious. "Not just spiders, William. All creatures of darkness will know your scent now. It permeates all realms and every wicked thing will be drawn to you. All planets will know it has happened, for those that are listening."

If Billy looked worried, it was nothing compared to the taut, drawn looks of horror etched onto Greyson and Ash-Lea's faces.

Greyson spoke next, his voice thin. "But, why did the spider know exactly where Billy's bedroom was? If that was monsters having a hard time finding him, we might as well quit already."

Mr. Diomed turned back to Billy. "The Spider King sensed your demonic scent because you accessed the power of your blood. When you participate in the stickball game, the demonblood enhances your perceptions and your strength, even though it is not fully awake. It is why you are superior to all the other mortals."

Billy felt his heart sink. "So, I cheat?"

"Not at all. You simply used the abilities natural to your demonic heritage. Where before your blood whispered to all creatures of shadow, it now sings to them."

Billy sank against the wall. He barely survived the first attack in his room. If it wasn't for something close to a dark miracle, the spiders in the forest would have finished picking their mandibles clean with his bones. Now everything demonic could smell him and the scent was getting worse. "Yep, definitely something you should have brought up."

Ash-Lea folder her arms across her chest, her teeth gritted as she spoke. "How many other little caveats have you failed to mention to us?"

"Us, little human?" Mr. Diomed cocked his head to one side.

"Yes, us," said Greyson as he stepped up next to Ash-Lea.

Billy planted his feet behind his friends. "They're with me, Seth. You need to tell them everything. Especially because I just hit the top of the McDemon dollar menu."

Mr. Diomed glanced from Greyson to Ash-Lea, his gaze finally resting on Billy. His eyes narrowed. Billy could see him process the situation, he crumpled his hat in his hand. The demon had his own idea of how training would proceed and Billy wasn't playing along. *And that's just fine with me.*

Mr. Diomed let out a low grumble. "Very well. The reason why I did not tell you is because there are things you would not understand until your blood was awakened. And as it stands, there are things your friends will never comprehend." He waved a dismissive hand toward Greyson and Ash-Lea.

"Try us, Hamburgler," Ash-Lea growled.

Mr. Diomed's eyes flashed with a furious fire, then faded. "As you wish. I shall tell you the basic rules of handling the demonblood."

Ash-Lea huffed and stepped back, allowing Mr. Diomed into the house. She led them into the living room. Greyson, Billy and Ash-Lea sat down in that order or the couch, Billy in the middle.

Mr. Diomed stood in front of the fireplace. "This power that has been given you is not for mortals, that is why you must be augmented with a drop of my blood to allow you to control it."

His voice took on that funny tone it did sometimes, like the sound reaching Billy's brain had nothing to do with the vibrating air molecules between the demon's lips and Billy's ears. It occurred to Billy that Greyson's mom was not going to be able to hear this part of the conversation.

Billy processed the information for a moment. "So, it's in my blood, right?"

"Yes, I think I have been very clear on that point," Mr. Diomed responded with the air of one practicing extreme patience.

"So, why me, and not Chris?" Billy asked.

"Do you recall the tale of the Patriarch?" He didn't wait for a response. "The spell cast on the demon blood is an amalgamation of the will of the Patriarch, and the souls of each sacrifice. It is a mindful and intelligent thing. It has chosen its host throughout the generations. It did not find your older brother to be worthy, and chose you instead as its vessel." Mr. Diomed folded his arms and waited with a placid look on his face, as if he'd just said something simple and obvious.

Billy shook his head. "My brother is much cooler than me. That doesn't make sense."

"He is," Ash-Lea volunteered in agreement.

The demon smiled slightly. "It knows more about your potential than you do, little one."

"No, we're pretty sure it picked the wrong brother," Greyson said. Ash-Lea flashed him a wide smile.

Mr. Diomed, unimpressed, continued his lecture. "The first rule, and it is of utmost importance—never allow anyone to take even a drop of your blood. It is powerful, it is willful, it can be used for great evil, and it can be used to hurt others. As my blood was a catalyst to awaken yours, your blood can be used to infuse the soul of a partaker with the force and will of a thousand humans. It can be used to control the mind and actions of others against their will. Imagine the power some demons possess to persuade mortals. Then multiply that by a thousand. Your blood is dangerous to others now."

"Don't bleed. Got it," Billy nodded. "Never really a fan of bleeding anyway."

Greyson sniggered.

Mr. Diomed looked Billy up and down. "I can see that your blood has indeed been awakened and your body is taking to the change rather well."

Billy patted his broad stomach. "I don't feel any different."

"It is how you were able to escape the Tremanchen at the cabin."

Billy shrugged. "Yeah, I was running away from them and then I just started running faster and faster. I don't know how I did it."

The demon smiled knowingly. "That is your body beginning to embrace the demonblood. An increase in your agility is the first sign."

Ash-Lea *ah-hemmed*. "But if everyone from Demonland is going to try to kill him now, I'm pretty sure he's not going to be able to run away from them all. Aren't there some pretty fast guys where you're from?"

Mr. Diomed inclined his head. "While William's scent is now permeating all realms of darkness, making those of fang, mandible, and wing drool at the savor of his blood, it comes with it a message of power. They are afraid of him now."

"So, super-tasty, but super-scary?" she asked, adjusting in her seat.

"Essentially. Also, he has the protection of my associates and I."

"You mean *we* have the protection?" Billy waved his index finger back and forth, including Ash-Lea and Greyson in the gesture.

Mr. Diomed scowled. "Yes, all of you."

"So, what's next?" Greyson asked as he picked up a cupcake from the table.

"As you have seen, initially you will find your agility has increased, followed by your strength. Eventually your mind will become sharpened and the channels of magics—the remains of your wizard ancestry—will be opened back unto you. You will be able to unlock portals as I do. The extent of your magic ability depends a lot on what the blood has to work with. That will require a great deal of work on your part if you wish to utilize it to the utmost of your potential."

"Cool," said Greyson.

"Wait, do you mean there'll be homework?" Billy asked with trepidation.

Mr. Diomed nodded. "Of course. I told you that this is not a free gift. What things of value in this world come without effort? Or reading?" He leveled a look at Billy and continued. "Finally your body will begin to adapt and you will adopt the form of a true demon."

Billy sat bolt upright. "Whoa, hold the phone. I'm going to end up looking like you?"

Mr. Diomed tightened his lips and shook his head. "Not necessarily. But you will obtain your true demon form."

"That's going to make it kind of hard to get a driver's license," Billy said, looking askance at Mr. Diomed.

"You will not be confined to the form. It is a willful thing. You will need to learn to control and contain it." He clenched his fists before him, an evil, greedy smile growing across his face. "And if you survive, you will master it," he finished with relish in his voice.

From the look in Seth's eye, Billy suspected there was something in this for the demon, once he mastered the Demonblood. He had no idea what that could be. "That sounds like an awful lot of work," Billy grumbled and settled back down.

Mr. Diomed smirked. "You will be challenged beyond what any mortal has faced for millennia. To say it will be work is a devastating understatement."

Billy felt his stomach sink again. "You should have mentioned all of this—any of this—earlier." *This doesn't sound fun at all. And for what? Saving a world that doesn't need to be saved. Well, not yet, at least.*

Mr. Diomed looked at him with a gravity that Billy felt on his shoulders. "What I offer you is the ability to unlock the power within you, William Blacksmith. If you chose, you may become the greatest warrior in any mortal or demonic realm. But if you chose not to, you may continue to live your life as you have been, and never reach your potential."

Billy eyed the man before him. "But if I do that the world will be destroyed, guaranteed?"

"Absolutely," the demon nodded once. "Then every world in this universe, in turn."

Billy sighed. "Not much of a choice then, is it?"

Mr. Diomed's eyes narrowed with an inscrutable expression. "The fact that you see it that way says a lot about who you are, William. May I offer you one piece of advice?"

"Hmm, kay?"

"This is a spell that combines the mortal and demonic. The will and soul of those that came before you have a power to influence and augment you, but it is based upon your mortal form, physically and mentally. And currently your mortal form," he looked Billy up and down, "is in need of a great deal of enhancing."

Billy frowned. "Hey, you're not so good looking yourself."

Ash-Lea guffawed and slapped her knee. Greyson hid a snigger behind one hand.

"Good, keep that fire close, William Blacksmith. You will need it for the battles ahead."

Mr. Diomed took on a serious demeanor that made Billy stop and look. Where the room sat muffled before, the air was now thick with silence. All sound drowned out except the breathing of his friends beside him. Billy could no longer hear the cars driving by on the distant highway, or the wind rattling through the trees beyond the gigantic windows. Across the stark void, Billy felt the demon's words ring in his ears.

"Finally," Mr. Diomed continued, "as I said, the blood is willful. Within your blood, the will of a thousand human souls have taken residence. In addition to the Patriarch, each is a mindful individual, each has a personality, each has a will. Although I do not know if the minds remain distinct from one another—I sincerely hope they do—their combined force is incredibly strong. It is the role of the Demonblooded to overcome and direct these wills for good. The Patriarch loved his maiden, but he was a demon, as am I. Indeed, he was far more powerful than I could ever hope to be. It is these one thousand and one wills that you must contend against. Do you understand?"

Billy felt all the blood leave his face as the weight of his words settled in.

The silence in the room slowly lifted. He could hear the clock ticking on the wall, then crickets chirped outside the window, and a car door slammed on the street. Billy stared at Mr. Diomed, going over the words in his mind.

There are a thousand humans in me? How is that even possible? And what if . . . his mind felt so full of questions he couldn't form another one.

Ash-Lea was the first one to break the silence, speaking in a small voice. "Is Billy going to go crazy?"

"It is a great possibility, little one."

15

Escalation

———◆——————————————◆———

K rios crushed the metal goblet in his claw and threw it against the wall. It slammed into the stone wall of the dining hall and rebounded over the second row of long trestle tables into the center of the room.

Krios faced the trembling Tremanchen across the table before him. "There is only one reason why the Demonseed should have been able to escape."

The spider, flanked by two huge guards, lowered his eight eyes, looking anywhere but his General.

Krios rose and paced away down the dining hall and past the tall arched windows that looked out upon the Sulfur Sea. The long dining hall, built to host several hundred of the king's subjects at a meal, echoed at the sound of his claws. He was the only one eating at this late hour. The vaulted ceiling disappeared into the dim light high above them. Hundreds of candelabras lined the walls and bathed the room in a sullen light.

Sir Ursus picked up the bent cup, careful not to touch the jagged shard protruding from the lip, and placed it on the table beside the General's supper.

Krios reached the wall by the entrance doors and took a deep breath. The guards standing by the door kept their eyes forward, maintaining a stolid, professional demeanor despite their General's frustration. Finally, Krios walked back and sat before his meal again—though he had no appetite.

"I sent two hundred soldiers to scour the city for the human," Krios growled, nudging the fleshworm steak on the plate before him. "That should have been more than enough legs to find a simple, fat human. Why have you failed me, Amyntas?"

Amyntas shifted backwards a step. The pair of Arachnis guards looming next to him moved closer. "We were closing in on him as he left his place of education," Amyntas stammered. "But there appears to have been someone assisting him. Before we could attack, he was lifted away and we could not pursue."

"No, no, no, no, NO." Krios spat, pounding a claw on the table, the cutlery jangled with the movement. "Why did you not take him while he sat idle at that place of education?"

Amyntas glanced up at Krios, his many eyes wide. "But, honored General, it is against the law. The humans are far more capable of defending themselves against us than they used to be." He swallowed, searching the stone under his claws for some explanation. "And the Threshold still seals the greater powers. We are not permitted to engage in any activity that may cause an incident. If there is to be war against them we shall surely lose."

A burst of anger exploded in Krios' thorax. He leapt across the table towards the soldier. Hooking Amyntas' mandibles with one claw, Krios stood on his back legs, jerking the Tremanchen off the floor. The guards beside him stepped back, allowing their General his educational privilege. Amyntas' eight legs flailed uselessly as he tried to steady himself.

Krios leaned close and snarled in the spider's face. "I do not need you to explain the law to me. You will not use rules as an excuse for your overt cowardice. We are dealing with the Demonseed and you allowed the law to stop you? If his blood is awakened, then the coming war against the humans is already lost."

Krios twisted his mighty body, hurling Amyntas through the air. The smaller spider slammed into the hard floor and slid across the stone, gasping in pain. He slowly rose on shaking legs, and bowed before his General.

"So, my incompetent Captain. You tracked him to where the accomplice took him, correct?" Krios asked.

Amyntas nodded.

Krios could not keep the red hot fire out of his words. "Then tell me how the Demonseed escaped you."

Amyntas shook, trying to stay upright on quivering legs. "He ran from us, honored General."

"And it is this piece of information that gives me the greatest concern. Please clarify something for me, if you would, Amyntas. Did he run away from you on his human legs?"

Amyntas swallowed. "He did."

"His fat, slow, weak human legs?"

Amyntas closed his eyes. "He did."

Krios looked down at his subordinate that had failed him, that had failed his king, so completely. He leaned in close and whispered, "Tell me why you think that is."

Amyntas gasped in a dozen pained breaths before he could speak. "Because the Demonseed's blood has been awakened," he whispered.

"BECAUSE THE DEMONSEED'S BLOOD HAS BEEN AWAKENED," Krios bellowed. "And you allowed that to happen."

Krios drew his sword from his scabbard and held the blade above his head. "As much as I regret losing a soldier as capable as you, for failure so great it equals treason, I hereby sentence you to death." He looked down at Amyntas cowering before him. This was a mistake of utter incompetence, and the repercussions would be impossible to ignore. But the spider himself was a good and loyal soldier to the king. Krios slid his sword back into the scabbard.

"You may rot in the dungeons until your final day."

Amnytas burst into tears. "Oh, thank you. Thank you, General," he said through his sobs. "You spared my life."

Sir Ursus waved to the guards by the door. "Please remove this coward. We don't need him weeping all over the floor."

The guards moved and dragged Amyntas away.

"The king will need to hear of this soon, General," Sir Ursus suggested.

Krios snorted. "The scent of the Blacksmith already begins to permeate this realm. If the king does not know the blood has been awakened, he will know in short order."

"I advise that you tell him yourself."

Krios gave him a sidelong look. "Naturally. How goes the gathering?"

"The ingredients are almost all in place. We have arranged them to be pooled so we may remove them from the earth at the same time."

"Excellent. A greater gathering of my soldiers will make it harder for the mortals to stop us if we are discovered." A memory stirred from when Krios first visited the human realm one hundred years earlier. "Sir Ursus, have you ever beheld a human gun?"

"No, sir. I have not been in battle against a human in almost five hundred years."

"They are amazing creations. They spit fire that easily passes through the lesser soldier's armor. It would be marvelous if the ants could investigate making such weapons for us. It would certainly even the odds when the war comes."

Sir Ursus nodded. "I will instruct them to begin researching."

"Thank you." Krios paused, raking a claw through the course hair on the back of his head. "A thought occurs to me. Perhaps we can use this opportunity to ensnare the Blacksmith. He is only new to his power, he will still be weak. If we can lure him to the place where we will remove the materials we have gathered, we can overpower him." Krios stroked his chin. "We shall behead two flies with one bite. I will see to the delivery myself."

"I have arranged for a full battalion to be stationed at the delivery point. I'm sure your presence would not be required. I would hate for the General of the Spider Horde to be in harm's way."

"It is my place to stand between danger and my king, Counselor." Krios shook his head. "I am obligated to show his majesty that I am dedicated to his cause. Especially after I have let him down so thoroughly by allowing the Demonseed to awaken."

Sir Ursus twisted his grey beard with a claw and stepped up beside Krios. "May I suggest we call upon the scorpions? They are known for their cunning and have often been useful in moving secretly about the Earthly Realm."

A smile stretched Krios' mouth. "Yes, I will send word to their General immediately. Get me parchment and a messenger wyvern."

Sir Ursus waved a claw to the young page by the door, who brought forth parchment and ink. The page placed parchment in front of Krios and he began to write. The Master of Communication arrived bearing a cage containing a small winged wyvern, the grey brown scales glinted below leathery wings. He opened the cage and the wyvern shot out, flapping around Krios' head and squawking merrily. It landed next to his claw and started nuzzling the paper, eager to deliver the message.

Krios brushed him aside with an amused grunt. "You picked an enthusiastic one." He continued scrawling, "I will offer the scorpions my ounce of the Blacksmith's blood as payment for his assistance."

Sir Ursus froze and looked at Krios with wide eyes. "That is a valuable gift. To give away even a drop of the Demonseed's blood sounds like madness."

The wyvern cawed impatiently.

"No, not madness. I gave my word to my king that I would bring him the Blacksmith. I would rather die than break an oath."

"A matter of pride?" inquired Sir Ursus.

Krios faced his advisor and glowered. "Not pride, honor. Honor is the most valuable item a soldier possesses. I ask no less from my warriors—to do as they have sworn to do. That being the case, I can ask no less of myself. That power would be meaningless if I could not be trusted to keep my promises."

"As you say, my General."

Krios rolled up the parchment and sealed it with his wax seal before slipping it into the canister tied to the messenger wyvern's back. "Take word to the scorpions," he told the small dragon. It squawked dutifully and flapped its leathery wings as it flew out of sight. Krios turned back to his counselor, a smile on his spider face. "I have a plan, Sir Ursus. The one useful thing Captain Amyntas provided before his untimely incarceration were the names of the Blacksmith's companions. Humans greatest weakness is their irrational need to save other humans." He strode out of the hall his appetite diminished. "Before this week has ended, I shall capture the Blacksmith and bring him before the throne myself."

16

Missing

•————————————————————————————•

Ash-Lea was already sitting when Billy entered the classroom. She held up her hand for a high-five. Billy slapped her hand before talking the seat next to her. Sun streamed in through the window, though the light seemed muted somehow—the sunlight was the wrong color. He stared at the grounds outside. The air appeared smoky, although he couldn't see or smell a fire anywhere. The kids bustled about the classroom making their way to their seats, their voices harsher than usual. The air trembled with a hint of nervous irascibility. So many people had gone missing around town, it was taking its toll on everyone.

He leaned forward eyeing the empty seat next to Ash-Lea with a curious glance. "Where is Greyson today? Did he tell you he was going to be out?"

Ash-Lea spun her pencil around her thumb. "I swung by this morning. His parents said he was sick in his room, that wuss." She leaned toward him. "And they were like, super rude. I think I ticked off Mrs. Ash last night."

"Really? I didn't know she could get ticked off. She's the nicest lady I know."

"I know, right?" Ash-Lea shrugged. "Hope not. I hate hanging out at my place. There is no cat hair at Greyson's. It's everywhere at my house."

It was Billy's turn to shrug. "I like your house. It's lively. The Fosters aren't really great company."

Ash-Lea huffed out a breath and rose her eyebrows. "Don't take the peace and quiet for granted, man. I would kill for some quiet. Or at least some sweet noise cancelling headphones. Failing that I'd settle for a septuple murder-suicide involving my siblings."

Billy gave her a dry look.

"Septuple means seven of something. I looked it up so I knew what to tell the news folks when it finally happened. Pretty sure it's going to be my sister on the phone versus my brother's music."

"Ashes," Billy sighed. "Don't take the noise for granted. Those people in your house are noisy and get in your face all the time. But there's a lot of love there. I'd love to have a family."

Ash-Lea looked away and settled down in her seat. "Sorry, man," she muttered.

Billy changed the subject. "Greyson didn't look sick yesterday."

"No." She shook her head. "Other than the normal sick you'd feel when a demon is telling you your best friend is going to go insane with demonic power."

There was a long pause.

"Pretty weird, huh?" Billy scrunched his face up, fearing the answer.

"If you think it's going to make me think of you any differently, you're going to be disappointed. But yeah, it's weird. Demon blood, huh? Wonder what that even means."

"I'm kind of freaked out. Seth seems like he's telling the truth, and I really did run away from those spiders pretty quickly. Something's going on, and I know I feel different."

Ash-Lea looked up at him and gave a small, sincere smile. "We're going to be here for you, Billy. You don't have to worry about that."

"Honestly, Ashes. That's the only thing I care about."

She punched him in the arm as the Strictmeister entered the room and hushed the students.

"Quinn's not here," lamented Ash-Lea under her breath.

"So, why would you care? I thought you hated her," Billy said.

"I think she's a bimbo, but Greyson hasn't signed up for the diorama contest yet."

"Isn't that tomorrow? I thought he signed up days ago."

Ash-Lea rolled her eyes. "Duh. Kind of slipped his mind when his best friend went missing."

Billy felt himself blush and smile at the same time.

Ash-Lea kept her eyes on Billy and counted down silently. "Three, two, one."

"Miss Gray," Mr. Strict said.

Ash-Lea smirked and straightened, her face falling into an odd look of concern.

Billy turned to see Mr. Strict eyeing Greyson's empty seat. "Is Mr. Ash, um," he coughed, stopping himself before he asked the question.

"He's just sick, sir," Ash-Lea waved a hand.

The man looked visibly relieved. "That's good news. I mean. It's better than what it could be, all things considered. Now," he said, his voice shaking faintly as he started writing on the board again, "expanding equations."

Billy looked about the room, a sinking feeling in his stomach. There were four empty chairs today. Too many people were missing.

This can't be a coincidence, he thought. *Seth, your friendly neighborhood demon just happens to show up right around the time insane amounts of people go missing in my town. But how are they connected?* Billy felt an urgency building inside him. He had to figure this out before someone got hurt.

As the day continued Billy just felt more frustrated. The school felt emptier than usual. It may have been the students clumping together between classes, or the empty seats in the cafeteria. *Like hell I'm going to sit around and let crap like this happen.*

Seth had to know what was happening, Billy was sure of it. He wanted to talk to the demon, force him to tell him what he knew. Billy had not seen any of his demon support team following him, let alone Seth. But when he did see any other demons, he'd beat the information out of them if he had to. By the time the bell rang a grey lull hung over the school; as if a cloud of depression was settling over the building.

When the last class was dismissed the unsettled sensation made his neck itch. "I have to go to baseball," Billy said to Ash-Lea, almost adding 'I'm sorry.' *Something is not right.* "I'll meet you at Greyson's later?"

"Yeah, if he's up to it." She waved over her shoulder as she turned towards her bike. Billy watched her go, a heavy feeling weighed in his chest, something he couldn't quite describe.

Walking across school to the diamond, Billy looked around from roof tops to trees, to the deep shadows between buildings. He didn't see anything or anyone—at least not anything demonic.

"Where are you, jerk?" Billy muttered to himself. "I know you're out there watching me. *Protecting* me." He snorted.

But if he's a bad guy, why did he wake your blood and help you escape those spiders? You couldn't run like that before, could you? An annoyingly rational part of his brain asked him. Billy shook it away, he liked being mad at the demon. It gave him focus for his helpless aggravation.

Cop cars dotted the streets about the school, keeping an eye on the children as they walked home. A uniformed officer stood at the entrance to the diamond, taking mental note of everyone that walked by. He watched Billy as he passed, chewing his lip debating. After a moment, he decided Billy was nothing but a student and returned to scrutinizing the afternoon.

An abundance of police officers aside, practice didn't even feel like practice any more. Baseball came easier than ever and Belle wasn't there to glower at him. When he focused on the ball, it appeared as if it moved in slow motion—not dramatic movie slow-motion, but boring, drawn-out slow-motion. The ball bent toward him through the air and he hit it perfectly every time. The ease with which he played was completely unfair to the other players. He didn't know if he could keep playing in good conscience. He wasn't even wholly human anymore—maybe—he honestly didn't know. He'd never seen any mention of non-humans in the high school sports rule books, but demon blood probably disqualified him.

While resting after his twelfth home run of the day, Billy looked up and saw Ash-Lea standing nervously on the grass. His friends would come to every game, but didn't typically attend practice. He took in the stress on her face and felt his chest clench.

Billy climbed out of the dugout and jogged towards her. "What's up, Ashes?"

"Greyson isn't answering. I think they're home. I can hear something in there banging around, but nobody is coming to the door."

The floor dropped out from under Billy. "I'm coming," he said. He had a gut-wrenching suspicion what had happened to Greyson, and did not want to believe it.

Billy ran to pick up his bag and slung it over his shoulder.

"Blacksmith!" Coach Schnurrbart shouted as Billy ran to his bike. "Where do you think you're going? We're in the middle of practice."

"I quit, coach," he took off his cap and tossed it to him. "I've got more important things to worry about,"

The man caught the cap, and started at Billy. He looked ready to collapse, but steadied himself on the shoulder of the player next to him. His lips trembled, flowing through a dozen things he didn't quite say. "You take some time off, Blacksmith. We'll talk about this tomorrow."

"Not likely," Billy said to himself.

They sprung onto their bikes and were off. Billy did not want to think of what awaited them—but he knew. Something in his blood told him that dark things were crawling around his town, preparing to do evil.

The smoke in the air that no one seemed to notice grew thicker—and something about it called to him, called to his demon blood. The atmosphere felt familiar to someone inside him, someone that wasn't him. Seth stated the people inside Billy might have retained their individuality. Billy suspected *someone* had, and recognized the demonic scent. It drifted across the neighborhoods between him and Greyson's house, an ethereal scent so rancid he could almost taste it. He ignored his pounding heart and started peddling as fast as he could. His instincts started screaming at him that he needed to get to Greyson five minutes ago.

"Hey, speed racer," Ash-Lea yelled, winded, from far behind on the street. "Don't leave me behind. You need me."

It took more restraint than Billy knew he had, but he slowed, allowing Ash-Lea to keep up. Ten minutes later, they pulled onto the lawn and let their bikes clatter to the grass. Barely slowing, they ran to the front door.

Billy slammed his fist against the wood. "Greyson."

Something inside the house moved, a shadow shifting across the closed curtains. Billy took a step back, pulled his bat from his bag and gripped it like a weapon.

"Stand back," he said.

Ash-Lea stepped down from the porch, but drew a throwing knife from inside her coat, holding it defensively in her hand. She nodded at Billy.

Bat in hand, Billy lifted his foot and kicked towards the door. The world slowed down again as his foot moved, allowing him the change to angle his cleat just right so he could strike the panel directly next to the lock. The wood shattered, the door swinging inward so quickly the handle struck the entrance wall with a gigantic bang. The force of the kick twisted the hinges and the door stayed open.

Billy moved into the dark house, the bat held up, ready to strike. Beyond the dark entryway under the stairs, he could see something thick and corded covering the windows. It didn't look like the usual blinds. Ash-Lea stepped up silently behind him.

"Greyson?" Billy shouted, trying to keep the fear out of his voice.

Something gave a muffled a response. His eyes adjusting to the dark, Billy saw what covered the windows. Two adult-sized figures were bound in spider webs, suspended from the ceiling and wall, their silhouettes framed by the muted light through the large windows.

Movement came at them from the top of the stairs. So focused on the figures hanging from the ceiling, Billy did not have time to react. A flash of silver came from beside him as Ash-Lea's knife left her hand. A monstrous squeal of pain echoed through the house.

Billy jumped backwards and looked up in time to see a spider retreating to the roof above the stairway. It reached up with one furry claw and plucked the knife out of its eye. Green goo leaked from the wound. "Blacksmith," its low voice rattled, "the one you call Greyson is not here."

"What are you doing here?" Billy asked, his voice shaking. The creature watched them from its perch by the ceiling. It was larger than the one that attacked him in his room, and more of a brown color than black. *Tremanchen, or Balchen, then.* He wasn't sure.

"We wanted to get your attention, Blacksmith."

"Oh yeah? Well you've kind of strung up my friend's parents. So if you want to talk, you'll have to let them go first."

The spider made a tut-tut noise. "I am not here to negotiate, fleshy mortal. I am here to deliver a message."

"You want to talk, you let them go," Billy growled, his fury overriding his fear.

The thing made an odd tittering noise that Billy supposed might have been laughter. "We will drink your blood. And if you refuse, we will drink the blood of those you love until you lie down and let us sup upon you."

"Not impressed with either of those options, hairy."

"You have no choice, Blacksmith. We outnumber you. We will not tire. Your soft human body will sleep at some time. You have no choice."

"What have you done with Greyson?" Ash-Lea insisted, more composed than Billy felt but still furious.

The creature's many eyes flicked to her. "Alas, he is not here. I was ordered to wait and give you this message."

Ash-Lea had another knife gripped in her hand. "What does Greyson's parents have to do with this?"

It shrugged, its many shoulders moving in a grotesque, rippling motion. "While I waited for you I thought making a meal of his parents would be a nice reward for my services."

Mr. and Mrs. Ash started to squirm, making muffled cries of panic. They were still alive, conscious, and terrified.

"Not if we can help it," Ash-Lea snarled.

"No, no," it said, its voice sounding like someone reproving a young child. "You will leave now. Greyson's minutes are numbered. You will not interrupt my supper. You will run along and save him. These humans are lost to you."

Greyson's parent's muffled shouts grew in volume. Though he couldn't understand them, Billy knew what they were trying to say, *please, go, save Greyson*. But he could not leave them there. Ash-Lea glanced at him, worry and fear painting her face. She pulled another knife from within her coat and crouched.

Billy turned back to the spider that leered down at them from the ceiling. "Dude, I'm pretty fast. I think we can fit everything in."

Ash-Lea flicked him a tremulous smile.

Without a sound, the spider leapt, lunging for Ash-Lea. Even prepared for it, the thing moved wickedly fast. But Ash-Lea was just slightly faster. She let fly with another knife before the spider reached her. The blade thudded into its eye, but the monster did not stop charging. Billy let out a shout, and lunged toward it, sweeping the bat underneath the spider's right legs as they tried to find purchase. The spider stumbled to its side, but sprung off the floor immediately, facing them as it slid to a stop in the formal dining room. The heavy table upended as the spider crashed into it, spilling a decorative vase of flowers and toppling the chairs to the floor.

Ash-Lea let fly with three more knives, each one landing in the spider's fleshy head. It squealed and glared at her with its mandibles slashing in its anger.

Billy took the opening, running towards it as the world slowed down around him. He could see the spider's head flick towards him, its front claw lifted off the tile attempting to swat him aside—but it wasn't fast enough for his demon-blood enhanced speed. His bat moved upward, sliding between the mandibles and cracked into the spider's head. Blood and goo squirted from the crevice and the spider fell to the floor twitching.

Billy caught himself and faced the monster. "That'll do, donkey," he said in a mock Scottish accent.

"Just in time, I was out." Ash-Lea panted. She inched her way toward the spider where she cautiously plucked the knives from the monster's face with two fingers. As she wiped the blade on her pants the blood morphed into what appeared to be white drywall and pink, puffy ceiling insulation. "You're pretty fast, Blacksmith."

"Yeah, don't call me that. It's one of their favorite nicknames. Not sure why." Billy turned to look at Greyson's parents, then the nausea overtook him. Before he could stop himself he sunk to the floor.

"You okay?" Ash-Lea's voice was full of concern. She knelt beside him.

"Yeah, just get really dizzy when I move like that. Help Greyson's folks."

"Okay." She patted him on the shoulder and stood. She walked under the stairs and into the living room-kitchen area, craning her neck to look at the webs that bound them. A man's eye, wide with fear and confusion, could be seen through a gap in the webbing. "How am I supposed to—?" she asked, turning around to face Billy.

Billy watched as Ash-Lea, framed in the arch under the stairs, looked towards the ceiling in the living room. Her expression shifted from relived tension into utter fear.

A dry, scraping voice echoed from the room in which she stood. "You don't think the messenger was left alone, do you?"

17

The Webbed Wall

"Great googly moogly," Ash-Lea stammered. She flicked her head back and forth, her eyes wide, counting things Billy could not see.

"It is an important message that the Spider King wanted you to hear," the rasping voice said. "But we do not hail to the Spider King. It is of no concern to us if you save this Greyson person. What we do desire is your human flesh."

Billy's skin crawled as the sound of a dozen claws scraping on tile and wood reached his ears. A chorus of excited breaths, rattling through alien throats, rose in tempo. Some monster howled in delight and Billy heard them rush towards Ash-Lea.

Ash-Lea let fly each one of her knives, save one. Five separate screeches of pain followed. She'd hit as many as she could. She bent, prepared to fight, her eyes darting about at the things attacking her. She raised the knife in a steady hand and narrowed her eyes.

Ignoring the nausea, Billy leapt off his butt and raced through the archway. Despite his supernatural speed, he couldn't make it into the living room fast enough. A black scaly, insect-like body the size of a Doberman, flew at Ash-Lea aiming its long stinger right at her. She brought the knife up, catching the thing in the abdomen, and twisted her body, throwing the demon to the side. The creature landed in a tangle of limbs on the floor and lashed out at Ash-Lea's leg with its stinger, missing her by an inch. It slid across the tile and into the wall of spider webs and started thrashing, squealing in panic as it entwined itself hopelessly in the sticky netting.

Billy reached the living room in time for two more scorpions—he guessed from their flicking tails and crab-like claws—to leap from the walls towards Ash-Lea, their spindly legs spread wide. Billy jumped, twisting in the air as the creatures dove towards her. He let out a cry of effort and brought the bat around as he spun, bashing one of the scorpions into the other. They flew across the room into the kitchen and slammed into the cabinets, scrabbling against one another as they fell to the floor. The iron railing on which Meredith Ash kept her heavy pots teetered and fell behind the island. The sound of scorpion screams was covered by the cacophonous clatter of cookware.

Billy backed up next to Ash-Lea and finally got a good look at what kept her so distracted. Eight more scorpions clung to the ceiling and walls; ugly, black and grey scaly things. Each had a red stripe running down their backs and tails, but the mark was not natural—it had been smeared on like some kind of war paint. The creatures looked down at Billy and Ash-Lea, their unnecessarily gigantic crab-like pincers snapping menacingly, each hissing and clacking. It took Billy a moment to realize that they were speaking. The largest one in the middle appeared to be giving directions, his stinger-tipped tail flicking back and forth as it pointed.

There were eight of them left, and according to Billy's calculations, he was going to end up dead very quickly.

"Get out of here, Ashes," Billy said, "I'll hold them off. You go find Greyson."

"Oh, okay." Ash-Lea scoffed. "Heroic dingus."

The scorpions began creeping slowly down the wall to the floor. They were not planning on jumping at him, which was unfortunate; he could handle objects being flung at his face, especially when he was holding a baseball bat. A sinking feeling told him exactly what the scorpions were thinking. Behind him, Meredith gave a low, muffled scream.

"It'll be ok, guys. Hold on for a minute longer," Ash-Lea said, sweeping her knife before her. "Billy totally has this under control. Right, Billy?"

He tried to respond, but instead made a noise somewhere between a cough and hiccup.

The scorpions fanned out on the floor, claws scuttling on the tile. They formed a semi-circle around Billy and Ash-Lea, trapping them against the wall of spider webs. Billy swallowed. Demonic speed was not going to help him here. If he ran for one, the others would close in on Ash-Lea. Looking quickly from one huge, black scorpion to the other, his mind raced, trying to figure a way out of the trap. The animals took a slow, synchronized step towards him, tightening the vice about them.

"Billy?" Ash-Lea asked, her voice rising in pitch. "You do have this under control, don't you?"

The largest scorpion, the one in the middle handing out all the instructions, continued to clatter and chirp. Small bony protrusions in its face, something like lips, grated against each other, letting out the unearthly noise. The scorpion stepped forward towards Billy, the others remained behind, their attention shifting to Ash-Lea. The message was clear. *I'll take you, and if you resist, they will kill her.*

Without preamble, the monster lunged at Billy, the stinger on its tail stabbing towards him. On instinct, he swatted with his bat. The leader scorpion retreated a step, the others scuttling closer to Ash-Lea.

"Don't think he's a fan of that," Ash-Lea cautioned.

Billy kept his eyes on the leader as he stepped up again. It tilted it head-like appendage in a condescending manner, its black eyes glistening.

"Die quietly," it instructed in a wholly alien accent.

Billy shivered, gripped his bat and planted his feet. "No."

It straightened its head. "Then you will watch her die noisily."

It lunged at Ash-Lea this time, keeping its body low to avoid Billy's swing. He thrust his bat out to the left, trying to get something, anything, between the monster and his friend. A great thwack sounded as the bat was nearly torn from his grasp. He gripped it with his other hand and held on as the scorpion backed away. He yanked on the bat, and the scorpion dug his claws into the floor. It took a moment for Billy to realize what had happened—the leader's stinger had become imbedded in his bat, and try as the monster might, he couldn't pull it free. Billy and the scorpion played tug-of-war for a few horrible seconds. The scorpion tried to wrench the bat out of his hands, Billy tried desperately not to be separated from his only weapon. The henchmen scorpions watched on with wide-eyes at the spectacle.

"Not sure how this is helping," Ash-Lea pointed her knife at another scorpion that tried to sneak in closer.

The leader scorpion scuttled on the tile as it strained against Billy. He took a step backwards and the scorpion scraped forward a foot, the rug under his claws sliding easily. Then something occurred to Billy; the demonic animals were light. There simply wasn't much more to them than the black exoskeleton. Billy stopped struggling against the creature and stood to his full height, stretching the bat out to the side. The scorpion hung from the end of the bat, twisting and spitting in fury. The henchmen scorpions looked at one another, and Billy thought he could hear some of them give a demon-scorpion version of a chuckle.

Billy twisted the bat around his head in an arc, the scorpion attached to the end screamed in futile fury. He brought the thing down on the nearest minion with a wet crack. The noise reminded the other scorpions why they were there and they stopped chuckling.

Two lunged for Ash-Lea. She caught the tail of one just below the stinger in her hand and sunk her blade into the head of the other. As she withdrew the knife, the henchman scorpion flopped to the floor, its body melting. Seeing his friend dispatched so easily, the scorpion wrenched his stinger free from Ash-Lea's hand and retreated.

Billy tugged on the rug as hard as he could. The scorpions instinctively gripped the carpet and rode it until he dumped them upside down. The lumps under the carpet hissed and bucked. He swung the limp body of the former scorpion leader into the last free scorpion and they collided with a snap. The impact wrenched the scorpion leader free of his tail. He wailed as he stumbled on the lumps of his companions still struggling under the rug.

Ash-Lea took the opportunity and jumped onto the leader, cutting it across what may have been its throat. The monster immediately started to turn into pink, fluffy ceiling insulation.

Then the remaining three scorpions finally extracted themselves from under the carpet. They glanced over the room, taking in the bat in Billy's hand, the tail of their former leader still imbedded in the metal, quickly dissolving into drywall. Without another sound, they scuttled down the hall, around the unconscious spider, and out the front door.

The nausea threatened to overwhelm Billy, but he swallowed it back, keeping the bat in his hand as he watched the retreating forms disappear into the darkening evening. "Looks like you scared them off, Ashes."

There came a muffled sound from the spider webs containing Greyson's parents. They started shaking and Billy saw Mr. Ash trying to nod; although, bound upside down in demonic spider webs, he only managed to make himself shake. Billy looked at the remaining scorpion, still trapped in the webs. He had become completely ensnared and gave up struggling. It, instead, hissed in defiance.

"Keep an eye on that one." Billy lifted his chin in the direction of the last scorpion.

Ash-Lea nodded without looking away from Mr. and Mrs. Ash, and extended a comforting hand. "Take it easy, Mr. Ash, we'll get you out."

"Mung fuu," Meredith replied.

Ash-Lea hooked her last knife into her belt and a look of fury crossed her face. "My knives," Ash-Lea spat furiously. "They took my knives."

"In their eyeballs." Billy laughed, letting out some tension. "I'll buy you some new ones."

"How? You still have a bedroom to pay for."

Billy's laugh turned into a frown. He inched towards the kitchen island. He'd been surprised by enough demonic insects for one day. In the dark kitchen, the pile of iron pots and pans covered nothing but cracked tile and a mess of insulation and framing beams.

"I bet they came in through the roof," Billy said.

Billy stood beside Ash-Lea and looked at the ceiling-tall webs then back to the spider in the entrance. Its body wasn't dissolving. Billy could see its chest rising and falling slightly, a rattling sound of labored breathing escaping its abdomen. But the thing was out cold, and going to die—but it wasn't dead yet.

"I wonder if he would know how to take down the webs. Bugger isn't dead yet."

"Isn't he?" Ash-Lea asked and looked back to the monster lying by the door. "Darn."

She walked up and touched one of the strands with an outstretched finger. It remained attached to her as she pulled away. "This stuff is sticky." She tried wiping it off on the carpet. "Really, really sticky. I'm not sure how we're going to get it off them without getting stuck ourselves."

A thought occurred to Billy. "They don't get stuck to their own webs, do they?"

Ash-Lea smiled, understanding what Billy was thinking. "No, they don't."

They turned back to face the monster. Behind them Mr. and Mrs. Ash started thrashing, shouting muffled cries of warning.

"Okay," Billy said as they slowly approached the spider, "if it dies, the body will disappear, then we'll have to think of some other way to get Greyson's folks out. So, we need the leg, but we need the spider alive."

"But if it dies won't the webs disappear too?" Ash-Lea asked.

Billy shrugged hopelessly. "I don't know. But if it doesn't we'll be stuck for sure. And," he lowered his voice, "I don't know how long they can survive like that."

Ash-Lea glanced over her shoulder at the two fingers suspended upside-down. She nodded.

As they walked into the entrance, the monster gurgled, green viscous blood leaking from its head, turning into powder as it struck the floor.

"How do you want to do this?" Ash-Lea asked.

Billy watched the monster for a moment, its abdomen rising and falling. "I guess they have lungs so they can speak."

"Uh, what?" Ash-Lea looked at Billy with a crooked eyebrow.

"He's breathing. I guess they have to breathe so they can threaten us and stuff. Normal spiders don't have lungs like humans."

"You're kinda getting off topic, buddy. You want me to like, cut its leg off?"

The spider shifted, the massive body dragging inches across the floor towards the pair. Ash-Lea let out a "Whoa, boy," and jumped away. Billy had his bat out in front of him. The spider gurgled once more, its breathing becoming even more labored.

"Right. So, um. Take its leg." Billy pointed to the closest hairy appendage. Ash-Lea looked at him with raised eyebrows. "Trust me, they pop off really easily if you hit it right. You hold it, and I'll hit it near the shoulder. It'll come right off."

The spider let in a stuttering breath, its razor-sharp mandibles scraping together.

Ash-Lea reached for the leg and took it by the ankle, just above the talon. She held it gingerly, just far enough in front of her so that the claw didn't catch her shirt. "Confound you and your schemes," she muttered under her breath. "This is so gross, Billy. Hurry up."

He looked at the monster lying before him and raised his bat above his head. He brought it down on what he guessed was the shoulder with a loud, wet, *thwack*. The spider twitched, almost pulling Ash-Lea on top of it as it moved. A low, agonized sound rumbled from its alien throat.

"Pop off easily?" Ash-Lea whispered through gritted teeth.

Billy gave her a sidelong look and struck the leg again. The spider coughed, goo shooting from its mouth, and Billy jumped away in surprise. The thing's eyes moved, rolling around behind closed eyelids.

Ash-Lea jerked on the leg, her lips pressed together tightly and Billy knew she was fighting back the urge to throw up. She looked at him with furious eyes. "Come on," she said through clenched teeth.

Billy lined up the strike once more, trying to remember what made the leg come off in his bedroom. *Well, the thing was standing on it, and moving, at the time.* He gritted his teeth, wondering if this would work with nothing but Ash-Lea's relatively small weight tugging on the limb.

He swung, putting as much focus and force into the attack as he could. His bat hit home and the leg came free with a fleshy crack. Ash-Lea fell to the tile, letting out a small yelp. She managed to stop the claw from impaling her in the stomach by twisting at the last second.

The spider stirred, a rumbling, groan rolled out from its broken head.

Billy backed away from the thing as the noise grew steadily in volume.

"Go, go, go, go, GO!" Ash-Lea shouted as she scrambled to her feet, snatching up the bony limb in her hands.

Billy backed into the living room, not turning away from the spider as it rose to its seven legs. Its remaining eyes focused on Billy. It let out a warbling, evil growl.

"Demonseed," it snarled, "I shall eat the limbs from your quivering body."

Billy planted his feet and faced the monster as it approached. Glancing behind him, he saw Ash-Lea hard at work on the spider web, raking the claw across the bonds. Slowly, too slowly, Meredith started to come free. In front of Billy, the spider advanced, its rage growing as it stalked towards him. It hit the archway and tried to duck through, but the narrow hall was too small for its huge body. Billy breathed a sigh of relief.

The demon snarled and focused on Billy like a missile. "Your blood is mine," it screamed.

The spider began thrashing furiously at the walls, the roar of exploding drywall and tile filled the house. A cloud of dust billowed into the room as the thing literally started to tear the place apart. The demon shrieked as it advanced, foot by foot.

Billy braced himself, his bat held before him. "We don't have a lot of time!" Billy shouted, though he doubted Ash-Lea could hear him over the monster's fury.

The spider breached the living room tearing the walls with manic slashes. Dust and chunks of wood exploded everywhere. The demon loomed above him and raised on its hindquarters as it emerged from the cloud of dust, letting out a guttural cry of rage.

Between the web and the spider, the room wasn't wide enough for a good swing with his bat, so Billy did the next best thing he could think of and tackled the thing.

The spider continued its bellowing, not expecting Billy to do anything that stupid. Unbalanced as the spider was, it stumbled backwards as Billy slammed into it, smashing into the wall. Billy gripped the spider's wiry pelt and rode the beast to the floor. Seven claws slashed at him and he hunched his shoulders reflexively. He cried out in pain as the spider's talons gouged into his back and tore into his skin. He swatted the attacking legs aside and rose to his feet.

Standing on the spider's chest, he cracked the bat down on the broken, bleeding head. The creature shuddered and let out a slow, hissing breath. It rocked back and forth, trying to shake the human off of him. Billy hit it again and again until the swaying stopped. The spider gave a long wheeze. Billy stumbled as he felt the body begin to dissolve underneath him. He jumped away from the demon and landed next to the thorax as it puffed into little pieces of pink insulation.

Turning, Billy smiled as he saw Greyson's parents—sweaty, filthy, but alive—kneeling on the floor next to Ash-Lea. She looked at Billy with a tired expression on her face. She suddenly seemed much older to him. In her hand, the spider's leg transformed slowly from a black, hairy limb, to a shaft of wood.

"I got them," she said, satisfied.

Looking up Billy could see the wall of webbing did not disappear with the spider. He let out an exhausted sigh.

Mr. Ash shook as he climbed to his feet and help his wife to stand. "Thank you," he breathed.

"Did it bite you?" Billy asked the couple.

Meredith shook her head. "No. But," she started crying and fell against her husband, "he said he wanted to eat us and hear us scream."

Billy and Ash-Lea exchanged disgusted looks.

"Yeah, they're into eating humans," Ash-Lea said.

Mr. Ash put a hand on Billy's shoulder. "It didn't bite me either. We're going to be okay. But we need to find Greyson. Now. That thing said they wanted to hurt him."

Billy eyed Greyson's parents. "You seem to be taking this pretty well. You do realize you were almost eaten by demons, right?"

"No, that hasn't really settled in." Mr. Ash stepped around Billy and studied the wooden beams that used to be a spider. He then looked at the hole that the spider tore in the hallway. "First day I try to take off in twelve years and this happens. Hell of a thing."

"I'm sorry," Meredith said.

"No, Meri, don't. It's not your fault." He held her close. "Just the luck of the draw."

Meredith smiled at Billy, then fainted.

"Meri," Mr. Ash exclaimed as he clumsily tried to catch her. They both ended up sitting on the floor, Meredith's head in his lap.

"Oh, no. How did I get down here?" she asked as her eyes fluttered open.

"You fainted, honey."

She considered that. "Maybe I'm not taking this as well as I thought."

With a pale, wan complexion, Mr. Ash didn't look far from fainting himself. "Me neither."

"Don't worry," Ash-lea said. "You guys hang tight. We'll go get Greyson."

"Please," said Meredith, looking from Ash-lea to Billy, "please find him. We don't know where he is. He didn't come home from school."

"He never went to school." Ash-Lea looked between Mr. and Mrs. Ash. "You told me he was sick this morning."

Mr. Ash's mouth dropped open. "No," he began slowly. "No, I didn't."

Billy's exhaustion from the fight melted away as renewed terror for his friend crept into its place. Greyson had been missing all day.

"It wasn't you I talked to this morning?" Ash-Lea asked, her words halting as if she couldn't believe they were coming out of her mouth.

"No, dear. You were here?" Meredith asked.

Ash-Lea shoved Billy. "What the hell, man? Can they, like, mess with our heads or something?"

Billy shook his head. "I don't know. But if you think about the kind of things we're dealing with, I can believe it."

Ash-Lea let out a genuine growl. "The things your buddy Seth is leaving out are kind of a big flippin' deal. He and I are going to have words."

"Maybe this guy knows where Greyson is." Billy glanced at the scorpion still suspended from the web. He found the creature's face and squatted down. "So, Pinchy, where did they take my friend?"

The scorpion wavered in the sticky netting. "Blacksmith. You are nothing more than a pitiful human and yet you have slain my kin. I deny your request. Greyson will suffer and die."

Ash-Lea stomped around to stand beside Billy. "Look, you ugly freak of nature. You don't exactly have a lot of choices here. Tell us where Greyson is, or your life on this plane will be very short."

"You are not even the Demonseed, little child. I have nothing to say to you," it hissed. "But I will say one thing to you, Blacksmith."

"Okay, shoot," Billy said, allowing himself to hope, just a little.

"Come closer. This is not for mortal ears. Only those who have demon blood in their veins can know this secret."

Billy glanced at Ash-Lea, who shook her head vigorously. He leaned in closer, near to the scorpion's mouth.

"This world will end," it whispered. "My kind will claim it, burn it, and then spread throughout the universe, feeding on all life. The thing that must happen first is for you to DIE."

As it said the last word its tail came free from the web and swept down towards Billy's face. Billy yelped and fell onto his butt.

Ash-Lea was there, grasping the tail in both hands, the muscles in her forearms straining against its strength.

"Don't you dare," she shouted, screaming out a cry of effort, her sneakers slipping on the tile. The scorpion fought against her, struggling to free its stinger from her grasp. She forced it down until the stinger pressed against the creature's head. It screamed in frustration, trying to twist its tail out of her grip. She redoubled her efforts and the needle-like end moved lower.

"Pitiful, worthless, meaningless human," the scorpion cried. "This world will end in fire and blood."

Ash-Lea, her voice thin from the strain, shouted, "Yeah? Well you first, buddy." She shoved down with her whole weight and forced the stinger into the head of the scorpion. It hissed out a breath and went slack in the web. A moment later, its body transformed into insulation.

Billy simply sat there, feeling very stupid. "Thank you," he said. His amazement at Ash-Lea's bravery and physical strength stopped his mouth from saying anything more.

"You owe me one," Ash-Lea winked. "But now we have no one to tell us where Greyson is." She looked at the grownups shivering on the floor. "Where was he seen last?"

"He left this morning for Quinn's house," Meredith said in a small voice. "Something about the diorama."

"Well, that's something," Billy climbed to his feet. "Don't worry, we'll take care of Greyson."

Meredith gave a sad smile. "He is a lucky boy to have you as friends."

"We're the lucky ones," Ash-Lea said. "Do you know where Quinn lives?"

Mr. and Mrs. Ash pointed to the house next door.

18

Human Reinførcments

◆————————————————————◆

sh-Lea rang the doorbell to Quinn's house and jumped in surprise at the sonorous chime. In Billy's estimation, the house ranked closer to the Mansion half on the residence qualification continuum. A door made of intricately carved wood and stained glass stood before them, so tall Seth in his demonic form, could enter without stooping. Billy would have considered the whole thing ostentatious, but his thoughts froze at the devastation he could see through the glass. Ornamental pillars were scattered in pieces on the floor of the entryway. The winding staircase that twisted up toward the second floor lay battered and broken, as if something large had fallen and rolled down the stairs. The long-chained chandelier hung slanted from the ceiling overhead.

Ash-Lea rung the bell again. Nobody answered.

When Billy knocked on the door, it swung wide open. He exchanged a serious look with Ash-Lea. She nodded, gripping her single remaining knife. With dented bat in hand, Billy stepped over the threshold and edged into the darkness beyond.

His boots crunched over the broken plaster and glass on the floor as he cautiously skirted around the slowly swinging chandelier.

"Quinn? Greyson?" Billy stepped over the twisted stair railing. No one answered.

"Déjà vu, much?" Ash-Lea whispered.

Billy smirked with one side of his mouth.

They crept towards the back of the house, kicking the remains of an ornamental statue to the side. The room at the back of the house could fit Billy's residence inside it twice. Made entirely of glass, the back wall gave a panoramic view of their huge backyard and mountains beyond. Long glass shards lay across the carpet glinting in the oncoming evening as a cool breeze blew through the completely open back of the house. Something with large teeth had eaten half of the couch, the white stuffing spilled onto the carpet.

An arched doorway to the right revealed a kitchen with a gas burner that was still alight. Ash-Lea walked over and turned it off.

"No one here, I guess." Billy picked up a dusty pillow from the floor and threw it back onto what was left of the couch.

"This is awful," Ash-Lea said, taking in the scene. "Quinn's family didn't deserve this."

Strings of spider web coated everything. Holes covered the walls and ceiling, much like the holes the spider left in his room on the night of the first attack. Large puddles of goo that looked like the remains of some powerful acid pockmarked the room.

"They better've made it out alright." Billy let out a shout of frustration and kicked over an end table. It clattered to the floor, spilling dust and glass as it went. "This is my fault. They're after me and they're using Greyson as a weapon against me. This isn't fair. And then Quinn's family gets roped into it for no good reason at all."

"Dude, come on," Ash-Lea said, waving her arms at the devastation surrounding them. "Like you knew any of this would happen."

"I should have." He pointed a finger at her. "I should have. Someone showing up, telling me I'm important. Me. Like that would ever happen without there being a big fat catch."

Ash-Lea punched Billy in the arm. "You dumb-ass," she said affectionately. "You were important before Seth showed up."

Before Billy could disagree, a door slammed open from the hall. A man-shaped figure rushed out of the darkness screaming a battle cry. He held something heavy-looking above his head and swung it toward Billy. He ducked to the side and batted the weapon away with one hand. With his other hand, Billy pushed the man into the large coffee table. His attacker shrieked in pain as he struck it and slid off, the large piece of wood slipping out of his fingers.

"Dad, Dad," a familiar voice shouted. "No Dad, I know them."

Quinn ran up to the man on the ground and helped him to his feet.

"Honey?" a woman's voice said from the entrance area.

"It's okay, Mom. These are friends from school," Quinn held up her hand in a *stand down* gesture.

Ash-Lea twisted her mouth in distaste at Quinn's word *friends* and shot Billy a dubious look.

Billy lowered his bat. "Hi, I'm Billy."

"Nice place you have here," Ash-Lea pulled a piece of drywall out of her hair.

A young boy with a preteen's lanky frame ran from the hall and took up a defensive position in front of Quinn and her mother. He glared at Billy, his fists balled, ready to fight the teenager at least four times his size. The woman put an arm over the boy's shoulders and pulled him close, her eyes full of warning.

Quinn's family stood together in their devastated home, lit gently by twilight filtering in through the windows. They looked frightened, and defiant.

"So," Ash-Lea kicked a piece of countertop with her toe, "you guys see anything unusual this evening?"

The adults glanced at each other, then looked to Quinn. Billy noted she had inherited her mother's looks and her father's athletic built. All their best features. She opened her mouth, but hesitated, unsure of what to say.

The little boy spoke first. "Giant spiders," he growled.

"They took Greyson," Quinn's voice quivered with panic. "Why would they take him?"

"It's me they want," Billy said. "I'm sorry. This didn't need to happen to you."

"It's not your fault, hon," said Quinn's mother. She spoke with a light Louisiana accent.

Billy grunted in response. "How did it happen?"

Quinn straightened her hair, pulling flecks of tile out of it. "Greyson showed up this morning to see if he could still get the diorama papers signed. I wanted to help him, but he missed the deadline. Poor guy looked totally bummed. He was just getting ready to leave when they came."

"The spiders?" Ash-Lea asked.

Quinn nodded.

"I don't know how many there were," Quinn's father looked at his family with worry in his eyes. "They were sitting in the trees in the back yard and just rushed in through the windows. There must have been about twenty of them. They kept us hostage for hours, just sitting around. They didn't speak, other than to tell us to stay put and shut up."

The boy shuddered and closed his eyes, shaking away some memory.

"They didn't even try to trash the house, not on purpose," Quinn's mother spat. She wore black jeans and a black t-shirt that were nearly made white from dust. "Just so many giant spiders moving around in here, knockin' everything over. Then they climbed up the walls. Sweet Mary. And when they got hungry, they just started eating my couches." She grimaced at the disgusting memory. "And no, we don't have giant spider insurance."

Billy found himself smiling at that.

Quinn's father sneered, adjusting his torn t-shirt over his muscled frame. He had blood seeping through in several places. "I tried to stop them, but there were too many. My guns couldn't even touch 'em. They just tore apart the house and left when some giant scorpion showed up and told them to go."

"When was that?" Billy asked.

"Only an hour or so," Quinn's dad said. "We've been bound in spider web, and only just managed to escape."

"Did they say where they're going?" Ash-Lea demanded.

"The Place of Learning. You said your name is Billy?" Quinn's father asked.

"Yes, sir."

"William Blacksmith?"

Billy nodded. He didn't need to ask how Quinn's father knew.

The man let out a significant sigh. "They said tell William Blacksmith they will be waiting at the Place of Learning. If he wishes for his friend to live, he must come alone." His face soured, as if the words were bitter in his mouth.

"No way he's going alone," Ash-Lea said.

"I'll drive," Quinn's father said. "I'll be right back."

"Baby," Quinn's mother protested, "you're a better Shotgun. I'll drive."

"What about Junior?"

The woman considered him for a moment, "He can load."

"Wait." Billy held his hands up and shook them. "I'm supposed to go alone, and you're talking about bringing a kid?"

"I'm eleven," Junior protested.

Quinn's father eyed Billy. "Son, a score of giant spiders just tore up my house looking for Greyson. One," he counted off on his fingers, "I am not letting them get away with it. Two, like hell I'm leaving any of my family behind. And three, my daughter's friend is in danger. That don't fly if I'm in any position to disagree." Quinn's dad ran into the entrance and upstairs.

Ash-Lea laughed once, "He's got you there, big-guy."

Billy groaned, feeling frustration and panic swirling inside him. Spiders were attacking people because of him, attacking his friends and their families. He didn't want to be responsible for more pain and damage.

Ash-Lea, Quinn, and her mother stood in a circle discussing their plan of attack.

"Guys, don't I get a say?" Billy asked.

Quinn's mom stopped talking only long enough to raise an eyebrow at him.

Loud thumping noises could be heard upstairs, like someone rummaging through an overcrowded closet "Got 'em!" Quinn's father called down the stairs.

Billy felt his back tingle and itch against the cool night breeze. He reached with the bat to scratch behind him.

"Might want to hold off on that," Ash-Lea reached out and took the bat. "The spider you just jumped on got you pretty good."

"What?" Billy froze.

"Let me take care of that," Quinn's mother waved her finger. She disappeared into another room and came back with a wad of paper towels and a bottle of rubbing alcohol. "Let's take off your shirt, honey."

Billy's face felt like it caught fire. He did not like taking his shirt off for anyone. "Oh, uh . . . um," he stammered. He'd rather take on another gang of scorpions than take off his shirt—in front of girls, too.

"Oh dear, you're being so cute," Quinn's mother said. "No need to be shy, I got boys of my own."

Ash-Lea chortled and Billy groaned. "Just, don't look. Please," he said, then waited.

Ash-Lea and Quinn giggled and turned around. Billy began lifting his shirt over his head. His arms and shoulders ached more than he expected. His skin felt tight, flashes of pain jolting up his back in ways he'd never experienced. Quinn's mother poured the alcohol on the paper and started dabbing Billy's wounds.

Agony hit his back like a spider's claw and he hissed with pain. "Ow."

Quinn's mother *hmm-ed*. "The spider at Greyson's house got your back pretty good when you jumped on him. You're bleeding."

"Really? Didn't know it was that bad," Billy said through clenched teeth. "Thanks, Mrs.?"

"Blouin, honey."

"Thanks, Mrs. Blouin."

She made a kind tutting sound and continued to wreak torture on Billy's back. He braced himself against the back of the couch, his eyes watering, and let her work. After a minute she said, "That's the best I can do for now. I've put some gauze on it, but it won't be enough for the long haul."

Billy grunted in thanks.

Mr. Blouin's footsteps clomped down the stairs. "I hear that right?" He came back into the room, heavy looking shirts draped over his arms. "You killed one next door by jumping on it?"

"Well, the bat to the head did it. I was just standing on him at the time."

"Well, I'll be." Mr. Blouin smiled widely.

The man started handing out the items in his hands. They appeared to be bullet-proof flak jackets. He handed one to Quinn and Mrs. Blouin, who slid into them easily. The one he handed to Junior hung too low on him, but would do the job.

"You should fit in Quinn's old one." Mr. Blouin handed a vest to Ash-Lea. He frowned at Billy. "I'm sorry I don't have one in your size, son. Looks like you could use it with those cuts on your back."

"I'll be fine," Billy said, noticing everyone had forgotten his request to not look at him with his shirt off. "I can be fast when I need to."

Mr. Blouin raised an eyebrow, but nodded.

"Hey," Ash-Lea said, after pulling the jacket over her head. "You wouldn't happen to have some throwing knives would you?"

An excited grin appeared on the man's face and snapped his fingers in Ash-Lea's direction. He ran upstairs and returned a minute later holding two assault rifles, a shotgun, and a bundle of heavy black canvas. He handed the shotgun to his wife and a rifle to Quinn. She checked the safety, slid out the clip, confirmed the presence of bullets and slid the clip back in. She obviously knew her way around a gun.

"You get the Boom Bag?" Mrs. Blouin asked.

"It's by the bed."

"Let me get that for you," she kissed Mr. Blouin on the lips and disappeared upstairs.

"You know how to use that thing?" Ash-Lea eyed Quinn, disbelief thick in her voice.

Mr. Blouin's face took on a proud, fatherly gleam. "My baby girl is state marksman champion for the under eighteens." He handed Ash-Lea the black canvas bundle. "And over eighteens come the competition next year."

"Huh." Ash-Lea looked at Quinn as if seeing her for the first time, her lips pursed. "Maybe Greyson isn't insane."

"Why do you say that?" Quinn asked, slinging the rifle over her shoulder, and tucking her long hair behind her ear.

Ash-Lea shrugged and looked at the bundle Mr. Blouin had handed her. She let out an excited noise and almost jumped with glee. "Smither Steel? Crikey. Now, that's a knife."

Mr. Blouin let out a satisfied chuff. Ash-Lea knelt on the ground and unrolled the canvas package. A dozen shiny metal knives in snug sleeves glinted in the moonlight. She began pulling them out and sliding them into the pockets on the vest. She then withdrew two especially long blades, complete with leather sheaths, and, with some adjusting of the vest, managed to clip them to her belt. When she rose, she was grinning like a kid on Christmas morning.

Mrs. Blouin came down the stairs, holding a large gym bag in one hand and a black shirt in the other. "I paint in this sometimes. It's a bit of a mess, but it's the only thing that might fit you."

She handed him the large smock and Billy slipped into it with relief, careful as he pulled the shirt over his back. It wasn't a terrible fit, only a little tight around the stomach, and he could live with the paint smeared all over it.

Billy looked about the room at the strangers, arming themselves for battle. "Thank you," he said to the room at large. "I know we all want to get Greyson back, and I know I'm going to need your help. But you don't have to do this. I don't want you to put yourselves in danger for something that's my responsibility."

Mrs. Blouin leveled a look at Billy. "Did you see what those furry critters did to my furniture?"

Billy nodded. The last thing he wanted was for anyone else to be in harm's way. And if being dragged down to the demonic spider's lair was the way it had to happen, so be it.

He imagined dark caves covered in webs that creatures like that must inhabit. He pictured being tied up as they stripped the skin from his bones, and drank his blood. He swallowed. *If it's me or my friends being killed, I chose me.* That was Plan A.

Plan B involved kicking their asses and taking Greyson back without their permission. Knowing demonic spiders, it was likely they wouldn't play fair.

"You're not alone, Billy," Ash-Lea said, smiling grimly.

Billy took a very deep breath. "Alright, but we're still missing someone." He kicked piles of broken glass aside as he stepped onto the back patio. "Seth," he called. "Get your leathery butt down here."

With a gush of wind Seth appeared in his demonic form, descending from the black trees above like a nightmare. He landed on the wooden deck with a reverberating thud.

Behind him, Junior squealed as several guns were cocked. He held up a hand. "Chill. He's a good guy."

"Are you sure about that, boy?" Mr. Blouin asked, his voice trembling.

"I'll answer that when this is over." Billy rested his bat on his shoulder. "We're going to the school to rescue Greyson. Follow this man's car and meet us there."

The demon's eyes flicked at what he saw behind Billy. "William. I am not permitted to interfere. It will compromise my associates."

"Dude, if you stand by and do nothing while my friends need help, then I want nothing to do with people like you . . . with demons like you. What is the point of your power if you can't use it for good?"

Billy did not wait for a response. He turned and walked back into the house. "Blouin family? Ashes? Let's go kick some spider ass."

19

Demønslaying 101

———————◆———————

T he Blouin's SUV pulled up across the street from the school. The occupants stared at the nearest building, the gym, which loomed black in the moonlight. The school simply did not look right. It may have been the empty yard and parking lots, or the gut-deep fear Billy felt throughout his body. More possibly it was the cluster of giant, demonic spiders crawling over the roof and up the walls of the gymnasium.

Yet there was something more ominous and intangible about the place. The moon did not shine as bright around the school, as if a black fog had descended specifically upon it. The scent of putrid, rotten smoke that had bothered Billy all day, now burned his nostrils with its phantom stench. There was something evil about that fog, Billy could feel it in his demon blood.

The seething mass of monstrous forms crawled about. Giant spiders scaled the walls and nearby trees, spinning disgustingly thick webs. Scorpions lined the grass between the road and gymnasium door, filling the night air with chittering mandibles and rasping scales.

"This place is giving me the creeps," Ash-Lea said. "More than usual, I mean."

Billy turned the aluminum baseball bat in his fingers. "You guys should wait here. This is worse than I thought."

"Billy." Ash-Lea backhanded his shoulder. "You can't go in there alone."

"Damn straight." Mrs. Blouin brought out her shotgun. She zipped open the Boom Bag and pulled out two disk shaped cartridges, loaded full with shotgun shells. She snapped the clips to the side of the shotgun, pumped the gun, and gave a satisfied nod. He didn't even know cartridges existed for shotguns.

Mrs. Blouin opened the door and stepped onto the street. Running around to the rear of the SUV she climbed up a ladder to the roof and flipped open a compartment mounted there. She pulled out metal poles and started assembling something that looked like a hunter's cage. "I'll stay with the car. You guys do what you need to do."

Junior climbed into the front seat and pressed buttons on the console. Metal slats descended over the windows. He climbed into the back seat and started organizing boxes of ammunition from the Boom Bag in piles. He then slid open the sun roof and thumped his fist against the roof twice. Mrs. Blouin stomped her foot twice in return.

Ash-Lea scanned the boxes and boxes of bullets. "Why do you guys have so much ammunition?"

"I'm a boy scout," Mr. Blouin replied. "I believe in being prepared."

Billy and Ash-Lea exchanged tense looks and turned to watch the demonic forms on the school lawn then slipped out of the car. Standing beside the Blouin's vehicle, he saw that metal plates now protected the wheels, too. Quinn and Mr. Blouin followed them out of the car and stood next to him.

Billy took in the scene. A thousand scorpions filled the yard, thousands of demon eyes fixed on him, their stingers lashing hungrily. The familiar sound of laughing spiders filled the air, their mandibles grating, sending a chill down Billy's spine.

"I hate school," Billy said.

A gust of wind surrounded the group. Mrs. Blouin flicked her shotgun towards the source of the sound. Seth descended from the blackness, his black wings flapping to slow his descent. He slammed into the street and Billy felt the earth tremble slightly under his feet.

"William, no," his deep voice rumbled with panic. "I cannot allow you to enter this place."

At the command Billy's desire to march right into the school shot up by about one thousand percent. "Greyson is in there," he said in a low voice.

"This is more important than the life of your friend. If you die here then the world is lost."

Billy looked up at Seth and saw him, really saw him, somehow he got a glimpse into the demon and understood him in a way he hadn't before. "What is the point of life without friends, Seth? What world is worth saving if I can't save those I care about?"

The demon did not answer. He clenched his giant fists, his eyes flicked about, unfocused. Billy could see an unbidden memory stir within them.

"Don't, William. Please." The demon regarded him with what looked like sadness in his black eyes.

"You can wait here too. Make sure Pinchy and his friends don't get to the SUV."

"The scorpion's poison is deadly to me too, William."

"Then I suggest you avoid the poisonous part if they come for you. Stay here and keep everyone safe. I'll be back as soon as I can."

Seth shook his head once. "No. You must survive this, William Blacksmith. I will go with you."

Quinn and her father cocked their rifles and set the stocks against their shoulders, training the barrel on the closest scorpions.

Ash-Lea flicked the two long knives out of the holsters and held them in both hands, the blades pointed downward.

"Good luck, Baby." Mrs. Blouin lay on her stomach on the SUV's roof. She leaned over and kissed Mr. Blouin before clamping down the last piece of the protective cage. She stood, her shotgun trained on the demons. Inside the car, Junior continued sorting the ammunition, ready to hand it up to his mother.

"Why do you even have that?" Billy asked, eyeing the cage.

Mr. Blouin glanced over his shoulder at the car with its slat-covered windows. "That's a long story, Demonseed. Perhaps I'll tell you some time."

Junior locked the car doors and flipped his father a thumbs up. Mrs. Blouin clicked on the laser sight on her shotgun and the red dot danced across the closest scorpions. The demons seemed to sense what the light meant, and scurried away when it fell on them.

Billy looked around at his friends, at the family of strangers that were going to walk into a swarm of demons for him. "Is nobody planning to listen to me?" Billy asked.

Ash-Lea gave him a flat look, then rolled her eyes.

Billy cleared his throat. "Just nobody get dead, okay?" He took in a deep breath. Then another. He walked forward slowly, approaching the line of scorpions, his bat slung over one shoulder. Behind him he could feel the hot, quiet presence of Selanthiel the demon towering over him. The unreasonably large insects gathered close, hissing.

"Out of the way," Billy shouted. "I've been asked to come. I understand someone in there would like to talk to me."

"It's the Blacksmith," the closest scorpion clacked. "Make way, make way."

Billy forced himself to put one foot in front of the other, trying hard to ignore the urge to run away screaming. Quinn, Mr. Blouin, and Ash-Lea kept pace, flanking him. Seth trailed reluctantly. The scorpions closed ranks behind them, but did not follow. He made his way toward the large doors of the gymnasium. As Billy approached he realized the doors had been replaced by a pair of heavy webs, parted like stage curtains for them as they neared. He hesitated, took a deep breath, and pushed through his fear as he entered.

Billy's jaw hit the floor. Beside him Ash-Lea let in a sharp breath. The walls were covered in spiders. Their hairy legs shuffled as they climbed up and down the walls and over the ceiling, drops of acid falling from their mouths like drool. The noise they made as they spoke in their spider language grated across Billy's nerves. Hundreds of human forms were stuck to the cinderblocks in uneven rows, some moved, screaming through the webs, pleading for help. He could not tell one bundle from another, let alone find which one held Greyson. Some humans lay in unconscious piles on the floor, some were being bound before Billy's eyes. Whatever the spiders were hoping to accomplish, they were in the midst of it. Slung unceremoniously from the ceiling from one wall to the other was a banner that read "Diorama Competition."

"This is the worst diorama I've ever seen," Billy stated.

"Tubberrrr . . . ers," a voice called weakly. Billy looked at one of the figures to his left. Patrick the jock was strung against the wall. "Get out of here, maaa . . . aaan," he wheezed. "These guys are bad news."

"Patrick?" said Quinn dolefully as she ran to him. "Oh baby, what are they doing to you?"

"Don't touch that stuff," Ash-Lea ordered. "You'll get stuck too."

Quinn skidded to a stop, her eyes wide, her mouth pulled into a desperate frown.

"It's going to be okay, Patrick," Billy called, although he wasn't sure he believed it. He turned back to the deep, dark room. "Who's in charge here?" he shouted over the shrill sound of a hundred raking mandibles.

The noise died down as a hundred spiders looked at one another in excitement. From the darkened stage at the end of the gym, a low, rumbling voice sounded.

"William Blacksmith," it said with relish. "I have called my minions from the blackest realms to find you here. We have traversed dimensions incomprehensible—"

"Stow it, four-eyes," Billy hollered. "You're going to let these kids go. Then you're going to crawl back into your dark, smelly hole. You're not welcome here."

The figure stepped forward, each hairy leg thumping against the ground as it moved. A sliver of weak moonlight, streaming in through a high window, revealed the demon's form. Its body was gigantic, a huge thing, covered in a thick plate of what looked like armor. The top of its head had to be almost twenty feet off the ground, a hundred eyes glistening from within his helmet, his gaze full of maleficent glee in the blue light. Billy did not need Seth to tell him that this was an Arachnis—the biggest, baddest spider demons around. Billy's throat clenched in fear as it approached, and he suddenly forgot how to breathe.

The ground shook as it stepped closer. "No, little human. *You* are no longer welcome here. We will take this realm from you and your kind will be but cattle to us."

"And you are?" Billy asked, his voice cracking.

"I am Krios, the Slayer of Bats, Holder of the White Flame, Champion of the Black Sands, General of the Spider Hordes of Hidden Corner."

"That's a cheery name," Ash-Lea said with one side of her mouth.

"Kay, Krios." Billy twirled his bat in a circle. "You guys like to use a lot of long words, but I think big spiders just like to eat humans. I've said it before, and I'll say it again—I have a problem with that."

Krios looked past Billy, his eyes flashed with simmering anger. "What are you doing here?"

Billy turned and saw that Krios was speaking to Seth. He held out his hands in a friendly gesture, but Billy didn't miss the way he widened his stance, ready to fight if he needed to.

"I am simply an observer of this realm. I am not here to interfere."

"You're not?" Billy and Krios asked in unison.

Krios smiled and a thin, serpentine tongue licked his mandibles. "Selanthiel Jakob Molef, the third of that name. Son of Selanthiel the Consumer. You are he that had provided aid to the Demonseed." Krios laughed. "Your grandfather would be most displeased to find you consorting with humans."

"As I have said, General. I am here to observe your victory over the humans."

Billy flinched as the Arachnis let out a hideous sound of amusement, its head bobbing up and down. "Oh, I'm sure your grandfather will understand. So you will stand by and let me eat this human?"

"Hey," Billy interjected. "I'm not sure what Seth is planning to do but if you intend to eat me, you'd better believe I'm going to put up a fight."

The wet, demonic eyes found Billy and they all blinked. "I hoped you would," growled Krios.

Seth stepped forward, next to Billy. "First, I think you need to consider all your options."

"Keep your feeble attempts to save this human to yourself, traitor!" Krios bellowed and lunged towards Billy, brandishing his wide, sword-like mandibles.

Billy positioned himself between the advancing monster and his friends. He felt the blood within him quicken as the world slowed down around him. He could see the spiders covering the walls, watching their General with anticipation, making hisses of delight at Billy's fear. The world shook under the weight of the charging monster. Waiting until the last moment he leapt forward.

The bat cracked down on Krios' armored head. The metal clang sent a shockwave through the bat, the impact painfully jarring his wrists. Billy landed behind Krios and slid, steadying himself with one hand on the floor, his bat held straight out to the side for balance.

Krios chuckled. The blow did not so much as rattle the Arachnis. He shook his head and his mouth contorted in a revolting smile. "I can smell that your blood has been awakened, Blacksmith. You have grown accustomed to it rather quickly."

Scraping metal rang as Krios' drew swords from the sheaths under his abdomen. Billy's face fell at the sight. *Yeah, that's not fair.* The weapons were brutal looking things, a dozen jagged edges on the front of blades as tall as Ash-Lea. The dim light in the room glinted off the hook on the back side of the hilt. An excited clacking sound rose from the spiders observing from the walls.

Billy swallowed. "Uh, Seth. Sure you don't want to reconsider the no-intervention policy there?" he called.

"I am confident in your ability to defeat him," Seth stepped back and folded his arms.

"Well, that makes one of us," Billy muttered.

Krios let out a wall-shaking battle cry and rose on his hind legs, his head lifting almost thirty feet off the ground. He whirled the blades in a show of skill intended to scare Billy. It worked. The blades whipped in wide circles sending a gale of wind that blew Billy's hair in his face.

A small smile tugged the corner of his mouth. All the spider's weight sat on his back legs. Billy focused in as an idea came to him.

Billy burst forward towards the spider, but Krios sensed him coming and dropped, charging at him. With barely a moment to react, Billy parried a sword blow off his bat as he dove under the sweeping arm. He slid on his knees under the spider and leapt to his feet behind him.

Billy's eyes widened as he saw the end of his bat. A small section of the tip had been sheared off cleanly, an oval hole revealing the hollow center inside the bat.

"Ready to give up?" Billy stood, panting, and readjusted his grip on the bat. His back throbbed, and he could feel the bandages being to peel away. He ignored the pain.

Krios twisted. "Oh, not quite," he hissed.

Billy rushed again, hoping he could move fast enough to outmaneuver the giant thing. Krios anticipated Billy's movement. The sword in the thing's right claw came down as Billy rushed forward. He parried the blow and leapt, landing a solid kick in the spider's armored side. He twisted away and stumbled backwards, barely managing to stay upright. Looking at his bat he could see another nick in the shaft.

"You are not even a challenge to me, fat thing. It is inevitable how this will end. Allow me to drink your blood and I will let this friend of yours go."

Billy knelt on the floor, panting heavily. He couldn't even scratch the spider. "What about the rest of them?"

Krios laughed, his voice suddenly furious. "You are in no position to bargain, human. I have need of these." He indicated the bodies clinging to the walls. "If I offer you your friend's life then you bow in gratitude and kiss my hairy abdomen."

Seth stepped forward. "For what do you require human children?"

"Nothing a traitor like yourself need concern himself about. Once I have killed the Demonseed I will report your presence to your grandfather, Selanthiel. He shall deal with you."

"Hey," shouted Billy, "you're talking to me." He rose, pointed his bat at the giant Arachnis. "It's all of them or none of them."

"You will have to drag them from the dead claws of my soldiers, human."

Billy gritted his teeth and glared at the monster. He had no choice left. Either everyone here would make it out, or he would die trying to save them. He clutched the bat in a batter's stance and faced the General of the Spider Horde. "So be it."

Billy raced forward, twirling around the spider, dodging the blades as they whipped down. The swords whistled through the air and hammered into the floor, scoring the wood deeply as splinters flew about the room. Billy bobbed and ran, driving his sharpened bat into flesh whenever he found an opening. As fast as Billy ran he couldn't keep up, it felt like Krios wasn't even trying. Billy's heart thumped heavily in his chest, his leaden legs burned like he ran through thigh-deep water.

The blade came towards him but Billy didn't see it in time. He screamed as he felt a blinding gouge of pain across his back. Billy fell to the floor, rolling away from Krios with the force of the blow. He could feel the wide wound across the whole of his back. He guessed he'd been struck with the flat of the blade or he would have been cut in half. An explosion of chattering and cheers arose from all around the walls. The soldiers were convinced their master had prevailed.

Krios raised a leg to his mouth, feeling his mandibles. One of the teeth-like things on his face was broken in half, hanging by a sliver of cartilage. Black blood dripped from his mouth to the floor and when he spoke his words were slurred. "You have challenged me more than I expected, Demonseed. I am pleased you will not live to realize the full potential of your blood. You may have eventually become a problem." The beast stepped forward slowly. "But now, you will simply be a boon to the power of my king."

Billy tried to scoot away from the Arachnis, but his arms crumpled as pain shot through his back. He cringed as Krios leaned over him, the one unbroken mandible quivering excitedly. Something loud and fast struck Krios' helm and he whipped his head around.

"No," Billy said.

Quinn and her father knelt by the webbed entrance, their rifles trained on the giant spider. Ash-Lea stood behind them, her knives held high against the Shadowlurks that eagerly eyed them.

"That's far enough, ugly," Mr. Blouin shouted.

Krios' legs thumped into the floor as he started towards them spitting furiously.

"William Blacksmith." Seth suddenly knelt over Billy. "Have you forgotten what is at stake? Why are you lying down to die?"

Krios stopped and looked at Seth, a malicious grin creeping across his face. "Oh, simply an observer? What is this treachery you speak of?"

Seth ignored Krios and placed the bat back into Billy's hand. The clamor about Billy grew muffled. When Seth spoke, it seemed as though it were the only sound in the world. "William, rest, allow me to assist."

Billy pushed himself to his elbows. "No, you can't risk your life just for me. It's not just about training me, is it? I know about Rose Bloom. I know about your wife. I know you're staying uninvolved to protect her."

Seth paused, sadness written in his demonic eyes. "No, William, you are everything. Take the humans from the walls. I will protect you."

"But they'll hurt her."

"For the sake of this world, difficult sacrifices must be made. If we cannot use our power to save our friends, then what is the point?" He smiled sadly. "Just promise me, small human. If I do not survive, that you will go to Rose and protect her. Please."

Billy looked in the eyes of the demon, and swallowed. The horrifying, giant monster looked close to tears.

"I promise. I'll take care of her."

"That is a promise I do not intend to allow you to fulfill." Sound flooded back into the room around them and Seth rose, facing the gargantuan spider.

Krios hissed, rapidly pounding his claws into the ground with deafening thumps. "I have waited two hundred years for this, Selanthiel the Betrayer." He lifted a claw to his face, tore the broken mandible off and threw it across the room.

Seth roared. The glass in the high windows shook with the sound. Seth stretched out his arm and the claws on his right hand grew and extended. They lengthened until at the end of his fingers he had four long blades the span of his forearm, the nails interlocking to form a single blade. The skin on Seth's left forearm twisted and writhed, spikes emerged from under the skin. The bone grew to form a shield, jagged spikes lining the edge.

Seth the demon, he hummed to himself. *More than meets the eyes.*

Krios reared, repulsive sounds of excitement rumbling from his demonic body. He twirled his swords faster than Billy could perceive.

The floor shook as Seth took two lightning fast strides and Krios charged. The demons clashed. A sudden gush of wind rushed through the room, knocking Billy down and making the diorama banner flutter like a leaf.

Krios bounded away from Seth and slashed a sword through the air. A gigantic portal, which reached from the roof of the gym to the floor, opened before the stage. On the other side of the portal Billy saw a huge, dark cave made of black rocks. The howl of a distant wind filled the cavern that lay beyond.

"Take the humans," the demonic spider roared as he came about and rushed Seth once more.

The demons covering the walls seethed at the command, boiling into motion as they gathered up their bundles. Billy's head spun as the walls seemed to flow, hundreds of spiders moving towards the opening at the end of the gym.

Shrieks of metal against demonbone echoed about the room. Seth and Krios attacked in a flurry of wings and hairy legs. The two monsters in the middle of the room were an unfathomable blur.

"The portal," Billy shouted, hoping his voice rose above the fray. "Stop them from getting to the portal."

20

The Pure Fire

———————◆———————

A sh-Lea appeared beside him, brushing his hair out of his eyes, wincing as she took in his appearance. "You are absolutely insane," she said, no trace of a smile on her face.

"You're only saying that because I'm attacking demons with a baseball bat." Billy grinned—it hurt. Ash-Lea stood and grabbed one of his hands, putting her whole bodyweight into it as she pulled him to his feet. "Help those people," he said, ignoring the fact that his brain was doing laps in his skull.

With his damaged bat gripped in his throbbing hand Billy started moving once more. Excruciating pain shot through his back, but he forced himself to put one foot in front of the other. Seth and the giant spider continued to battle, the weight of their unearthly bodies sending tremors and cracks through the boarded floor under their feet. The demons' blades met again and again, shaking the air. It felt like trying to sprint during an earthquake.

Seth let out a violent shout of surprise and Billy turned in time to see him lifted in the air by four of Krios' legs. The spider bellowed as he slammed Seth into the floor. The impact knocked Billy off his feet and he fell, Ash-Lea stumbling and swearing behind him. Wood splintered from where Seth had struck. The shock wave vibrated through the walls and onto the ceiling, dislodging a trail of dust in its wake.

Seth rose from the circle of demolished wood about him, his demonbone sword flashing in the dim light.

"William!" he bellowed. "The portal!"

Billy saw helpless forms wrapped in spider silk being dragged by scores of Shadowlurks. They scurried directly towards the hole in the universe at the end of the gym. Some figures were as small as children, some as large as adults. Hundreds of spiders moved towards the breach, each holding a little package of human in their hairy arms. There were too many—too many to follow, too many to save.

"Hey, Billy." Mr. Blouin ran up beside him, not taking his rifle from his shoulder. "You going to join this party or not?"

He let loose a round and green goo exploded from the head of one of the spiders. It fell slowly off the wall, as if its legs hadn't realized what had happened and were still trying to hold on to the cinderblocks. It landed on the floor with a whump, spilling its silk-wrapped bundle onto the basketball court.

There was another rifle shot, and another spider fell. Billy watched Quinn join her father in what he imagined was the biggest, most horrifying skeet shoot of her life. They knelt on the floor, side by side, taking down spiders as they approached the portal.

"Billy-boy, you take the left, we'll take the right," Mr. Blouin shouted.

"I'll watch their backs," Ash-Lea said, twirling the knives in her hand. She fumbled one and it almost dropped on her foot. She glanced at Billy, then gripped the knife like nothing had happened.

Billy took in a deep, aching breath. He'd used all his strength to not get killed. He needed more time, more strength. Hundreds of lives counted on him being better than he was. The horde of spiders was just too much. *Come on, dummy. You can't afford thoughts like that.*

Billy emptied his mind of the pain in his back, of the noise all about him, of the heavy fear he felt in the pit of his stomach as he looked at such an overwhelming fight. He let out a breath. In the clear, white space of his thoughts he saw Ash-Lea teasing Greyson, the sun shining on her dark hair. The way her mouth moved when she laughed. The way she cried for him when Billy was sad. He thought of Greyson and how he was always there, no matter what. When you needed Greyson, he would give up time for you. And then there was Chris. He really had been a father to him through all this. Chris protected him through the foster system. Nobody cared about foster kids as people. You were just a case number or a pay check. But Chris had held on to him, reminding him that he was a person, all the time teaching him and being there for him. The gym walls were covered in people, young and old. They were Ash-Leas and Greysons and big brothers. People were waiting for them to come home and he couldn't let them down. Inside him Billy felt something stir, a smoldering pile of ancient ash that took flame once again.

And then he *ran*.

Within an instant Billy leapt off the floor towards the wall, the bat clutched in his hands. But he could feel each step, he could see each spider move, he could hear the heart of each human in the room. The severed end of his bat acted as a blade and Billy sliced through the legs and thoraxes of the nearest spiders, each would scream and drop their living bundle.

One lunged at him. Billy sprung from the wall, bounding towards the ceiling. The spider missed, flying through the air under him, its legs flailing as it fell. Far below he saw Ash-Lea spin away from the falling beast, her knives glinting in her hands. The spider screamed and spilled onto the floor, sliding away from her.

Not until then did Billy realized he was watching this scene from the ceiling, the toes of his shoes touching the lip of the high windows, one arm gripping the supports beam of the roof. Quinn and her father continued their skeet shoot. A rapid pop, click, pop, click. The spiders were falling, dropping their prisoners, but there were still too many; some spiders were still making it through, their innocent captives on their backs.

A monstrous screech rose from the center of the room and Billy looked to see half of Krios' helm sheared away with Seth's demonbone blade. Seth's shredded shirt revealed deep gouges of red blood running down his chest. The demons screamed in rage and were upon each other once more.

More spiders detached their captives from the walls and attempted to make it to the portal. Billy let himself fall. The spider under him did not see him coming. He landed on the spider's back and drove his bat through the spider's head. It didn't even scream. He kept moving, taking out spider after spider. But there was no time left. If something didn't happen now, then the spiders would keep stealing the humans.

"Seth," Billy called in desperation.

Without looking, Seth understood and leapt forward. Krios raised on his hind legs once more, his swords spinning about him with lightning-fast speed. Seth ducked in to Krios' right, driving his demonbone through the spider's shoulder. Krios shrieked as he brought his other sword down to slice through Seth's back. But Billy was there, slamming his bat down on the spider demon's limb with all his demonblooded might. Krios screeched and his swords clattered to the ground.

Seth stepped forward but Krios ran. He turned to the portal and fled. Billy let out a wild, high laugh of triumph.

"Ha. We sure showed him." Billy looked at Seth to join in the celebration. He didn't.

"That is only the beginning if we do not seal that door," Seth bellowed as Krios disappeared into the portal he'd made. "William, take the humans."

It was then that Billy noticed the spiders were moving much faster. Without their master, their leisurely exodus became a rush. Billy moved.

Not caring about killing or even hurting the spiders, Billy ran from place to place, snatching the bundles from the spider's arms.

They didn't even seem to care. They kept running faster and faster toward the breach, sensing that something was coming. Billy quivered; he didn't want to find out.

Seth faced the interdimensional escape route the spiders were pouring into and closed his eyes. The demonbone sword and shield that had grown from his arms retreated. Ash-Lea, Quinn, and her father were dragging the bundles away from the breach. Goosebumps prickled up Billy's arms as a deep, ominous rumble, like a stampede echoed from the other side of the portal. Spiders were dropping their humans now and fleeing towards the gate. Whatever was coming, no demon wanted to be here when it arrived.

Billy turned to ask Seth what they needed to do, but Seth stood still, his hands clenched by his side. His lips moved, chanting something in an old language that Billy did not understand. As he did, a light formed within the demon's chest, a glow that Billy could not name. The demon planted his feet firmly on the ground, drew back his fists, and then howled.

Fire billowed from Seth's open mouth, a white hot flame that Billy could feel from across the gym. The stream of fire shot from Seth like a demonic flamethrower, warping the atmosphere about it with its heat. The edges of the portal caught alight, as if the air itself was burning. The spiders unlucky enough to be retreating through the gap at that moment burst into flames. They fell to the floor screaming and writhing in agony. The spiders not through the portal saw the flames and fled, dropping the humans and pouring out the windows and doors into the night. Unfortunately, everything else in the room caught on fire too. The wooden floor exploded like gasoline on kindling. The curtains on the stage lit up, the flame racing to the roof, the bottom half of the burning rags dropping to the floor, igniting the stacks of stage props stored out of sight.

Seth closed his mouth and the stream of flame abruptly ceased. He wiped his lips with the back of his hand. "Get the humans out of here," he ordered.

Not for the first time tonight, Billy thought, *There are too many.*

Ash-Lea, Quinn and her father had managed to rescue maybe five or six humans by dragging them, still in their spider silk, into the night. At the rate the building was going up, they were not going to get even half of the captives out in time. Billy moved, running as fast as he could to pull the unconscious people away from the flames. He almost let himself feel despair when he looked up and saw Seth with the cocoons of three humans linked on each hand. He ran, dragging them to the door and then threw them unceremoniously into the night. They landed with soft thuds on the grass outside. They weren't going to appreciate the aches when they woke up, but they'd be alive.

Billy and his friends stopped trying to drag people out of the burning building and instead settled for moving them just far enough away from the raging inferno to keep them alive. Then Seth would come, grab six or seven and throw them through the door. Somewhat worse for wear, but not burned, and not dead.

A shout of rage erupted behind Billy, nearly forgetting the portal burning closed behind them. Krios' scarred face loomed through the closing gap. But not just him, a hundred more spiders, each as large and just as heavily armored stood on the other side. They rattled and stomped, shouting in rage and anticipation.

"The Threshold," Krios screeched. "Selanthiel the Betrayer has burned the Threshold. You are sentenced to oblivion, traitor. No demon will rest until your head is at the feet of the Winged King."

But behind it all voices thick with excitement and loathing muttered, "William Blacksmith. Demonseed. Demonblood. Blacksmith."

The flames finished licking at the air with a twist as the portal burned closed.

As they dragged the last of the people from the building, Billy turned back to the gym. The entire stage was ablaze now. The smoke forming into a thick cloud by the ceiling. The portal, when it was open, sucked out the smoke from Seth's, well, Seth's hellfire, now that he really thought about it. Without the dimensional hole, the smoke billowed straight up, rapidly filling the vaulted ceiling of the gym. The heat scorched Billy's face, and he was having a hard time breathing. A mighty creak came from the wall somewhere close to the flame.

"Everyone out," Billy called.

Ash-Lea, Quinn, Mr. Blouin, and Seth all retreated, making sure there were no lingering spiders. Billy glanced around the room one more time to see if they had left any humans. He couldn't see any.

Billy stepped out into the night. The air felt cool compared to the growing inferno in what was soon to be the old gym. He took in the scene on the school yard. A hundred or more white, human-shaped lumps lay strewn across the grass. He hoped Greyson was among them. More than a few spiders had made it through with their cargo. He felt his chest hurt with desperation, his neck muscles clenching. If he'd lost his friend he would not be able to live with himself.

He looked across the dark street. In the distance, he could hear the whirr of fire engines. Movement over the nearby houses caught his attention. A black, eight-legged shadow crawled over the rooftop, and in that shadow, were eight red eyes glaring at him. Then they were gone. Not everything had escaped through the hole that Seth had burned closed. He clenched his teeth as he wondered how many other spiders were now running unchecked about the city.

Billy stepped up to the closest bound human. He tugged on the sticky white spider silk. The silk was tough. Getting stuck to the web wasn't an issue, everyone's hands were now covered in it. But he had no idea how to cut it. Seth approached, his hand outstretched. In his palm lay several sharp spider claws.

"Just something to be mindful of when you're battling spiders, Demonseed," Seth said. "Keep a few souvenirs."

Billy took a claw and grimaced at the hundred bodies lying about the grass. He let his head fall back as he let out an exasperated groan.

Ash-Lea ran up and snatched a claw from Seth. "Look for Greyson. Everyone look for Greyson."

She rushed from person to person, cutting away the webbing with quick, careful strokes. Some of the figures stirred, sitting up weakly. Others were still unconscious, suffering from the effects of the spider's tranquilizing venom. Quinn and Mr. Blouin each took a claw and started to help.

Mrs. Blouin still stood on the SUV, shotgun in hand. The bodies of a dozen scorpions lay around the car, disintegrating into piles of dirt and leaves. Their pristine SUV now had a giant scratch that ran the entire length of the car. She lifted her head as the sirens wailed and passed her shotgun through the sunroof to Junior. She then began dismantling the cage with amazingly swift, practiced movements.

"I should not be here when they arrive," Seth said.

Billy looked up at him. He stood, tall, bleeding, his wings half extended behind him in a nervous sort of way. Behind him the gym blazed. There can't be much to burn in a building of cinderblocks and steel, but burn it did. Tall red and blue flames danced high into the night. He was struck with the majesty of the sight. Seth glanced into the distance, a concerned look on his face.

"What about us?" Billy asked.

Seth nodded, a trusting look in his eye. He extended his wings, flapped once, and was gone into the clear, dark sky above them.

"Holy gee," Mr. Blouin shook his head. "That's quite a friend you've got there, Billy."

Billy nodded. "Yes, sir."

"I should probably put my rifle away before the police show up," Mr. Blouin said as he walked towards his truck. "Quinn," he shouted, then whistled twice—a loud, rapid, distinct noise.

Quinn reacted to the sound as if it were a command. She slung the rifle off her back, emptied the chamber, removed the clip and threw the gun to her father. He caught it in one hand and kept moving towards the truck. Mrs. Blouin walked casually around to the back of the car, opened the door, and unlocked a hidden compartment. Mr. Blouin placed the firearms within and clicked it closed as three police vehicles and two fire engines screamed around the corner. They were joined by an ambulance.

They'll need more than one of those, Billy thought.

Billy felt a lump form in his throat as he saw Quinn kneeling on the ground next to a body. Ash-Lea knelt on the other side. Dread rose in his chest as he thought of what he might see as he approached. The fear evaporated as he came around Quinn and saw Ash-Lea wiping some of the webs away from Greyson's face, a smile lying underneath.

"You rescued me," Greyson said to Quinn, his voice rich with gratitude. It was as if he didn't even notice Ash-Lea.

Ash-Lea looked up at Billy, stuck her tongue out like she was going to be sick.

"Of course I did," Quinn said, smiling at Greyson. Her black ponytail hanging over her shoulder. She placed a hand on his chest. "You're such a good friend, I couldn't leave you."

Quinn bounced off the ground and ran to join her mother as they cut free more cocooned victims.

Billy nudged Greyson with the toe of his shoe. "We found you."

Greyson didn't answer. He sat up, looking at the burning school. The fire had spread from the gym to the adjoining building. The long hall surrounded by the classrooms was now beginning to go up. Billy didn't understand how it was spreading so rapidly. But then again, it wasn't normal fire.

Greyson stood and started towards the inferno. "Well, I'm off. I'll see you next life."

Ash-Lea grabbed his shoulder and spun him around. "What the fudge do you think you're doing? I just spent my entire evening rescuing your sorry butt."

"Did you hear that?" Greyson spoke tonelessly and looked at Billy. "She said I'm a *good friend*. I was better off when she didn't know who I was. You might as well of left me in there."

Ash-Lea punched him in the shoulder, hard. Greyson barked in surprise and stepped away, tripping on an unconscious person that lay behind him. He fell onto his butt and yelped again, wincing and grabbing reflexively for his tailbone.

"You're an idiot," Ash-Lea announced. She looked like she was going to turn and stomp off, but then reached out a hand to Greyson. "But I still think you're okay."

Greyson smiled and took her hand.

A hiss of steam sounded as the firefighters began spraying water on the blaze. Billy wasn't sure what Hellfire was made of, but it was strong enough to close inter-dimensional portals and burn cinderblocks. He had a feeling the water wasn't going to do much good.

A man wearing a white emergency medical uniform approached and started asking them questions. Billy tried to ask the paramedic to help Greyson when the man swore. Billy gave him a questioning look.

"What?"

"Are you aware of how much trauma you have on your back?"

Billy tried looking over his shoulder. "No."

Ash-Lea stepped behind him. She hissed. "You got beat up real good in there. It's actually, pretty damn bad, man. You owe Mrs. Blouin a new t-shirt."

"Phil," the paramedic called. "Let's get this guy stable." He looked about at the hundred or so unconscious or groggy people. Mr. and Mrs. Blouin, Quinn and Junior were just cutting free the remaining few. "And call this in. We're going to need a lot of help."

He let the paramedic lead him to the ambulance, but sat him down on the curb. The man looked at Billy's back, the one stretcher in the ambulance, then at everyone else by the burning school. He sighed.

"You first, I guess. We'll stop the bleeding, but you're conscious, so you can wait it out here."

The man had Billy lie stomach down on the stretcher and started attending to the wounds on his back. He cut Billy's shirt off, first. The pain of the anesthetic was close to unbearable. He clenched the stretcher and gritted his teeth. It was a while before Billy realized someone was asking him a question. He opened an eye to see an officer with long brown hair. She was sort of pretty.

"Son, what happened here?" The police officer asked again.

Billy bit his lip. More paramedics had arrived, and with the firefighters they swarmed over the people on the grass, but there were too few. Someone was by a police car shouting into a radio for more ambulances. A second fire truck pulled around and began spraying down the burning art rooms. Quinn was under Patrick's arm, helping him limp towards an ambulance.

"Gas explosion, I think," Billy said.

The officer looked around her and nodded. She walked away quickly, grabbing the radio on her shoulder and shouting.

The paramedic attending him taped something that felt like a doormat to his back and said, "Can you get yourself to the hospital?"

"Sure," Billy said, rising.

"Great. Get your back properly attended immediately. I'm going to need this stretcher for people in worse shape than you. Scoot."

"Thanks," Billy said as he slid off the stretcher. The paramedic handed him a blanket then walked away, wheeling the stretcher onto the grass. He shouted to the closest emergency medical technicians.

Ash-Lea walked up to Billy and almost slapped him on the shoulder, but instead patted him on the head. She was no longer wearing the flak jacket and the knives. They both watched as a paramedic gave Greyson the once over, blood pressure, light in the eyes, uncapping a bottle of water and handing it to him.

"You seem to have made it out of this pretty well," Billy said to Ash-Lea.

She let out a mirthless 'heh' and pulled up the sleeves on her shirt. Bloody gashes covered both forearms up to the elbows. "The risks you take as a knife fighter, I guess."

"You need to get that checked out."

"You need to stop finding new hobbies," she said. "First baseball and now this. You're ruining our group dynamic, you know that?" She flashed Billy a smile.

Billy stretched his shoulders, feeling a painful pull in his muscles. "You might be right about that one."

"You know why I love us?" Ash-Lea asked, her hands resting on her hips. Her black hair hung over one eye and shoulder, the ends looked a little singed. She had a strangely grown-up look to her that Billy had never seen before.

"Why?" Billy challenged in a gruff, playful tone.

"If it was any of us wrapped up in that spider's butt-string, the rest of us would come."

The ominous gloom that had descended on the school was gone now. He smiled widely and took her in a one-armed hug as they stood on the grass in the middle of the night, watching their school go up in gloriously bright, demonic flames. "Every single time, Ashes."

21

Home Is Still Home

◆────────────────────────────────────◆

B illy stood on the mountainside looking out over the valley. He faced away from the cabin in which his blood had been changed; along with so many other things. Ash-Lea stood next to him, her arms folded tight across her stomach. Mr. Blouin held Quinn under his arm, she leaned against him, her eyes closed. Mrs. Blouin and Junior were asleep, snuggling in the back of the SUV. Greyson sat on the ground sipping from another bottle of water. Something about the spider venom left him very thirsty.

Patrick the jock was still sick, so Mr. Blouin took him to the hospital. Quinn hadn't had much desire to stay with him. Greyson took that as a positive sign and perked up.

The school burned all night. Before the end there were eight trucks battling the inferno. The rumor was that they didn't actually put out the blaze. The fire just ran out of things to burn and then decided to stop. The school had been devastated, nothing survived. The few remaining piles of charred bricks would have to be bulldozed.

In the distance the thick black smoke still rose from the smoldering ruin of the grounds, a broad, dark pillar that reached all the way to heaven. The sun warmed the sky over the eastern peaks. They'd been awake all night, but that didn't matter. Billy guessed there wouldn't be any school that day.

"You sure he's coming?" Ash-Lea asked, glancing away from the column of black smoke briefly to look up at Billy.

"I'm sure," he replied.

On cue, a rush of wind caught them in the face and they all looked up. Seth beat his wings laboriously as he descended. Billy squinted as the hurricane whipped into his eyes.

Seth hit the ground hard, but managed to remain standing. He folded his wings behind his back and gave Billy a warm smile. Bandages wrapped crisscross around the demon's chest and shoulders, his right hand stretched across his body applying pressure to the left side of his stomach. He walked up to Billy and placed the other hand on his shoulder.

"It is done. For now."

"That's good, but you kind of burned down the school." Billy nodded in the direction of the smoke.

Seth shrugged, nonplussed. "I imagine that outcome is preferable to being eaten?"

Ash-Lea snorted. "Darn tootin', it is."

"Greyson isn't doing too hot, is there anything we can do for him?" Billy asked.

Seth walked slowly to Greyson and knelt before him, studying his eyes. "The poison itself cannot exist in this dimension if the Will that created it is no longer here. But even with the poison gone, the dehydrating, sickening effects will remain. However, that is only true with the poison that is formed when the spider first crosses the Threshold."

"Is that why the webs didn't disappear?" Billy asked. "Because they made them after they arrived, with stuff they ate?"

Seth nodded. "Yes. If they feed while here and produce more venom or webs, they will not disintegrate when the Will leaves this Realm. But I do not think Greyson is in danger. They did not want any of their captives killed."

"Why can't they just open the gate again?" The thought hadn't occurred to Billy until right then. "They got into my bedroom, around here, the school. What's keeping them from coming back?"

Seth rose, a grave look on his face. "I damaged the Threshold, for now. But it is not destroyed."

"But that was just one spot in the gym." Billy pointed to the column of smoke.

Seth shook his head. "All gateways from my realm have the same genesis if you wish a significant power to cross through. It is the will of those who cross the Threshold that determine where they emerge. And it is the Threshold that I devastated. Think of it as the only bridge between our worlds that can support any respectable amount of weight."

"Significant power?" Ash-Lea interjected. "What does that mean?"

"There are lesser gates—cracks between our worlds—that smaller powers can squeeze through. It is how the weak Shadowlurk entered your room. Nothing more powerful than he can cross over for now; and even that is unlikely until repairs begin on the Threshold. However, most Shadowlurks lack the knowledge to open portals. Many that survived my fire are stranded here."

Billy dug his fingers into his temples. "So, there is one major Threshold, which you burned, but it opens up in many different places. Does that work both ways?"

Seth nodded.

Billy felt something like concern creep into his chest. "You came all the way over, didn't you? You couldn't have done that and kept one foot in your world."

Seth watched him for a moment, an unreadable look on his face. "I did, William."

"Can you get back?" Billy asked.

"No. Not while it is burned."

Seth's face fell and Billy realized something that made his heart feel heavy. "They're going to go after your family, aren't they? Just to get back at you."

"It is their nature, William. A head in exchange for a lost eye, a life taken for an insult given."

The demon raised his head and took in the valley. Seth stared away for a while, his arms folded, watching the sun rise over the city. He had the demeanor of a man, of a demon, rather, judging what he looked at. Billy couldn't tell if he blamed the humans or loved them.

"There is something that you did not think of, William," Seth said without turning. Billy's eyes flicked back and forth as he searched for a piece he'd missed. He couldn't think of anything. Seth continued, "The Spiderkine love human flesh, and human blood. They come and take it when they can."

Billy considered that. "But if that's the case—" he swallowed, "why take so many humans at once, just this week? Are they getting ready for a party?" He felt his stomach drop into his toes and wanted to vomit. He understood what Seth was saying.

A sardonic smile grew on the demon's his face as he watched Billy catch up mentally. "This is not about spreading fear, or drinking your blood. Demons feast on humans frequently without drawing any attention to themselves. That many humans would be required for something very specific." Seth's eyes seemed to glow a brighter red with each word he spoke.

"Specific like what?" Quinn looked between Billy and Seth in confusion.

Billy heard himself say the words, even though he didn't want to. "Specific like a ritual. A very large ritual."

"It's a good thing we stopped them, then," Mr. Blouin insisted victoriously.

Billy could feel the terror in his own expression, no hope in his eyes that Quinn's father was right.

"We did not stop them," Seth said. "We slowed them down for now. But to gather that many sacrifices so blatantly, they are most certainly planning something. And they want it done soon. The spiderkine are not typically known for their propensity to work together, as you saw at the end. Someone is directing them. And I don't imagine whomever it is will give up easily."

Billy had the very distinct impression that Seth knew what the ritual was for, but didn't ask. He didn't think that was something Greyson and Ash-Lea needed to hear just yet.

"How long do we have?" Ash-Lea eyed Seth from behind lowered brows. "Until the Threshold is opened? You burned it down, I get that. But how long until it opens again, or they repair it, or whatever?"

"I do not know," Seth said simply, an apologetic note in his voice.

Ash-Lea rolled her eyes and threw her hands up in the air. "You useless lump of demon. That doesn't help us."

"On the contrary, small one. When this begins, in earnest, you will never rest again until it is done. Enjoy this small reprieve."

Ash-Lea looked at Seth with wide, frustrated eyes, her mouth pressed flat. "That helps me even less. I'm not going to be able to sleep because a spider is going to bite my head off any day. Thanks."

Seth grinned at her.

"What about the ones that got away?" Billy remembered the red-eyed shadows running into the night.

Seth shrugged, the motion seeming to pain him, and he touched his ribs again. "They will not be of concern to you. They are scattered and few in number. Likely they will hide and feed from the humans here until a gate opens once more."

"Hey," Greyson called out from where he sat, weak but insistent. "Could we please decide on a name. I hate inconsistency, it's confusing. You've called it the portal, the gate, the threshold. I vote the Threshold, it's the coolest one." He coughed and took another sip.

Ash-Lea smiled at her friend's exhausted doggedness. "Threshold it is."

Seth opened his mouth to protest, but then shook his head.

Billy resumed the conversation. "So, there are giant spiders in the Salt Lake Valley that will be killing people until their big brothers show up again?"

"Essentially," Seth agreed.

Billy eyed Ash-Lea and Greyson, they looked back, grins growing on their faces. "Looks like we've got our work cut out for us, then."

"Me too," said Quinn resolutely.

Greyson gave a wry smile at the announcement.

"And I'll drive," Mr. Blouin offered.

"Team Demonic Spider Hunters, hoo, hoo, hoo!" Billy spun his fist in a circle.

"No," Ash-Lea insisted. "If we have to name our team, let me sleep on that, at least."

"That is the most sensible idea I have heard all night. I must rest." Seth wavered, his face pale, almost a rose color.

"Don't you have magical demonic speed healing or something?" Greyson asked dubiously.

Seth raised one eyebrow, his mouth curved into something that was almost a sneer. "Where in the depths did you get a ridiculous notion like that?"

Greyson shrugged, a wide-eyed, innocent look on his face.

Billy patted his own shoulder, then took Seth's hand and placed it on the spot he just tapped. It stung like spider claws, but he didn't complain. "Come on. I'll take you inside." The demon must have felt miserable. He accepted the guidance without comment.

Billy could feel his friends watching him as he led the demon to the cabin. Seth's limp increased as they walked, and he could hear the demon's breathing becoming more labored. By the time they reached the cabin steps, Billy had to practically pull the huge creature up them. He slid the glass doors open and Seth lumbered through. He collapsed onto the floor into the middle of the ritualistic pits that were on fire a lifetime ago.

"You gonna be okay?" Billy asked.

Seth stirred weakly, but his eyes remained closed. "Come see me tomorrow. If I am alive, then the answer is yes."

Billy did not like that answer at all. "You're not going anywhere. You said there's a lot of training to do."

Seth gave a weak shrug.

"What would Rose say if you died?" Billy said, hoping his tone was playful.

Seth smiled—a full, toothy, genuine smile that lit up his weakened face and made his eyes sparkle. "She would be most displeased."

And still, with the smile on his face remembering something that Billy was sure he would never know, Seth fell into a deep sleep and began snoring immediately. Billy backed out of the room making a mental note to always avoid a snoring demon. He sounded like a growling bear with a chainsaw.

Billy walked back to his friends. Greyson was still on the grass with his bottle of water. He held out a hand towards Quinn for assistance. Quinn's father gallantly jumped forward and helped him stand.

Ash-Lea slugged Billy in the arm and nodded in the direction of the cabin. "Is he going to be okay?"

Billy looked back the way he'd come. "I think so. He's just tired."

"That makes five of us," Quinn said with an exhausted sigh.

"Who wants pancakes?" Mr. Blouin asked.

Billy placed a hand on his shoulder. "I like you."

Billy fell to sleep as soon as he sat down in the back seat. Apparently, Meredith Ash had been apprised of their arrival, because there were hot pancakes, fresh muffins, cut fruit, cold milk and a chilled case of Mountain Dew waiting for them when they arrived.

"Because you deserve it," she said, beaming at Billy and Ash-Lea. They ate at the table by the giant broken windows in the Blouin's house. Mr. Ash didn't join them, however. After he'd heard Greyson was fine, he left for work.

"Man gets strung up by gigantic spiders and still goes into work the next day," Mr. Blouin said through a mouth of pancake and with a shake of his head.

Greyson put down his fork and pushed his plate away.

Mrs. Ash provided Billy with a gigantic pink sleep shirt that passed as a tight t-shirt on him. It felt ridiculous, but was better than sitting around bare-chested. Breakfast tasted amazing. Quinn left for her room with a lot of thank-yous and hugs. Billy, Ash-Lea and Greyson left for the Ash's house shortly after. They could hear the sound of Mrs. Blouin sweeping glass and debris up on her patio from across the fence. Greyson walked weakly off to bed almost immediately after they arrived, and Ash-Lea crashed in one of the spare bedrooms. Billy didn't know what The Fosters would think of him staying out all night and then coming home to sleep on the floor of their formal dining room during the day. While he mulled over what he was going to do, he walked into the living room, sat on the edge half-eaten couch, careful to avoid bumping his back, and flipped on the television—which miraculously had survived the spider siege.

The school fire covered every news station. The police stated that several teenagers were seen but then later disappeared. Some expert appeared on the screen and explained about the gas leak. His speculation on why all the people went missing—they became overwhelmed by the gas and fainted. Some were undoubtedly lost in the blaze, but miraculously, most made it out alive. They didn't mention, or try to explain, the tons of spider web all over the grass. Billy could only imagine what was happening to the people that were dragged over the Threshold. Perhaps death in the flames would have been kinder than whatever the spiders were doing to them now.

Billy woke up, face down on the couch, around three in the afternoon with a blanket on him, not remembering falling to sleep at all. The Ash's couch was far more luxurious than the one owned by his foster parents. His neck didn't hurt in the slightest. Meredith told him that Ash-Lea had been driven home by Quinn's father hours ago. Billy figured he might as well go face the music—the screeching, hideous music that awaited him.

He rode his bike home slowly, in no rush to hear whatever The Fosters would say about staying out all night. Turning onto his street he could hear the typical sounds of a suburban neighborhood. Someone slammed a car door. Someone called a friend in the distance. Then they called once more. Billy looked up to see Chris standing in the street waving his arms.

"Billy," he called again, and began running to him.

Billy brought his bike to a stop as he reached his brother. Chris had a frantic, yet relieved look on his face.

"Where have you been? I missed work today looking for you. I swung by and Belinda said you were probably at school. But by then I knew the whole place had burned down."

Billy smiled and hugged his brother. Chris slapped him on the back.

"Ouch,"

"You okay?"

"I guess. I'll get to that. Didn't mean to worry you."

Chris stepped back and held him at arm's length. "I'm just glad you're alright. You look like you've been through hell . . . and a woman's wardrobe."

Billy glanced at his reflection in a nearby car window. His eye was yellow from where the spider punched him. On top of that, his hair was all over the place, soot covered his face and arms. His t-shirt was pink and ridiculous.

"I've had worse," Billy smiled.

"What the hell happened? I haven't seen you since Tuesday," Chris exclaimed.

Billy gave him a quizzical look.

"It's Thursday, man," Chris said.

"Guess I lost track of time." Billy looked at his shoes, not able to stop himself from feeling a kind of sadness at worrying his brother. "Let's talk."

Billy left his bike on his foster parents' front yard and told his brother the whole story as they hiked around the neighborhood. Chris listened in silence, too amazed for even a 'wow.' Finally, after what felt like the tenth time around the block, Billy finished his story and they were sitting on the tailgate of Chris' truck.

He looked at his brother, his eyes drawn down in concern. "So, you're like a super hero now?"

Billy shot a look at Chris, his eyebrows furrowed. He began slowly shaking his head. "No, man. I'm just me. I'm just helping Seth out for now. I'm not a hero." He looked down at his big, fat hands. He felt his stomach sitting on top of his legs as he slouched. "No. I'm just me."

Chris patted Billy on the shoulder once and Billy gasped.

"Sorry, man. What did you do?"

"My back? Spider claws and demonic blades," he explained.

"Oh, right." Chris nodded. "Hey," his voice taking on a serious tone. "You know I hated that you were so good at baseball?"

Billy's face twisted in confusion at the confession. "What? I thought you liked playing baseball with me."

"Well, I wanted to like it," he leaned back and pulled his legs into the truck bed. "I always wanted to play baseball with my little brother, but you were always on your video games. You remember how many years I bugged you?"

"No. Feels like you were always bugging me."

Chris laughed once. "It does feel that way, doesn't it? But then you agreed to come out and play that one day. You remember that?"

Billy did. On a comfortably warm Autumn day, only a few months prior, the snow had just left the field a few blocks down from their house so Chris dragged Billy down there. Chris handed Billy the bat and ran twenty yards away. *You ready, Billy?* Chris beamed as he asked the question. Billy gripped the bat, but didn't really want to be there, he just wanted Chris to stop bugging him and leave him alone for good. *Let's just get this over with,* Billy thought. Then Chris threw the ball underhand and Billy saw it coming to him. The ball appeared like it was walking through the air. He knew where it was, where it would go. He felt the bat almost buzz in his arms and something savage bubbled up inside him. Something that saw the ball as a threat, as an enemy that needed to be slain. And in his hands he held the weapon that could slay the enemy. With a jolt of adrenaline, he swung the bat. He thought it was his imagination, but he felt an energy thrum through his blood. He cracked the bat into the ball, and the ball disappeared into the distant grass. Chris spent five minutes recovering it, chuckling the whole time. Then Chris pitched again, overhand that time. Billy saw the enemy and slew it again. Laughing from the joy of not sucking at something for the first time in his life. Next time Chris threw the ball as hard as he could. It wasn't even hard for him to kill that small, white, round foe. Something inside him rejoiced at the release, at the victory—like there was someone else in his blood, and they were rejoicing at the challenge. Billy felt dread slowly darken the memory. There were people in his blood, and he did not understand what that could mean.

And then, out of nowhere, Ash-Lea's quiet question came to mind.

"Is Billy going to go crazy?" She had asked Seth.

And the demon looked at Ash-Lea with such sincere sadness. *"It is possible, little one."*

Billy came back to Chris's question. "Kind of," he lied.

Chris' mouth quirked up at the memory. "I've always tried to be good at baseball. It's what I really wanted to do. I wanted to be a ball player." He gazed longingly at the sky, like an invisible jumbo-vision displayed scenes of a show called 'This Could Have Been Your Life.' Chris sighed. "But I handed you a bat and you were better than me. I still thought I might have a chance, maybe try out for the minors. But you were just such a natural I knew I had to give up."

Billy watched his brother with growing horror. He had no idea he'd done that to Chris, his only family left in the world.

"I'm . . . I'm sorry."

Chris laughed and punched him in the leg. "Don't be. I didn't know you were cheating." He smiled widely and slid off the bed of the truck onto the asphalt.

"Cheating?" Billy felt a little offended.

Chris grinned. "You have magical blood infused with the power of an ancient demonic ritual?" The question intoned in a just-to-make-sure kind of way.

Billy shrugged, bobbed his head side to side, then finally nodded. "I guess."

"There you go. I didn't have a chance against you. Maybe I will try out for the minors after all." He swung an invisible bat and the invisible ball cracked the screen of that invisible jumbo vision. "But it wasn't fair of me."

"What wasn't?" Billy asked.

"I should have been happy for you." He looked at Billy with a trace of sadness on his tanned face. "You're my brother. If you were a natural at baseball I should have been happy."

Billy shook his head. "Hey, Chris," he said, lowering his voice. "Some of the spiders got away."

Chris dropped the invisible bat. It clattered soundlessly to the pavement. "They're loose in the city?"

Billy felt an awful guilt rise in him. He should have stopped them all. "Just be careful. If you see any, let me know."

Chris nodded solemnly. "I will. I'm actually thinking about mounting a Demon-Signal spot light in the back of my truck. Shine it on the clouds when I need you."

Billy took a playful swing at his brother. Chris jumped away to avoid it, but he wasn't fast enough. He barked in pain and grabbed his shoulder reflexively. He eyed Billy as he massaged the muscle.

"That hurt, buddy. You might want to take it easy with that."

Billy looked at his fist, not sure what had just happened. "I'm sorry."

"It's all good. Things are different now. We just have to adapt and survive."

Billy hugged his brother and Chris climbed in his truck and drove away. He walked up to the house and let himself in.

When Billy walked into the living room Belinda was arranging the beer on the table in ice for her and Steve to drink all evening. She looked at Billy as he walked into the room. She stopped what she was doing and straightened, looking Billy up and down.

"All night?" she asked.

"Well, there was a bit of a situation."

"And all day?"

"Yes. I should probably start at the beginning."

"Don't you dare try to talk your way out of this. Mr. Ash called and explained you were cleaning up after the burglars broke into his house. Let me make something clear. Your education is part of our responsibility as your foster parents. If Greyson's house burned down, you comfort him until nine, and then you come home. He'll still be homeless in the morning, and then you can go comfort him again. But you will not stay out all night again. I don't care what happens to your friends." Billy opened his mouth to respond, but Belinda made a zipping motion with her hand. "No excuses. Do you understand me?"

"Yes, Belinda. Loud and clear."

"You're grounded for a week."

"What? Things broke into his house. I had to help. I can't leave my friend hanging—"

"Do you want to make it two weeks?" she snapped.

"No," Billy muttered.

"Get your filthy shoes off my carpet," she said, before turning back the couch and recommenced getting things just right for the evening's activities.

Billy showered, the water and soap stinging the cuts on his face and lacerations on his arms and back. The pain helped dissipate the anger he felt towards Belinda.

He flopped the pillow sized bandage over his back, dressed in a huge white t-shirt and black track pants. He grabbed four cupcakes and the gallon of milk and started heading to his room before remembering he wasn't allowed to sleep in there anymore. He stood in front of his door for a minute, swallowing his frustration before heading back into the formal dining room and taking a seat at the table.

He sat alone, eating cupcakes and thinking. He thought about Seth. He thought about if Greyson would be okay. He thought about the new friend they'd made in Quinn and the Blouin family, and their fantastically convenient arsenal. He thought about how Ash-Lea had said if it were any of them trapped or lost or in trouble they would all come—every single time.

And the thought made Billy smile.

An old leather-bound book sat on the table only inches from Billy's hand. Billy stared at it for a long moment, sure it hadn't been there when he sat down. It was black and looked at least eight inches thick from cover to cover. Placing his cupcake down, he slid the book closer. It took more effort than he expected—the thing was heavy.

Etched into the cover with gold lettering were the words—
The Essential Arcane. Part One.

Billy was surprised to see the title scribed in English. By contrast, a very new looking sticky-note stuck out from the pages. He opened the book to the note, the binding creaking as he did. The book, or tome Billy supposed, appeared to be more than a thousand pages long; each page made of heavy parchment, not modern, thin sheets of paper. The writing inside appeared to be written by hand; the tiny cursive script crawling beautifully across each page. Billy took out the sticky-note and as he read it, his heart sank.

This is your homework for the week—I believe that is the human expression. Read and retain it all – Selathiel.

Billy let his head fall to the table and he gave a weary moan. *Demonic spiders I can handle, but I have homework too?*

22

The Spider General's Shame

━━━━━━━━━━━━◆━━━━━━━━━━━━

"Say that one more time," the Spider King slowly growled. He placed his goblet on the black oak table next to him. Two spiders cowered at the foot of the throne, their heads bowed.

Krios watched from the back of the throne room, stripped of his armor and beaten. Eight of his own guards stood about him, spears painfully penetrating his hide. Every time he breathed the spears dug deeper into his flesh and his breathing stumbled. His broken mandible hurt, they had not taken the time to bandage it. He would likely lose the whole thing.

The wide bowl-shaped throne, sat at the far end of the black marble hall. Twelve tall, intricately carved pillars rose in regular intervals against the walls, six on either side of the room. Long black and red drapes hung down between each pillar, the royal sigil depicting a spider with a human on a spear woven onto each one. Beside the throne stood four huge, armor-clad spiders, each holding a long wooden spear. Each of them held their gaze upward, away from Krios. None of them dared look at their disgraced General.

The king rose slowly from his throne, draining his goblet of wine onto the floor, and looked at the two servants kneeling before him.

"The Threshold is burned, my King," the spider at the foot of the throne repeated.

The Spider King descended the steps slowly, unclipping the cloak from his human shoulders and tossing it to his wife. The queen caught the garment and looked at her husband uneasily, a hand held defensively on her stomach. Her daughter, Patricia, was nowhere to be seen, and for that Krios was grateful. He did not want the princess to see him defeated and held prisoner. The two servants that knelt before the King shrunk away when they saw him approaching. He stopped when he reached them, tilting his head to the side.

"What is your name?" he asked.

"My na . . . name is Eudoxia, my Liege."

"Do you know what the destruction of the Threshold means, Eudoxia?" he asked softly.

"No . . . no, your majesty," the spider muttered.

"What is your friend's name?" he asked him, inclining his head towards the spider beside Eudoxia.

The spider looked to his left at the soldier that joined him on the mission. "That is Arcadius, my King. He is not a friend; we are simply soldiers in the same regimen."

"So he is not your friend. Does that mean you would like to see him die?"

Arcadius looked up at Eudoxia, alarm written clearly in his eight eyes.

"No, my King. He is a good soldier. I harbor no ill will against him."

The Spider King grumbled loudly. His queen looked at him and he nodded.

"Guards, bring Krios forward."

Krios fought back the urge to cry out as the eight spears bit into his flesh. He rose onto his legs, but collapsed immediately, too weak to stand.

"Bring him," the king roared, his voice echoing through the chamber.

Krios felt claws dig into his forelegs as they dragged him across the throne room floor. He wished to die in that moment, the humiliation was too great. Guards shoved Eudoxia and Arcadius to the side and left Krios to slump before the slender, black legs of the king.

The king glowered when he saw his general. Krios looked up at him weakly.

"You failed to protect the Threshold, General," King Theron boomed, stomping his claws into the stone floor.

"I did, my King. The demon, Selanthiel Jakob Molef has sided with the humans. He burned it with Hellfire," Krios rasped. "He is now known as Selanthiel the Betrayer."

The guards behind Krios shifted uncomfortably at the revelation.

"Truly, the highest form of treason," the queen observed quietly. "Against all demons."

"The Knights of the White Spire will blame us, you incompetent fool. It would have been better to die there than to let his happen." King Theron drew his sword. Krios eyed it, but did not flinch. "Who are these spiders, General Krios?" the King asked calmly, pointing his jeweled sword at Arcadius, and Eudoxia.

Krios looked up weakly, scrutinizing the hairy faces of the trembling soldiers. He told his king their names.

"Do they deserve to die?" he asked.

"No," Krios said immediately.

The King of Spiders stooped and placed the goblet into Krios' claw. He then walked over to the two cringing soldiers. He looked between them carefully, then took Eudoxia by one mandible.

He shivered, as if he wanted to pull away, but did not dare offend his king. He stood, forcing the smaller creature to rise until he was standing on the points of his claws. With one hand he held his mandible, with the other he pressed the flat of the blade against his cheek and gently turned his trembling head. Eudoxia let out a quiet sob, knowing what was coming.

The king's sword flashed in his hand as he drew it against Eudoxia's flesh, opening up the spider's throat. Eudoxia screamed. The king watched intently with a pleased smile on his face. He held his hand out to Krios.

"General, my cup."

The spiders surrounding him withdrew their spears and took a pace back. Krios rose on quivering limbs, and limped the leg's length to his king. He handed him the goblet before collapsing to the floor. Theron pushed the cup against the wound and let the blood drain into it. Eventually, the spider struggled less and less as its blood spilled and finally the spider's lifeless body fell to the floor. The king turned, his hands inky with Eudoxia's blood.

"Do you think that needed to happen, Krios?"

Krios watched the king, clenching his mouth shut, his eyes wide.

"For all your training and battle experience, you don't know what the right answer to my question is, do you? Is it a riddle, or isn't it? Did Eudoxia deserve to die? I recommend you choose to speak what you believe to be the truth." He held the cup of Eudoxias blood aloft, allowing the whole chamber to see it.

Krios let his gaze fall. "No, my King. Eudoxia was a good soldier. He did not need to die like that."

King Theron tightened his blood-covered fist on the goblet in his hand, his face growing red with anger. "If you do not think your soldiers must die needlessly, then why, in Aberdem's name, did you allow the Threshold to burn?" He swept the sword towards Krios' face, barely missing by an inch. "We were permitted to gather the humans for the ritual as an act of faith in our ability to be equal to the winged demons. And you let the Threshold burn! The Knights will be upon us as soon as they hear, and thousands of your soldiers will die for *no reason*." With every word he slashed his sword towards Krios' face, chips flying out of the stone floor and into his eyes.

Krios had nothing to say, so he remained quiet, enduring the king's furious rage in silence. Finally, after the echoes of the king's cries around the chamber died, he spoke. "Yes, my King."

"His blood is upon your head." Theron poured the still-warm blood over Krios' face. It ran into his eyes and stung. "All of their blood will be upon your head. Go and begin repairs immediately," the king said gently, his hand still black with blood. "You may have a chance to avoid a war."

Krios rose, shaking, still weak from the fight. He straightened and held his quaking head proudly. "As you wish, your majesties."

"And once the Threshold is repaired," Theron said with a quiet, controlled fury, "I will go drink the blood of the Demonseed myself, and no Demonic nor Earthly creature will dare to look down upon the Spiders again." He crushed the goblet in his fist, the metal groaning as it collapsed. "William Blacksmith will be mine."

Acknowledgements

I want to thank my amazing wife for her patience through this journey of bringing Billy from my brain to the page. I can't express how much I love my kids for daydreaming with me.

The staff at Ireland Ink have been wonderful, and I thank you for your encouragement and tolerance of wholly unacceptable working conditions.

And lastly, I want to thank Billy for jumping into my brain one day without my permission. I don't know where I would be without him.

About the Author

Ben Ireland is the author of many things, including the dystopian Kingdom City series (2014, 2016, 2017) and several short stories: Kissed a Snake in A Dash of Madness: a Thriller Anthology (July 2013), and Fairykin in Moments in Millennia: a Fantasy Anthology (January 2014).

Born and raised in Australia, Ben is uniquely qualified to write about horrifying spiders and how much they would like to kill you. The concept for Billy Blacksmith came to Ben when Billy jumped him in his kitchen and hit him in the face with his baseball bat.